DIE-OFF

A John Marquez novel

Kirk Russell

Severn House Large Print
London & New York

This first large print edition published 2015
in Great Britain and the USA by
SEVERN HOUSE PUBLISHERS LTD of
19 Cedar Road, Sutton, Surrey, England, SM2 5DA.
First world regular print edition published 2013 by
Severn House Publishers Ltd., London and New York.

British Library Cataloguing in Publication Data

Russell, Kirk, 1954- author.
  Die-off. – (The John Marquez series)
  1. Marquez, John (Fictitious character)–Fiction.
  2. Government investigators–California–Fiction.
  3. Murder–Investigation–Fiction. 4. Detective and
  mystery stories. 5. Large type books.
  I. Title II. Series
  813.6-dc23

  ISBN-13: 9780727870353

Severn House Publishers support the Forest Stewardship Council™
[FSC™], the leading international forest certification organisation. All
our titles that are printed on FSC certified paper carry the FSC logo.

DIE-OFF

Further Titles from Kirk Russell

The John Marquez series
SHELL GAMES
NIGHT GAME
DEADGAME
REDBACK*
DIE-OFF*

The Ben Raveneau series
A KILLING IN CHINA BASIN *
COUNTERFEIT ROAD *
ONE THROUGH THE HEART *

* *available from Severn House*

Judy, your courage and gentleness in the face of everything are my inspiration.

Acknowledgments

This is the fifth Marquez novel and, as with the earlier novels, many thanks go to Nancy Foley. When I wrote the first book, Nancy was a member of the Special Operations Unit and would go on to lead it and later to become head of the California Department of Fish and Game. I wish my writing career had an arc like that. Nancy is now retired, as is Kathy Ponting, long-time patrol lieutenant of the SOU, and often a great source for this author. Thanks go to Kathy as well as Stafford K. Lehr, Chief of the Fisheries Branch, and to warden pilots, Ron Vanthuysen and Gavin Woelfel. Thanks also to Detective Rick Jackson of the LAPD. As of 2013, the California Department of Fish and Game became the California Department of Fish and Wildlife, but the challenges remain the same. All the best to those who take on that fight.

ONE

When the call came Marquez was in a conference room at California Fish and Game headquarters looking at photos of elephant tusks and glass jars of ground rhino horn emailed that morning by an LAPD homicide detective. The mix of live animals and animal parts stockpiled at the warehouse were a good fit for the trafficker he was searching for and he was close to booking a flight to LA.

The tip call changed that. The caller refused to give her name but insisted it was urgent she talk with Lieutenant John Marquez. An office tech found him in the conference room and Marquez hesitated a moment then slid his laptop aside and reached for the phone. The woman's voice was immediate, intense, and strong.

'I have nothing to do with any of this. I'm just passing on a message.'

'Okay.'

'No, it's really not okay, but it's what's happening. Hold on a minute.'

Marquez heard a car door slam. He heard rain on a windshield and an engine start. When she spoke again she was on speakerphone and harder to hear.

'Don't worry about how well you can hear me. It doesn't matter. We aren't going to talk long anyway and all you have to do is listen. I'm going

1

to tell you where the gun is that was used to kill those two girls a couple of years ago along the Klamath River.'

Marquez was on the thirteenth floor of the Water Resources Building in Sacramento. He turned and looked out the window at sunlight through broken clouds and guessed she was well to the north along the Oregon border and probably somewhere near the Klamath, where it was raining today.

'Go ahead, I'm listening. Where's the gun?'

'It's buried along the White Salmon River three quarters of a mile down from Condit Dam on the road side. It's at a bend where two large gray rocks lean out over the water. They're side by side and he says you'll know the spot when you see it.'

'Who says?'

'We're not going there.'

'Are we talking about Terry Ellis and Sarah Steiner?'

'Yes.'

'Are you aware of what's going on at Condit Dam tomorrow?'

'He told me this morning.'

It could easily be a hoax call. It probably was and still it affected Marquez. He shifted in his chair and heard a low murmur, definitely male. He guessed the cell phone was on the dash and the man was listening and in control.

'If anyone in law enforcement is going to look for a gun buried along that river with such short notice it'll take more than an anonymous call. Who is it that told you it's there and why are you calling California Fish and Game? Why not

2

call the FBI or the local police in the area of the dam?'

Marquez spoke to the man.

'Whoever you are, talk to me.'

There were several seconds of silence and then she spoke again.

'You'll need a shovel and a metal detector.'

'Should I also pack a lunch? Look, you've called a California Fish and Game officer with a tip on a homicide cold case two states to the north. You need to call the people working on the case. The murders were in California and Rich Voight at the Siskiyou County Sheriff's Office is the investigator in charge. Call him. He'll know who to get in touch with in the state of Washington to get a search going.'

Even as he said that he knew he'd be making the calls and reached for something to write with. Terry Ellis and Sarah Steiner were twenty-four, young, idealistic, and part of a movement to remove dams along western rivers. Sarah Steiner would have started Columbia Law School that fall. Terry Ellis worked for a social media start-up in San Francisco, but through family both knew the north coast. Ellis' brother Jack still guided rafting trips in the Six River area. Steiner's father was a lawyer in Redding.

They traveled along the Klamath in a pickup with a home-made camper shell that belonged to Ellis' brother. Instead of a single door at the rear of the camper shell, it had two doors that opened out, a modification Jack Ellis made so he could slip a pair of kayaks in and out easily. At night Ellis and Steiner slept in sleeping bags on a piece

3

of four-inch foam with the back doors of the camper open. The river country was generally safe and family and friends said they were careful where they parked.

The sleeping bags, with Ellis and Steiner inside them, plus the foam underneath, everything got dragged out the back. They hit the ground in their sleeping bags and fought—or that's what Voight, the Siskiyou County investigator concluded.

Steiner was shot and stabbed and never made it out of her sleeping bag but did make a 911 call from her cell phone and talked eleven seconds with a dispatcher before the phone disconnected.

Ellis took off running. Her body was found in the Klamath River half submerged about a third of a mile away. She ran most of that distance with a bullet wound in her right upper hip and another high in her left shoulder.

'How does the man with you know where the gun is?'

'He's not with me.'

'I can set up a meeting with the Siskiyou County investigator if he wants to come in and talk. That's what should happen. Why don't we do that? I'll meet you in Yreka at the sheriff's office? If you're good with that I'll leave Sacramento in the next ten minutes.'

'He wants you to back off your investigation.'

'What investigation?'

'He wants you to stay out of Vancouver and LA and says you'll know what he's talking about. He said to tell you that you had a close call a month ago in the Washougal Basin and that you were lucky.'

4

'If I'm going to do anything about this call he needs to start talking.'

'We're about to lose connection, Lieutenant.'

'Then pull over to the side of the road. I need more before trying to convince anyone to search for this gun, and here's my message to the guy in the car with you. I'm coming for you. I'm getting closer and I will find you.'

Marquez heard the jarring thud of a car wheel hitting a pothole. The tire sound changed and he guessed they had turned onto dirt road and this was where cell connection would end. But he was wrong. There was one last thing said, a man's voice calm and so quiet Marquez had to replay the tape of the call several times before he was certain of what he had heard.

'This is Rider and the tip is real. I'm giving it to you as a last warning, Marquez. I'm not going to let you keep looking for me. What happened to those two women could happen to you. You'll drive down a dirt road one day and just disappear. Back off now or that's how it will end.'

Marquez didn't get to respond. The caller broke the connection. But that didn't matter; he would have said the same thing again.

'I will find you.'

TWO

At dawn Marquez was seventy miles north-east of Portland at Condit Dam standing in gray light

5

and cold with a Washington Fish and Wildlife warden named Donna Kinsell. A Klickitat County deputy was also there, though Marquez doubted the deputy would get out of his car again. He had already reminded them they were allowed four hours, not a second longer, to search the riverbank. He followed at a distance now as they left in Kinsell's truck, backtracking on the dam road to a steep trail that led down from the road to the river.

Marquez didn't get anywhere with the FBI. His guess was they Googled the river, saw plenty of rock and bends and, after weighing the likelihood that the call was a hoax, decided to offer expedited ballistics testing should anything turn up. In the bed of Kinsell's truck were a metal detector and a folding shovel. After they parked, he slid the shovel into his pack and cinched it tight enough to keep the shovel handle straight. He picked up the metal detector and Kinsell clipped a radio onto her belt and explained the rules again, pretty much a repeat of what the deputy said at the dam but with an edge of her own.

'When we get the radio call we leave. If we don't get the call we leave at eleven thirty.'

Marquez left that alone and they started down. The land was wet from recent rain, the trees pungent despite the cold, the trail rocky, narrow and slippery. He carried the metal detector in his left hand and gripped tree branches with his right as he descended. As they reached the river Kinsell waited for him to lead.

'You're the man with the tip.'

They started upriver, Kinsell monitoring her

GPS and pushing for more information on why the tip call came to him. He told her about Rider's animal trafficking and the investigation a year and a half ago that led to a failed Special Operations bust and how when the SOU pulled back he took over the open file.

'How big is this smuggling operation?'

'Big. Rider runs the Wal-Mart of wildlife trafficking. You can get just about anything.'

On her Garmin she had the river and the dam and when they reached the point where they were exactly three quarters of a mile from the dam she called it out.

'We're where your tipster said the rocks are, so what do you want to do?'

There was no bend, no rocks jutting, and it was cold. Her cheeks had two red spots. He checked his phone and saw they had burned an hour and twenty minutes of the four hours they were allowed.

'Let's keep going toward the dam.'

'So we're going to forget about the three quarters of a mile your tipster told you?'

'Maybe they were a little off.'

'Or maybe your anonymous caller made it all up so this Rider could talk to you.'

'Maybe, but we're not going to leave yet.'

As they got inside of a third of a mile from the dam, Kinsell was ready to call it off and climb the bank to the road.

'The directions you got don't match up with anything here. We're wasting our time and we've only got another half-hour anyway. We need ten minutes just to climb out of here.'

The radio call came not long after. He watched Kinsell pull the radio from her belt.

'Roger that, we're pulling out now.'

She hooked the radio back on and her voice took on more authority.

'We're done. It's time to back away from the river. Follow me.'

Marquez pointed upriver to the next bend where a bench of gray rock leaned into the current.

'I'm going to check that spot up there first. Those rocks look like what she described and I think we've got a safe fifteen minutes. That call to pull out was early.'

'Don't even go there.'

She squared off and faced him, her body language like something she would use making an arrest. A bright blonde ponytail fell between her shoulder blades and Marquez saw the confrontation coming, but he was still going to check out the rocks ahead.

'We gave our word, and that might not matter to you because you'll fly home, but this is where I live and work, so we leave together. If you screw with what we agreed to, you're messing with me and you don't want to do that.'

Marquez waited to see if there was more and then let her know he was going to the next bend. He tightened the pack straps. He looked at her face flushed from clambering over rocks and wading through brush looking for something that probably wasn't here and listened as her voice became loud and firm.

'Let's go, Lieutenant. You don't make the calls here and the way I hear it you're not running the undercover team in California anymore either. We leave now.'

Marquez turned from her. The comment bothered him and he didn't want her to read that on his face. It also would not take long to sweep the small sandbar ahead with the metal detector.

'You're out of state here, Lieutenant. You're not pulling my reputation down with yours.'

'Then take your reputation with you up to your truck and radio and tell them I wouldn't leave. I'll be up on the road before noon. You don't need to wait for me. I'll walk back to the dam.'

'I'm ordering you.'

'I hear you and I'm still going to check one last spot.'

She threw the radio to him with an underhand motion then turned away with a look of disgust, her face scarlet with anger. Marquez picked up the radio and moved upriver. At the next bend a muddy sandbar lay behind gray rocks leaning into the river. He switched on the metal detector and swept the sandbar but there was no ping and he stepped back and thought about where he would dig if it were him. He looked at the dam up ahead, gray-white in sunlight, 125 feet tall, and then looked again at the boil of water behind the gray rocks and stepped back onto the soft sandy mud.

He sank a few inches with each step and this time worked his way up closer to the bank so the arc of the metal detector swung up over the rocky soil of the riverbank. He got a ping just as the radio came again, static, and then, 'Are you both clear of the area?'

9

'This is Marquez and I'm still on the river. Warden Kinsell should be almost to the road. I'm on one last spot and then I'm out.'

'You're still on the river?'

'Yes.'

A different voice came over the radio, somebody higher up, a supervisor, he guessed.

'Are you trying to stop this from happening, Lieutenant? Get your ass out of there.'

'You got it.'

Marquez figured he needed five minutes, maybe less, to climb up from here to the road. He swung the detector again, got the ping, and then narrowed down where to dig. He marked the spot, turned off the metal detector and pulled the folding shovel out of the pack, tightened it, and started digging.

The riverbank was wet and the sandy mud heavy but easy to get through. He widened the hole and knew it could be anything down here, a piece of rusted iron, anything. The hole was two feet wide and a foot and a half deep when his cell rang. It was Kinsell.

'Are you on your way up?'

'I got a hit on the metal detector. I'm digging and then I'm on my way up and out.'

'I don't want to drive away until you're out.'

'I won't be long.'

'Didn't they call you?'

He broke the connection and the shovel scraped on what felt and sounded like metal. He cleaned off the top and found the lid of a metal box with a handle and tape sealing it shut. He dug around it and then lifted the handle and pulled hard. Now he was looking at an aluminum tackle box of a style he hadn't seen in years. Sturdy and more a box you would leave in garage with the ties and lures you weren't taking to the river that day. The kind of box a fisherman could hand down to a son or daughter.

He packed up the folding shovel and picked up the tackle box and metal detector and started out. All of the seams and the hinges on the backside were taped with what looked like waterproof tape. There was some weight in there, not a lot but enough, and something slid around as he climbed. He gripped the metal detector in his left hand, along with the tackle box, and with his right he used tree branches again, this time to help pull himself up the steep slope. As he reached the asphalt he called Kinsell.

'I'm out.'

'Stay where you are.'

He heard the word 'asshole' before she broke the connection and then caught his breath looking back down at the gorge of the White Salmon. It wouldn't be long now. He looked down at the river at the quiet water and tried to picture the change coming.

Kinsell came in close alongside him, her passenger-side mirror not more than six inches away from him and a steady stream of cars going around her and on toward the dam. He laid the metal detector in the pickup bed and put his pack alongside it in a way that would keep the detector from sliding around, then unzipped a pocket on the pack and felt around for a knife. The tackle box would ride with them and he

11

wanted to cut the tape free and get a look at what was inside.

Marquez put the tackle box on the floor of the passenger foot well and got in. 'Thanks for waiting.'

'I was never going to leave you here.' She stared down at the tackle box. 'That probably belongs to some fisherman.'

'Do you know a lot of fishermen who bury their tackle boxes along the river?'

Instead of answering, she radioed that she had him and they were on their way. She made it sound as if she was bringing a suspect in. He unfolded the knife, leaned over the tackle box, and cut and peeled back the waterproof tape. He tried the lid now and it was free. Kinsell looked down as he lifted the lid. She saw the trout flies and line and crimpers and floats and said, 'There you go. You just stole some guy's fishing box, or maybe the guy who called you buried it there for you to find. Today would have been my day off. I had plans my husband and I made two months ago. If my captain wasn't such a jerk he would have sent somebody else. He says you've known each other a long time.'

'We have. Look, I'm sorry you missed whatever you had planned.'

'You're really good at apologizing.'

Marquez studied the upper tray of the tackle box before using the knife blade to test lifting it out. He listened to the radio chatter. The Secretary of Interior was inbound with a police escort and was late but didn't need to worry. No one was holding their breath for his speech. The headliner

12

was the dam. He lifted the tray now and found himself looking at a box of ammunition; with the knife blade he opened the box and confirmed they were nine-millimeter bullets. Using the knife he peeled back white cotton cloth wrapped around the object alongside the ammo and stared at the grip of a hand gun.

Kinsell was probably expecting more fishing line or weights and was ready to comment. Seeing the gun changed everything for her. Marquez put the tray back in and shut the box and as they reached the dam and parked a klaxon horn sounded. Seven hundred pounds of dynamite were packed yesterday. Guards were stationed last night. As a second warning horn started, Marquez moved the tackle box to the trunk of his rental car and then like everyone else he focused on the base of Condit Dam.

When the blast came the sound enveloped them. At the base of the dam dirt and sediment and concrete blew out and upward in a boil of dark black smoke. Chunks of concrete rained down and with a roar water surged from under the dam. People nearby cried out as the flow became a churning torrent, rolling and boiling downstream.

Marquez kept an eye on his car but stood transfixed along with everyone else. Then near him, an older guy who looked like an engineer, possibly an employee of PacifiCorp, owner of the dam, lowered his cell phone with tears streaking his face. He looked at Marquez and said, 'Twelve thirty-five.'

'What's that?'

13

'That's when the first wave reached the Columbia River. I just got the call.'

He touched his phone as if confirming it again with his fingertips and Marquez nodded that he understood. For the first time since 1913 the White Salmon River was running free. He moved away as his phone screen lit with Rich Voight's name, but with the roar he couldn't hear Voight so he got in his car to take the call.

'Where was the gun?'

'Buried near the two rocks the caller described.'

'I've asked a detective from Portland to come get it from you.'

'I'm leaving here inside an hour. I can drop it off with the Portland Police.'

'He's already on his way.'

Marquez thought about that a moment before asking, 'Did you get any of my messages yesterday afternoon?'

'I got all of them, but I was tied up with a new homicide.'

'Why didn't you call me back last night?'

'I just didn't get to it. If the gun checks out we'll talk about everything. Thanks for searching for it.'

The Siskiyou County Sheriff was in an ongoing war with the Department of Fish and Game – and indeed all government except his own branch, Siskiyou County Sheriff's Office. He viewed himself as essential to Siskiyou County and his attitude rippled through the department.

When Voight started in on why an anonymous call to Fish and Game didn't make his list yesterday, Marquez cut him off.

14

'Tell the Portland detective I've got a white Toyota Camry.'

He killed the call and dropped the phone in his pocket. Then he walked down to get a better view of the river.

THREE

The estimated time to drain the reservoir was five hours and Marquez watched more of it than he expected to. When the Portland detective finally arrived it was with a Washington State Patrol car leading him, its light bar flashing. The detective was genial and after looking at the water surging into the gorge revealed that he was a fisherman, though with mixed feelings about dam removal.

'This dam has been here a long time. I hope they know what they're doing.'

'Why would they start now?'

That got a smile and then they were onto the tip and tackle box and why Marquez, after getting a call yesterday afternoon, made the decision to fly to Portland then drive here and search for the gun.

'There's a tie to a Fish and Game investigation I've been working for a year. Didn't Voight tell you that?'

'I'm not sure he did.'

'I'm sure he didn't.'

The detective didn't react to that. Instead, as

15

Marquez pulled the tackle box out of the trunk, he said, 'Rich Voight told me you were there when the girls' bodies were found.'

'I was in the area on an undercover operation and when Siskiyou County put out a BOLO on a vehicle the next day I went to where they were killed to see if I could help.'

'You were that close by?'

'I was.'

The detective nodded then stared down at the white water boiling from under the dam and asked, 'What are we going to do for electricity if we knock down all the dams? We'll be back in the Stone Age. Isn't there a group in California trying to tear down the Hetch Hetchy dam? What the hell is that about? What would San Francisco do for water and how many billions beyond the initial estimate would it cost to do it? Some of the ideas that come out of your state I can't get my head around.'

'Can you get your head around me leaving four or five messages for your friend Voight yesterday that I got a tip call saying the murder weapon was buried here and then not hearing back from him?'

'It sounds as if you two haven't always gotten along, and Rich can be difficult.'

'Maybe I'm just tired but it gets under my skin that he's got time to call you and ask you to probe for whatever you can find out as you take the tackle box from me. Why did I go by the murder scene and offer to help? I went because my daughter knew Terry Ellis and Sarah Steiner and I had just met them the day before. They

16

struck me as two well-meaning young women who cared enough to try to help solve a big problem. Voight asked the same questions that day. We sat in his car and talked.'

'He told me.'

'Told you what, that he had suspicions then?'

'Don't you think this tip call coming to you and you finding the gun should provoke some questions?'

'Listen to the tape of the call and then see what you think. We got a copy out to Voight this afternoon. Ask him to email you the file. If he won't, I will.'

Marquez handed him a card and looked at the tackle box in the detective's hand. The box was crusted with river mud and it was quite possible this was nothing more than a hoax. Terry Ellis and Sarah Steiner as he remembered them were warm and light-hearted and on a summer road trip in addition to bringing their idealism to the Klamath water debate. He took in the detective's balding gray head and tired face, the detective just doing his part.

'Voight doesn't think much of Fish and Game. He thinks we should issue hunting licenses, help clean up road kill, and generally stay out of the way of real cops like him. But that isn't your problem. Thanks for making the drive here to pick this up.'

'The Washington warden here says you were alone when you found the tackle box.'

'I was.'

'Time ran out and you refused to pull back from the river.'

'That's right. She kept her word and went up to the road. I stayed because the call to leave came early and the rocks up at the next bend up ahead looked like what was described to me.'

'You dug in just the right spot.'

Marquez was done with this. He leaned forward and in a confessional voice said, 'You know how it is, you bury your gun along a river and then go back years later and try to find it. It's not so easy to find anymore and the warden made me carry the pack and the shovel and the metal detector and that slowed me down. Then I had to wait for her to leave so I could retrieve it and get on with my scheme. Now you've got it and if it checks out, Rich Voight, who is already spread too thin in that giant county, can put more energy into investigating me. That's my secret plan, to have Voight on my ass.'

'How deep was it buried?'

'About two feet down.'

'Could you find the spot again?'

Marquez was unsure if the detective was serious and then decided he was and pointed at the churning white foam below the dam.

'The rocks should still be there. I think they're big enough to take this, but I wouldn't spend a lot of time looking for the sandbar.'

'Did the warden here watch you open the tackle box?'

'She did.'

'Did you touch the gun?'

'No. I used a knife to push back the cloth it was wrapped in. I'm going to head out now. Have a nice drive back.'

18

Before Marquez could turn away the detective said, 'Rich Voight is a good man and a persistent investigator. Persistence is how cases get solved.'

'Tell him Terry Ellis and Sarah Steiner were young and energetic in the way you can be when you still think everybody cares at least a little. And they were fighters. They would have done some good. Sarah Steiner managed to make a 911 call and couldn't say much but gave the dispatcher the river road. No one got out there to check until near dawn. Why don't you ask Voight why he hasn't looked into that?'

'Maybe he has.'

'Ask him.'

Marquez left soon after the detective and his phone started ringing about an hour later, more or less when he thought it would. It was Voight and he called three times in quick succession. He didn't leave a message until his fourth call. The message was he wanted to debrief with Marquez at the sheriff's office in Yreka tomorrow.

Marquez might have done that just to get clear with Voight if something else hadn't happened first. He returned the car, flew from Portland to Oakland, and drove home. Late that night a pickup carrying four eighty-gallon coolers loaded with fingerling fish rolled and pinned the driver near an abandoned boat landing off a dirt road along the Sacramento River. Marquez got a call from the warden whose area it was in. He recognized Grace's voice immediately.

'John, I've got something that may be what you've been looking for, a pickup truck that was loaded with fingerlings. The driver was backing

19

down to the water and rolled his truck. I don't think he had his lights on and I don't think these are fish we want in the Sacramento River. Do you want to come take a look?'

'I do. Where's the driver?'

'He's still trapped and he's in a bad way. They're trying to get him out, but the truck is wedged between trees and his arm is pinned under it. He had his window down and was probably leaning out trying to see in the dark as he backed off the slope. When the truck rolled his left arm and shoulder got caught under the driver's door. He also took a bad hit to the head. Paramedics are working on him and a tow truck is on its way here to try to get the pickup off him.'

'Who found him?'

'Someone made an anonymous call to 911.'

'Text me how to get there. I'm on my way.'

FOUR

A late-model white Ford 150 lay on its left side and brightly lit by lights powered by a generator. Marquez heard the voices of the first responders trying to get the driver freed above the sound of the diesel generator. He saw the pickup's windshield was out and they were working on him through the opening. Their breath showed in the glare of the lights. It was cold and still an hour to dawn. A low fog lay over the river and Grace Headley, the area warden, stood with him and gave him her take, which seemed to be the right one.

The driver had tried to back down to the river with his lights off using only brake lights and moonlight. The truck slid in mud from the recent rain and the right rear tire ran up on a rock. Marquez's flashlight beam illuminated muddy tire prints on the rock and he saw how as that tire rode up on the rock the other rear tire dropped into a rut. Then the truck rolled. The weight of the fish and water-filled coolers didn't help.

Fish and water flowed out of the upended coolers and the truck, now on its side, slid down into a stand of trees and got wedged there. Getting it back onto four tires meant pulling it free with a tow cable. But that meant dragging it along its side and with the man's arm pinned under the driver's door they couldn't do that.

He saw where they had cut five or six saplings down so they could get enough access to dig around his trapped arm. He watched as a tow driver repositioned his truck and ran a wench cable down.

Headley shook her head and touched Marquez's back.

'They found his wallet and I've run him. I'll give you what I've got so far. Do you want to go down there first?'

'Yeah, let's go take a look.'

They followed the pickup's tracks down the steep slope to where it rolled and fish flowed into the brush as the coolers spilled. That flood of water carried fingerlings almost to the river. Marquez shined his light on a red plastic cooler

21

lid caught in a young bay tree and beneath saw hundreds of three-inch fingerlings. The smell was strong.

'Over here, John, and you've got to walk around to the right. You're not going to believe how many of them almost made it. They must have sloshed out in one big wave. What was he thinking, trying to back all the way down here?'

Marquez thought he had a pretty good idea of what the driver was thinking. Each cooler weighed somewhere around 650 pounds. Two orange-colored five-gallon buckets were downslope from the nose of the truck and were probably thrown out when the windshield popped loose. Good chance he was supposed to park and ferry the fingerlings down to the water two buckets at a time, more or less ten trips per cooler, and he figured it would be a lot easier to back down the overgrown dirt track to the edge of the river.

He brought his light back to the fish lodged in the brush and then worked his way over to Headley, where the fish had washed out and over rocks. He took in the flow of fish and estimated there were more than a thousand, and he didn't have any doubt about what they were.

When he looked up Headley asked, 'Ready to wake up a biologist?'

He was. He squatted down close to the water with the flashlight and picked up the largest of the fingerlings nearest him and laid it in his palm.

'What's going on with those fins?' Headley asked.

The pectoral, the front-most fins, were cut short and damaged. So were the pelvic fins.

'Whoever raised them fed them with pellets and they all race each other to get to the pellets. When they do that they get crowded in and bite each other's fins. It happens in the feeding frenzy.'

Marquez looked at the dark line along the back, the start of speckled color along the sides, the long snout. He was sure but wanted to hear the biologist confirm it. He dropped the fish and with the light followed the rest of the wash of fish and saw several that had been crushed and, as Headley said, just a few feet from the water. She moved one with her boot.

'I stomped these. They were dead when I got here but I wanted to make certain. My father's family was from Michigan and we used to go there in the summers and I would fish with my father. It's not the first time I've seen northern pike fingerling.'

She moved another with her boot.

'Most grow to two feet but I've seen them as big as three. When I was seven I was watching a mother duck and a line of ducklings and then one of these came out of the water and the duckling at the end of the line was gone. After that my father couldn't get me to put a toe in, at least not on that trip. This is what you've been afraid of, isn't it?'

'It is.'

She was quiet for a moment, then said, 'There are enough northern pike here to start a colony. Are we looking for sport fishermen?'

'I don't think so.'

'Who else would do something like this?'

'That's what I'm working on.'

23

'John, really, what's going on here? This is an awful lot of pike and I know what these fish can do. There won't be any other species left. Why would anyone want that?'

'The usual reasons.'

'But where's the money in this?'

'I don't know yet but it's in there somewhere.'

'Well, I don't get it.'

Marquez moved his flashlight beam over the fingerling pike at their feet.

'You don't have to get it. This is all we need to know.'

They worked their way back up to the truck and then to her rig where she gave him what she had on the driver and the pickup that was registered to a corporation. The name on his license was Enrique Jordan and it was clear he was in bad shape. They were working to keep him conscious and there was urgency in their voices. He was almost free, almost on his way to a hospital, but not out yet. It sounded as if they hit a rock trying to dig around his arm and now were having to work around it.

Marquez and Headley moved back up to the levee road and were there as Enrique Jordan was freed. Four first responders supported his body and they brought him up the slickened muddy track on a backboard. He was unconscious but alive when they loaded him and left. Marquez got the name of the hospital where they were taking him and watched their lights disappear down the dirt road.

The pickup got dragged out of the trees and

winched up to the road and he and Headley retrieved items thrown from the truck and went through everything inside it. Marquez searched for an hour for a cell phone. He swept the brush with a light trying to find it and criss-crossed the slope as the sun rose red over river fog. He was there as a DFG biologist arrived and took samples and confirmed the fish were northern pike.

Before the pickup was loaded and hauled away Marquez went through it one more time. He searched a wider area around the crash site, refusing to give on finding a cell phone. Everyone carried one. The driver wouldn't be out here without one. He stood at the edge of the levee road reluctant to leave without finding it.

'John, when did you first hear about pike?'

'Three weeks ago from a guy who called me with a tip but no real information. He's danced around and is looking for something for himself and I'm not sure what that is yet.'

'I grew up on this river,' Headley said and Marquez got it. He understood.

He copied down the address of the impound yard and walked the slope once more with Headley and gathered a few pike samples of his own.

'What are you going to do with those?'

'Fry them in oil and have them with scrambled eggs.'

She smiled, but not much of a smile.

'I'm going to freeze them. We may need more samples later. Did you and your dad fish the Sacramento?'

'We did and it's lucky we had that. I was out

of control when I was fifteen and my dad was real smart. He knew if he couldn't get me to do anything else he could get me on the river with him, and if he could do that he could get me to talk. He talked me through some mistakes I made. I miss him a lot.'

She waved at the spilled pike.

'I'm glad he's not here to see this. He wouldn't understand someone trying to take out the salmon and trout. He wouldn't get it.'

'But you get it.'

'I don't know what I get or don't. It's like the world has turned into one big shopping mall, an open market where everything is up for grabs. Everything is for sale. To say something like a river is sacred is a joke to people. Nothing is sacred. Rivers are for drinking water and having fun, and if they grow fish great, and if they don't we'll get the fish somewhere else or grow them in factories like we do with chicken and hogs. We can probably screw that up just as well as we did with them. You know what I'm saying – when they stop being fish or anything living they'll just be product grown to eat. What are we going to do about these assholes that are behind that kid in the pickup? It wasn't his idea. He's probably all of nineteen.'

She paused then turned to him. 'You know he's going to die.'

Marquez was afraid she was right. She shook her head. 'It's overwhelming. I can't get my head around how we're going to stop something like this.'

He couldn't help her with that. He'd been

skeptical about the pike tip but wasn't anymore. He pulled his phone and after finding the hospital address said, 'I'm going to head to the hospital.'

Forty minutes later he was on the surgery floor among the anxious waiting to hear the results. At the desk the woman seated looked up and asked. 'Are you family?'

'No.'

'His brother is here.'

She pointed out a big man who looked like he was in his early thirties, so an older brother and maybe one with a different mother or father – or, on closer look, maybe a man who wasn't Enrique Jordan's brother at all. The man was quietly on his cell phone and Marquez moved out of the waiting lounge to the corridor and then to an empty corridor where he still had a good view of the carpeted opening to the Family Resource Center.

He called Captain Waller as he stood near a window in sunlight in the corridor.

'If I'm right about the guy in the waiting area, I'll need help following him when he leaves here. Right now he's waiting to hear surgery results.'

'Maybe he really is his brother.'

'He may be.'

'But you're sure he's not.'

'That's my gut feeling.'

'All right, let's talk again when you actually know something. In the meantime I'll find out who can back you up. How many pike spilled this morning?'

'I'm guessing a thousand.'

27

'That's an awful lot but it may just be some sport fishing nutcase.'

'And maybe the guy in the waiting room is his brother. Get me two SOU wardens if you can. I'll call you when I know.'

FIVE

A bloodstained surgeon and a woman that Marquez guessed was a hospital administrator came through the stainless clad doors of the surgery area. The surgeon looked tired and trailed a step behind. The administrator's face was grim but she walked with a take-charge step and continued to the reception desk in the Family Resource Center. The surgeon stopped in the hallway and checked his phone. He looked like he was ready for a smoke or a drink or both.

Marquez focused on the administrator. She leaned over the counter in front of the woman at the desk, who then turned and pointed toward the guy sitting in a corner, the brother. When he realized they were talking about him he sat up and appeared attentive and concerned. The administrator made her way to him and he rose, stood towering over her in a baggy white T-shirt and loose-fitting jeans.

Whatever she said caused his face to twist in pain and she put a hand on his back and guided him across the carpet and out toward the surgeon. The big man moving with the small well-dressed administrator made Marquez think of a tug pulling a cargo ship across San Francisco Bay, but he had that thought without any real humor and drifted back as they approached.

The surgeon crossed his arms and shifted as if preparing himself. They moved closer to the wall and the brother's back was to Marquez. Still, his deep voice was easy to hear.

'How can he be dead? Where is he? I need to see him.'

The administrator started on hospital rules and how that wasn't going to happen and the man ramped it up and got loud. Neither the surgeon nor the administrator liked that much and it drew attention from people waiting for the elevator, and everybody got a little agitated.

'I'm sorry,' the surgeon said, his voice more in command now. 'We did our best but he went into cardiac arrest. We did everything we could to try to save him.'

'Take me to him.'

The administrator stepped away and made a call and the surgeon shook his head. No doubt he knew something of how Enrique Jordan was injured and the sanctimoniousness of the big man was probably wearing thin. Either way, there was no enthusiasm for showing the brother the body, but they did finally relent and led him into the surgery area.

When that happened, Marquez rode the elevator down and walked out through the lobby and into cold air. He was in his car in the wide lot watching the doors along the white stucco face of the hospital building when the big man came out.

He was light-footed, a boxer rolling on the balls of his feet, ready for the fight, talking on his phone, gesturing with his right hand. He had passed quickly through the stages of grief and smiled and laughed at something which the person on the end of the phone had said.

Then he was off the phone and scanning the lot before getting in his car. He backed out slowly and sat idling as he made another call and was on the phone as he pulled out of the lot on to the street, accelerating hard but after less than a quarter mile pulled over to the curb and killed his lights. Nothing very subtle to that. It said he expected to be followed and he wasn't too clear about how to spot them.

Marquez talked with Waller and waited for the black Honda Civic to move again. He called the local police and gave his location and model of the Honda. He asked for help and then the big man made it easier. He came off the side of the road and back into the rightmost of three lanes on the boulevard as if coming out of a pit stop in a NASCAR race. As he approached the next green light he let it go to yellow before gunning his engine and shooting through the intersection as the light went from yellow to red.

The Honda was registered to an Emile Soliatano. It was lowered and ran on expensive chrome wheels and run-flat tires and the Fairfield Police didn't have any problem picking up on him. He went through two more lights with the same trick and just before the road reached the interstate he got pulled over and ticketed. The name matched the car registration. What Marquez drew from this was that Soliatano was inexperienced. He showed some chutzpah at the hospital, but he had no real cover and his efforts to avoid being followed were clumsy. He was probably scared.

When the two SOU wardens checked in, Marquez asked, 'Where are you guys?'

'Coming down the freeway and almost to you.'

'Go slow. He just got a ticket and turned law abiding, but he's getting on I-80 westbound right now and wherever he's going, we're going with him.'

SIX

Soliatano drove toward San Francisco. When he reached the bay he tracked down the east shore and broke left at the maze, hurtling through the bend onto 580 with his car drifting hard right. That move read as adrenalin-fueled paranoia to Marquez, but might also be a burst of action before getting off the freeway. When Soliatano dropped down the off ramp at Oakland Avenue and made the left back under the freeway, Marquez said, 'Fuck, it can't be.' He went to speaker on his cell and conferenced in both of the SOU wardens.

'For three weeks I've been talking to a climatologist named Matt Hauser who works for a firm called ENTR. He's the one who called me with the northern pike tip. Soliatano is bee-lining toward Hauser's house in Piedmont.'

31

'Who is this Hauser, again?'

That was O'Brien, the warden passing Marquez now on his left.

'ENTR is the business I'm looking at with this illegal hatchery scheme. Hauser claims an internal group at ENTR has a secret project going and has built three hatcheries in California, two in Oregon, and two more in Washington to grow northern pike. Until this truck flipped today there was no proof and Hauser is flaky. He's avoided meeting. It's all phone conversations on his terms and each one ends with something he immediately has to get to or another call coming in. You'd think the guy was a Hollywood producer.

'He does five-, ten-, and fifteen-year micro-climate projections for ENTR and told me a biologist also working for ENTR tipped him to the pike scheme. He got my cell number from a retired FBI agent I worked with in Argentina. That agent won't vouch for him and I've been digging into who he is. That's how I know where he lives.'

'What's he want?' O'Brien asked. 'Is he looking for money?'

'Probably, but he says no, it's his reputation as a scientist he's worried about and also some forty-page non-disclosure agreement he signed that leaves him vulnerable whether or not the company is engaged in something illegal. Like I said, he hasn't come across and he can never talk too long. They have an internal security group in the company and he goes on about how he's afraid of them, but if Soliatano goes to his house now then all bets are off.'

32

Marquez broke away three blocks later and was now into tree-lined streets where he could park and kill the lights as O'Brien and Liu reported Soliatano driving random blocks but looking like he was circling Hauser's house. The house was white-painted and big, with trees in front that had to be a hundred years old, and Marquez remembered an offhand and bitter comment Hauser made about his wife and the house and living in Piedmont. Marquez's phone buzzed. O'Brien.

'Heads up, he's coming your way.'

Soliatano passed Hauser's house and two blocks down turned around and came back, his headlights sweeping over Marquez's car. He pulled over but didn't get out of his car. Marquez could see him holding his phone to his ear.

'He's calling Hauser,' and Liu answered quietly, 'Yeah, I see him. He's on the phone and there's a tall guy coming out from the back.'

'Should be tall and thin, but I'm getting that from Internet photos.'

'Yeah, tall and thin, that's what I'm looking at.'

Marquez agreed as he watched the man cross the street and get in Soliatano's car. Soliatano pulled away from the curb though he didn't turn his headlights on until he was half a block away. Then they did a slow tour of Piedmont streets and, following, they gave them a lot of room. Marquez's best guess was that Hauser was calming Soliatano down and making some sort of plan to deal with the death of the driver.

Fifteen minutes later Soliatano and Hauser

returned to the house and Marquez got a better look at Hauser as he passed under a street light. He disappeared behind the same garden gate and Marquez and the SOU stayed with Soliatano who returned to the freeway and got on eastbound, probably headed to the Vacaville address on his driver's license.

But that's not where he went. When he got out of the Bay Area and into the Central Valley he took the 505 north cut-off, exited at Winters, and parked in front of a house on a suburban street that looked a lot like home from the way he got out and unlocked the front door.

'What do you want to do, Lieutenant Marquez?'

'Go home.'

'You sure?'

'Yeah, we're done here tonight.'

On the drive home Marquez's cell rang and it was Hauser.

'It's late, Matt, what's up?'

'I was just watching late local news and they're saying a pickup rolled over near the Sacramento River and the driver who was killed was carrying an invasive fish. They're quoting Fish and Game but the type of fish is unidentified. Was it pike, Lieutenant, and am I credible now?'

'We've been talking for three weeks, Matt. What have you given me?'

'Were they northern pike?'

'I don't know. You're the first person to call me about it. I'm driving back from up north. Where did this happen?'

'I didn't get that. I came into the room too late. I heard the last half of the report and I'm surprised you don't know. How come you don't? Doesn't your department communicate? They're saying this happened this morning.'

'Was it ENTR?'

'If it's northern pike it's them.'

'Let's meet tomorrow.'

'I'm not sure I can do that. I've got to check.'

'Go ahead and check, I'll stay on the phone. Who else have you talked with about this pike project?'

'My wife.'

'Anyone else?'

'No, the risks are considerable to my career. I'm looking at my schedule now. Tomorrow isn't going to work and I need some assurances first. I need protection and I don't mean from physical harm. I saw what happened to Nora Beloit who used to work at ENTR. She quit and took ENTR contacts to her new job. They sued her. They got her fired from the new job and then attacked her credibility as a scientist for two years as she tried to go back into academia. You can Google her name and see where they left it. She can't get hired anywhere now. I saw her about six months ago and she looks ten years older. I don't want to end up like that.'

'If you deliver, we'll back you up.'

'Get the head of your department to call me and put it in writing and I'll deliver enough information to find the hatcheries. Get him to call me.'

'He's going to want to know what you've done for us.'

'It's what I *will* do for you that matters.'

'You've told me there are two secret hatcheries

35

in Washington, two in Oregon, and three here, and that the ultimate goal is water reallocation. You say they're looking ten years down the road and trying to eliminate a slew of future lawsuits by introducing a fish species that'll wipe out the salmon, trout, smelt, and all the natives. Maybe if it were in a theater I might watch it for a while, but no one I work with is going to believe that without a lot more information.'

Hauser's voice hardened.

'You're not going to believe it because you can't picture it. Get your chief to call me.'

'I need a face-to-face with you first, Matt. I need proof. Let's meet tomorrow.'

'Less than five minutes ago I told you I can't.'

'Then Saturday.'

'I can't do that either.'

'Monday.'

'I'm booked all next week. Get your chief to call me.'

'All right, I'll see what I can do and thanks for all your help.'

Marquez killed the connection and switched the phone to vibrate. It was a gamble, but Hauser was a high-strung guy and manipulative and had to be nervous after today. But Hauser didn't call back during the rest of the drive home. He did call later in the night when Marquez was in bed with his wife Katherine and his phone was on a nightstand.

The phone vibrated as the call came and it was enough to wake Marquez. He looked at the screen but didn't answer it. Hauser called again a few minutes later and again after half an hour and Katherine asked sleepily, 'Who keeps doing that?'

'A source that is trying to play it two ways.'

'Why are they doing that?'

'That's what I'm trying to figure out.'

'Can it wait until morning?'

Not really, he thought and picked up the phone.

'Now what are you doing?'

'Texting him.'

'Seriously?'

She rolled away from him and Marquez typed, 'You're in or you're out.'

'I'm in.'

'Then help us.'

'I'm trying to.'

'Take the chance.'

'I want to but I could lose everything and I'm scared.'

SEVEN

When Voight called the next morning Marquez was outside with his laptop sitting in the cold at the back deck table drinking coffee and reading about Mathew Hauser. Twenty-three Google pages linked Hauser's name in some way to climate science. He was best known for efforts to refine microclimate forecasting, but he wasn't ringing warning bells about the coming changes of global warming or doing battle with deniers. Hauser had a different angle. He was selling the business community a message of adapt or perish and specializing in adaptation analysis.

A newspaper article summed up Hauser's decision to leave academia as 'a decision spurred by a lucrative offer.' Hauser called it 'a chance to apply my modeling to real-world problems.' That was the move to ENTR in 2003.

Voight was out of breath and before Marquez could ask why, he said, 'Marquez, my doctor smokes a pack a day. His car and his office smell like an ashtray and his teeth are stained yellow-brown, but he lectures me about my health. He says lose weight or plan on diabetes, so I'm walking four miles every morning. But I'm really not calling to chit-chat and this just happens to be my best chance to call you today.'

'Do you want to call back when you can breathe?'

'Fuck you.'

'I'm still coming up Tuesday, so what's up? Has something changed?'

'I want some questions answered before you get here, starting with the tie between whatever you're working on and my homicide investigation. What's going on in Vancouver and LA?'

'An animal trafficker I've been chasing hubs out of those cities. Vancouver is how he accesses his Asian market. It's also a good place to be if you're a buyer of bear gall and paws, and he is. In the south he's got a Mexican cartel that feeds South American and African animals both live or in parts. No one likes the hassle of shipping live, but as long as the money is there the cartel will move the animals along. He may

38

also have something going at Long Beach Harbor. Our problem has been finding where he operates from in the LA basin, and then tying it to him.'

'Yeah, yeah, you chase animal traffickers and it's all mystery and hard, but what does that have to do with the murders of two young women along the Klamath two years ago? I've listened to the tape a dozen times and I still don't hear the reason you flew up there and walked the river.'

'You heard the man in the car.'

'Who is he?'

'I think he's who I'm looking for with this trafficking operation.'

'Why is he calling you with the location of a murder weapon?'

'I don't know.'

'You don't know, but you flew up there.'

'Who else was going to search before they blew the dam? You weren't.'

'Why did your friend Rider engage you about this gun?'

'I don't know why.'

'You can't think of a single reason?'

'To taunt me.'

'I don't believe that's all.'

'We can talk about it Tuesday.'

'Don't hang up yet. The ballistics are a match. The gun you turned over was the gun they were shot with. I found out last night and now I need this Rider character. Do you have any kind of real name on him?'

'No.'

'You've got something I'm sure, rumor, something?'

'I'll bring what I have.'

'Okay, and one last thing and I've got to be blunt. There are questions about your involvement, and I know I'm not springing something new on you. We had a conversation when their bodies were found. You sat in my car, Marquez.'

'I did, so why are we talking about it again?'

'Questions have to be asked and I don't want you to be surprised or to walk out angry after you're here fifteen minutes. Understand?'

'Is this your idea or the sheriff's, or did you come up with it together?'

'I'm going to look at everything, so if in looking for Rider I cause you to lose some nurtured contact with a Korean selling bear paws, I honestly, truly, swear it on a Bible, don't give a shit. What happened to Terry Ellis and Sarah Steiner comes first and you should get that, but I don't know if you do. I've never understood who you are or why you're doing what you're doing.'

'You got drummed out of the DEA or you quit, I don't know which. That record is buried. When you left the DEA you vanished, and then came back and got yourself hired onto the Fish and Game undercover team, which as near as I can tell roams the state with almost no oversight. The last time we got into it with your SOU you were setting up a sting with no notice at all to anyone here at the SCSO. That was you making that call, so how can we trust you?'

'We didn't call you because the man we busted

40

was a hunting buddy of two of your deputies. If we had told the Siskiyou County Sheriff's Office I don't know if we would have gotten him.'

'Fuck you, again. You put animals ahead of people.'

'No, we just give them a chance.'

'My Portland homicide friend who picked up the gun from you, I know who he is. I know what he is. I don't know who you are. I know you were half raised in the woods and lived in a tent with a dirt floor and your mom was pretty well traveled in Humboldt County before she went off to India to find herself. I know your dad was a dope peddler and people said his mixed blood helped him make other connections. Those were your parents, not you, but yours is not a common law-enforcement story. How old were you when you and your sister got dropped at your grand-parents' doorstep?'

'You're way over the line here, Rich.'

'I know I am and I think we're all going over that line in the next week and I don't want to pretend. I did a lot of looking into you and where you came from after the murders when I didn't have any good leads. All that is going to come up, and you're right, the sheriff is involved. Best thing you can do is help me find this Rider and the woman who made the call.'

'What else can I do for you?'

'We have an opportunity here that hasn't been there – and yes, you found the gun, and thank you for that, but you didn't do it for Terry Ellis and Sarah Steiner. You did it for—'

41

'You're wrong.'

'I want everything.'

'I'm not going to hold back, but if you're looking at my files I want the same from you.'

'There is not a single investigation your department conducts that's equal to a homicide investigation, not anything close.'

Voight's role in Siskiyou County was broad. His track record was good and though they hadn't gotten on well together they really didn't have to. But this conversation was taking it somewhere new. Voight had done a strange thing coming on about his childhood and Marquez wasn't sure what to make of that. Voight's own story was a hard one, so that made it a little surprising that he came on this way.

Rich Voight was a career LAPD homicide detective who got warned not to take down a gang leader for the murder of another gang-banger. He made the arrest and a week later his ten-year-old boy disappeared. The boy was never found and connection to the gang never proved. It tore Voight apart and his career and marriage didn't last. When he moved to Siskiyou he was divorced and alone, a man with a deep hurt and a fierce anger.

'Be here at ten Tuesday morning, Marquez, or I'll come find you. Stonewall me and I'll run over you. Bring your files. See you then.'

'I'm looking forward to it.'

'Sure you are. We'll see you here.'

EIGHT

Marquez slid onto a bench across from Hauser who was alone at the table, eating a sandwich and squinting against the sunlight as he read emails on his cell phone. Up close, he had a bone-rich face, all slashes and sharp lines, an aquiline nose, long, almost effeminate eyelashes, square-framed glasses, and short dark hair cut modern and going gray fleck by fleck. He was startled to be interrupted. He looked unhappy and then covered that.

'Who are you?'

'John Marquez.'

'You can't do this. I'm not joking about ENTR security.'

'Then let's take a ride in my car and I'll bring you back. Bring your sandwich. How's the food here?'

'It's good.'

'Great. Let's go.'

In the car, which was a gray Ford sedan today and comfortable, Marquez said, 'I've been reading about ENTR and I'm not getting anywhere. Their website says they're going to remake the world, but how do they make money?'

'By turning research and information into businesses. They're very successful at that.'

'Then why seed western rivers with pike?'

'I told you it's nothing the main company is

43

backing. The project is segregated and secret.'

'But you know about it.'

'And I already told you how I know and I'm not going to say more until we have an agreement. But if you're asking more generally "why seed western rivers with northern pike?" then let me ask you this: how many salmon would be left in the Sacramento River or any of these rivers if northern pike colonized successfully?'

'Only a few.'

'And could anything be done to eradicate northern pike once they colonize?'

Marquez paused a moment. He didn't have much interest in this question and answer game. He needed the name of the ENTR biologist who had tipped Hauser to the pike plot. He stared at Hauser before continuing. 'If the pike colonized there wouldn't be anything we could do.'

'So they would become the dominant species.'

'They would.'

'And if salmon and other natives such as trout or smelt are no longer viable due to an invasive species, the fight over water diversion becomes less complicated. A number of environmental lawsuits will seem frivolous, especially in a country scrambling to cope with the changes global warming will bring. That's why they're doing this or that's the main reason. But it isn't the main company. It's a small group inside and I'm trying to identify who they are.'

He adjusted his glasses and went quiet for a moment before confessing, 'I've been paid well at ENTR, but I wish I never left the university.'

Marquez didn't go there. He moved on and so did Hauser.

'They're patient. They look ten and fifteen and sometimes twenty years out. They see a big fight over water rights coming in the west. They pay lobbyists millions a year so that as it arrives they'll have some influence with those who make policy. They identify people and establish relationships. They think on a long horizon.'

'Good for them. What's the name of the biologist who tipped you?'

Marquez remembered reading an article about a paper Hauser wrote, the text of which suggested that Hauser's microclimate models were confirming what was already feared, that the melting of the Artic ice would interrupt air circulation patterns and greatly reduce the rainfall in large areas of the United States. Droughts would become semi-permanent in large swathes of the country.

Hauser continued as if he hadn't heard the question.

'These are the opposite of climate deniers. These are people looking to get even wealthier by capitalizing on the change, and in their view if some goofball in Congress doesn't believe in science, well, all the better for them. It means they have more time with less restriction to make their own plans. They love the deniers and the conspiracists. Those are their downfield blockers. They know those guys will get swept away as the change really hits, but for the moment they're making it easier by keeping the country from acting and ENTR is getting a first mover advantage.

'I've sat around the table and seen them with tears in their eyes laughing over something that Senator—I think he's from Oklahoma, but I can't remember his name—said. But none of this stops them from donating to these same senators and congressmen. They also figure those guys actually know the truth and will roll over when it's politically correct and excuse themselves later from any responsibility to their children and grandchildren by claiming at the time no one knew whether global warming was real or not.'

'Put them aside, I'm looking for pike hatcheries. If you have information it's time, Matt. We're doing a weird little dance that's making me question where you're going with everything.'

'You're not going to intimidate me. That isn't going to happen, but I do want to stop the pike project before it's too late.'

'How many people inside ENTR would you guess know about the pike hatcheries?'

'Are you recording this?'

'No.'

'I'd guess less than five people, all of them very well compensated to keep quiet.'

'Does that include your biologist friend?'

'Lieutenant, I have to protect him. I can't just give you his name. His career is on the line the same as mine.'

'Tell me again exactly what you do.'

'I predict with some accuracy the future climate in specific areas with a focus currently on western states. ENTR is ramping up investment in water rights and want to know what they'll be dealing with climatically in ten years. They're investing in fish pens in Chile and in Thailand and Indonesia, and the questions are similar. They're growing salmon and targeting solving the pen disease problems within eight years. That's where the research at the legit hatcheries here can help out. They'll road-test virus vaccines in hatcheries here.

'I have to tell you I have wondered if ENTR is correct in looking at the coming reality with western rivers. That big die-off of salmon, thirty-two thousand or whatever it was on the Klamath some years ago, was about low water and warm water, and that's what's coming. Are you married, Lieutenant? My wife is one of my problems. She works for ENTR and she's not going to be on-board with this.'

'What does she know about the pike hatcheries?'

'Nothing.'

'Why are you bringing her up?'

'She's a lawyer for ENTR and she knows me. She knows I've got something on my mind and issues with the company. She told me last night I'd better not do anything that compromises the non-disclosure agreement, and between you and me, Lieutenant—and now you'll think I'm crazy—I came up with an algorithm to describe the process of our marriage and it wasn't pretty. We argue about everything and our conversations are dotted with code words. When she hears one of those or even the slightest vibration

47

of one, down she comes from her spider web.

'If I try to talk with her about whatever I'm working on, it's always too much information for her. She shuts me down. If I go quiet, it's my fault we don't communicate. I'm too tall and getting thin and work too much. I'm getting old faster than her. Don't ask me how she figured that out, but she's certain of it. Other complaints: I should have stayed in academia and would have made a name and be safely tenured. I know you don't want to hear about my marriage but it affects my decision to commit with you. She isn't going to like it.'

He continued on about his wife for a while and deflected questions and skipped through a variety of topics. He was bright and articulate and for all Marquez knew he had the name and number of the biologist in his cell phone. If not for last night and Soliatano's visit with Hauser, Marquez might have pushed it to the line with Hauser now. He came close then backed off. He dropped Hauser at the deli and watched him walk back to the ENTR office with sunlight on his back and San Francisco Bay a dark blue beyond him, and decided that Hauser was a cynic and working on a trade with Fish and Game. He wasn't going to quietly turn over a name and phone number of a biologist, and that wasn't a moral wrong, but it was a choice. He watched him cross the street and start down the next block, thinking *I know you're planning something. I know that and I don't have much time to figure out what it is—and we still need your help.*

48

NINE

For more than a decade Marquez ran California Fish and Game's undercover team, the Special Operations Unit or SOU, where the mission was clear: disrupt the black market flow of California wildlife and penetrate as high up the chain as possible, while at the same time projecting enough presence to make a skipper of a salmon trawler hooking an urchin bag filled with illegal abalone second-guess himself. It took luck, patience, and long hours to build the case a District Attorney's office couldn't find an excuse not to prosecute. It required teamwork and timing and knowing how to utilize momentum.

Now was different and quieter and in many ways more complex. He picked up the loose threads. He chased the lead once sure that had vanished, the investigation too slowly unfolding for the SOU to focus on, too expensive or time consuming, or the case where a key witness recanted at the last moment and disappeared into hiding. Or the black marketer who picks up on the surveillance and folds up shop temporarily. These came to Marquez.

He also worked with the Feds as a task force officer with the FBI and a deputized US Marshal. His passport breezed him through airport inspections and he was a burr to global traffickers. He often worked alone and that took a toll. He was alone this afternoon as he knocked on the door of Emile Soliatano's house. He knew now there was a wife and a dog and that Emile worked swing shift in a new factory in Sacramento where you needed the skill of an engineer to operate the robotic equipment. He knew the pay was very good there.

When Emile opened the door he blinked at the sunlight as if he'd never experienced it before and waited for Marquez to speak with an expression of curiosity and trepidation. Perhaps he hoped Marquez was a window salesman about to hand him a business card and propose measuring and pricing replacement windows. Yet it was in his eyes that he was afraid of this knock.

Marquez identified himself and slowly showed him his badge.

'I'm sorry about Enrique's death. I'm here on a follow up.'

'How did you find me?'

'You gave your cell phone number to hospital staff and they gave it to me.'

They looked at each other. Emile was a big guy. He filled the doorway. He blocked the door. Behind him a TV was on and no doubt he knew the Department of Fish and Game was very interested in talking with anybody who was a friend, associate, or family of Enrique Jordan. Local police were also canvassing.

'I don't feel much feel like talking about my brother and I've got to go to work real soon.'

'How soon?'

'Soon, and I've got to get ready. What's the big deal talking to me?'

50

'Your brother was trying to dump a thousand fingerling pike in the Sacramento River. That would have been bad news for the river.'

'I don't know anything about that.'

'Who called 911?'

'What do you mean?'

'After the accident a call got made to 911.'

'How would I know who called?'

'Haven't you wondered?'

'I hadn't even thought about it. I guess I'm not thinking clearly.'

'His phone was nowhere near him. We couldn't find it anywhere.'

'Maybe it got thrown out of the truck.'

'Yeah, maybe we should go look for it together. In fact, that's what I want to do. Let's go there together and I'd like to hear your side of things before we do anything with you.'

'What does that mean?'

'What it sounds like.'

Soliatano blinked at the sunlight again, said, 'I don't understand.'

'What if talking to me was your best chance of dealing with this?'

'What the fuck? What have I done? Is this because I said he was my brother and he's really my cousin? If it is, big fucking deal. I needed that nurse to talk to me. They're going to talk to immediate family and I wanted to know he was okay.'

'You already knew he wasn't. You were just making sure.'

Now Soliatano moved to shut the door.

'You can do that. You can close the door and

51

I can come back with a search warrant and question your wife. That's your call, Emile.'

Soliatano shut the door and Marquez walked back out to the street. He didn't turn or look back and was close to driving away when Soliatano hustled out to stop him, raising a hand, walking toward his car, signaling him to wait. Marquez lowered the passenger-side window.

'Enrique was a good friend and I'm freaking out. Like I said, I'm not thinking straight.'

'Were you with him when he picked up the coolers with the fish?'

'I don't know anything about that.'

'I think you do. Two undercover operatives and I followed you from the hospital and I know Enrique didn't make the call to 911. If we have to run a voice analysis I can get the taped call compared to your voice, or you can just talk to me.'

Marquez couldn't get a voice analysis done and didn't know anything about the 911 caller other than he was male and Soliatano was a good fit, but from Soliatano's downcast expression he knew he had hit home.

'Start with the pike.'

'I didn't know what kind they were and he didn't either. It didn't matter and I only sort of know where he goes to get them.'

'How many river trips with pike did Enrique make?'

'This was the second time. All the fish in the first drop died of a virus – or that's what they told him. He was going to have to go back there again.'

'I need you to show me where the first drop happened and where you think the hatchery is.'

'Like I said, I don't know where it is. They're super tight about only the drivers going in.'

'How many drivers?'

'Enrique and one other guy. What's so bad about these fish?'

In Soliatano's version there was the same one guy at the hatchery every time his distant cousin, Enrique Jordan, showed up which was once every two weeks, so four weeks in on a schedule that might or might not go through the winter. At the hatchery they told Enrique they would plant young fish in the rivers all winter if it was warm enough. He got a thousand dollars for each river stocking and the job came through a friend of Enrique's that Emile couldn't remember the name of.'

'But you rode with him each time?'

Emile nodded.

'What did your cousin say about the man at the hatchery?'

'The guy never talked to him. He made sure Enrique knew where he was going and never said what type of fish or anything. Enrique did training before he got hired and the job was different and then this part for cash came along after about six months. It was all super legit at first.'

'Give me a description of the man at the hatchery.'

'I never asked.'

It went like that. Marquez got close to the hatchery but never quite touched it, though Soliatano led him back into the house and showed him on his computer where he thought it was, between Chico and Sacramento but east into the foothills. The area he vaguely outlined was about a hundred square miles.

At some point it hit Marquez and he looked at Soliatano.

'You were the connection. You're the friend that got him the job.'

They went back and forth on that and when Soliatano admitted to that it still didn't feel right.

'I didn't know these guys. I just knew they were looking for a couple of drivers and my cousin drove everything.'

'How did you know they were looking for drivers?'

'I don't remember how.'

They kept talking past the time Soliatano was supposed to go to work and Soliatano came up with new numbers. Enrique was really making five grand per delivery, which was really good money. They both knew it was illegal what he was doing, but he stuck with not knowing what the fish was and Marquez believed that might be true.

'Dumping fish in a river at night with your lights off? You're trying to tell me you thought that was legit? Give me a break. What about the man you met last night? Was Matt Hauser the one who hired you?'

Soliatano adjusted to that, paused, and then reframed his story.

'Hauser hired me to ride with Enrique.'

'Ride with Enrique when he dumped fish in the river?'

'Yes.'

'How much has Hauser paid you?'

'That money is all gone, man. My wife is pregnant. We're doing the baby's room. It's spent. I can't give you the money.'

'I'm not asking for any money. I want to know how much he paid you.'

'Two thousand each drive.'

'Two thousand dollars each ride you took with Enrique?'

'Yeah, and he wanted to know about everything.'

'Did he say why?'

'No.'

'What did he give you when you drove down last night?'

'He doubled it. He gave me four grand and said four more if I didn't talk to anyone who questioned me later, so I'm giving that up.'

Marquez thought that over and said, 'Tomorrow we'll take a drive and you show me everything you know and everywhere you went with Enrique.'

Soliatano shook his head as a wave of emotion came over him and Marquez read it as real.

'I know I fucked up, but my wife is six months pregnant and I've got a good job. I can't go to jail.'

'Just keep working with me. What about Enrique, did he know Matt Hauser?'

He shook his head.

'How did you meet him?'

'Somehow he got Enrique's number and left this weird message and Enrique wanted me to listen to it. So I called him and he laid out the deal.'

'Did Enrique know Hauser was paying you?'

'No, but he wouldn't have cared. We were good friends.'

The drill was he called Hauser after each delivery and he took photos and sent those to Hauser. He pulled out his cell and showed Marquez the number and Marquez entered it in his phone.

'I'm supposed to call that number if we're going to a river with fish. When my cousin calls me I call Matt and I give him a report and send photos.'

'Let's see the photos you've sent.'

They went through those and Marquez asked, 'What about this last time? Where are the photos for that?'

'It was too dark and it was fucked up.'

Marquez got it.

'You called 911 from Enrique's phone and then left him there. Is that what happened?'

'I called 911 first.'

'Then you left.'

'I went down the road to wait to make sure they found him.'

'Did you talk to any of the first responders?'

'No, they drove past.'

'Okay, let's go back to dumping the fish in the river. He was driving the truck and you got outside to direct him.'

He nodded, emotion gathering on his face again. He felt responsible and guilty. He called 911 and did something with the phone afterward, possibly threw it in the river before he left Enrique and drove to where he could watch the first responders drive by. Or more likely he drove away and later went to the hospital. When he learned Enrique was dead he was so overwhelmed by grief that he hauled ass to the Bay Area and collected twice the usual payment from Hauser. Soliatano was more than he appeared to be. *I misread him earlier*, Marquez thought.

Perhaps he still had the phone and maybe there was a reason. Marquez asked about it again and Soliatano remained evasive.

'I don't know, man. I thought I left it with him, but maybe I didn't. I don't know where it is now.'

The 911 dispatcher thought she was talking to an injured man who kept repeating in Spanish that his arm was trapped and that was the same big guy standing across from him now. Marquez was six foot one, about the same height as Soliatano, maybe an inch or two shorter but close enough to be eye to eye as he rested a hand on Soliatano's shoulder.

'Hang in there. I'll see you early tomorrow and we'll talk as we drive. We'll get this figured out. It would be a really good thing if you remembered tonight where the phone is. You think it all through, Emile, and I'll see you in the morning.'

TEN

Before dawn the next day Marquez eased over to the curb a block down from Soliatano's house and turned his lights off. A lone streetlight shone at the far end of the block; it was dark here and he sat there with the engine idling, then turned it off and thought about what he knew and didn't. He tried to get at what he sensed and watched as lights came on in Soliatano's house and the sky whitened in the east and cold seeped into the car.

Not long after the front door opened and Soliatano came out with a dog. Here was a guy with a specialized, highly skilled job in a manufacturing facility that paid him well, who had gotten involved with illegal fish stocking to make side money. It didn't seem to mean anything to him that the pike would kill off everything else in the river or that he left Enrique Jordan trapped in the pickup. He showed some emotion yesterday but that was probably born of fear of having his life disrupted and less about feelings for Jordan.

Soliatano was about money and staying out of jail and not getting charged with anything. His claim of sending documenting photos to Hauser might be true. Those he forwarded last night to him were shots taken at night and not much as photos go, but they had the same truck and the date of the first drop last week stamped on the photo. Good chance they were real and Soliatano was documenting to earn his money. Did that mean Hauser was legitimate and building his own case?

He watched Soliatano and the little terrier turn back this direction and work their way back down. Soliatano dropped a plastic bag with the dog's poop in a garbage can and went back into the house. Marquez gave him fifteen minutes before calling.

'You're early.'

'We'll pick up coffee somewhere.'

When Soliatano got in the car Marquez asked, 'How long have you lived here?'

'About a year but it was my wife's mother's house. Stacey is six months pregnant and we're going to raise our kids here. I rent where I used to live in Vacaville.' He added as if he'd thought about it, 'It's better for a kid here.'

Then he went on: 'I talked to my brother-in-law last night. He's a lawyer. He said I shouldn't do this ride with you and that you can't charge me with anything because there aren't any witnesses.'

'How much does he know about Matt Hauser?'

'Not much.'

'Hauser could turn on you and testify against you. That's a reason to talk to me now.'

Soliatano processed that then said, 'I watch TV cop shows. I know you don't control everything, but I need to know you're not going to fuck me.'

'I'm going to take care of you like you did Enrique.'

Soliatano didn't like that but didn't respond and they drove and talked and Marquez followed his directions to where the first stocking occurred and the fish allegedly died of a virus. Then they left the highway and tracked dirt roads, drove past almond orchards and down to the river to a forgotten boat landing where Soliatano and Jordan had backed up and emptied fish into the river.

Soliatano took him through the drop, bringing the pickup truck's rear wheels all the way down to the water's edge, opening the first cooler and bailing water out of it until they could tip the rest of the cooler water and fish into the Sacramento.

'Those fish were swimming way too slow. They were already fucked up. We could tell.'

'You realized they were sick?'

'Yeah.'

'This was the first drop and there's only been one other?'

'That's right.'

The river was green and gray and lapped at rotted pilings. The ramp was in bad shape, cracked and broken and closed. When Marquez felt like he had all Soliatano was going to give him here, he turned back to the second fish stocking.

'What happened when Enrique got killed?'

'The truck slid on mud. It went sideways.'

'Why didn't you leave him the phone?'

'I wanted to have it in case I needed to call again. You know, if they didn't show up. That's why I waited down the road.'

'Okay, let's drive there and you show me where you waited.'

They drove to the second site. In daylight the small trees and broken brush and the muddy tracks from the truck looked raw. It looked like something bad had happened. A cold wind was blowing and they did the same again, Soliatano taking him through the whole thing, and then they moved down the levee road to where he had waited after calling 911.

'Did you hang up on the 911 dispatcher when she was asking for directions?'

60

'No.'

'She thinks you did.'

'That's bullshit, the connection broke.' He said that and then revealed, 'I know where the third drop was supposed to happen – and pretty soon.'

'Do you have a day?'

'No, but the fish are almost big enough. The guy at the hatchery told Enrique that. Hauser knows.'

'Knows what?'

'Knows the next batch is almost big enough.'

They drove thirty miles to the next spot and it was different in that they followed railroad tracks and drove a railroad road very clearly marked with No Trespassing signs. The tires crunched through gravel and the fall air carried the smell of creosote from the rail tracks. A little dirt cut-off road took them down into cottonwoods and they were staring at the Sacramento River again. On the way back, Marquez was frank with him.

'I'm just going to lay it on the table. I think when you left Enrique there you thought he would die and when he didn't you went to the hospital to reassure yourself he wasn't going to wake up and start talking about you.'

'You're fucking cold, man.'

'I think you hung up on the dispatcher but the first responders drew enough from your description to get there. They know the area and put it together. You knew it was over once the truck rolled and you went to collect that night so Hauser couldn't change his mind. You got the money and came home. The money was all that mattered.'

'Fuck, let me out right here.'

61

'Not yet, we've still got to get a statement from you. What did you take from Enrique's wallet when you took the phone? The first responders said it was down in the driver's footwell and it looked like someone had gone through it. There was no money.'

'He didn't carry money.'

'Not even a few bucks?'

'He carried some money in his jeans. Someone in the hospital probably stole it.'

Marquez took him to headquarters instead of the American River District Office. He interviewed Soliatano with Captain Waller sitting in. The video equipment was small and on a stand and Soliatano looked at the camera from time to time but he never complained and did another revision and refinement, telling the camera he thought that he and Enrique Jordan were stocking native fish in the river.

'I thought the guy who hired Enrique was growing fish to help the rivers but couldn't get a permit to do it so was doing it on his own.'

He stuck to his story of never having seen the hatchery and added, and this was a good touch, 'He told Enrique it was safest for the fish to introduce them into a river at night.'

He now denied having made the 911 call and maybe that was on the advice of his attorney brother-in-law who he had talked to just before the interview. Maybe the brother-in-law told him a voice analysis wouldn't be conclusive. He also denied knowing Matt Hauser or having met with him, ever communi-cated with him or received money from him. It was quite a turnaround from the truck ride and he did it all calmly as if the conversations with Marquez never happened.

He looked at Marquez and said, 'I made up the other site I took you to. When you knocked on my door yesterday morning I got scared and I was trying to give you some answers so you would go away.'

Marquez nodded as if that made complete sense.

'Anything else you'd like to tell us?'

'One thing and that's I won't need a ride home. My brother-in-law is picking me up.'

'Tell your brother-in-law we'll have some follow-up questions.'

Soliatano grinned as if Marquez had told a good joke, but said it was fine to call his cell and that he was up early every morning. Marquez called close to dawn the next morning and a recording said Soliatano's cell phone was no longer in service. When he stopped by Soliatano's house his black Honda was parked along the curb, but no one answered the door and the dog didn't bark. He knocked again and waited and walked around and looked in a window on one side of the garage then saw a neighbor come out of his house across the street.

'They left in the middle of the night,' the neighbor said. 'I hope it's not a problem with the baby being premature. My wife is worried.'

'I don't think it's the baby.'

'Are you a friend of theirs?'

'We just met but I'm hoping to see a lot more of him.'

'I see.'

Probably not, but that was okay. Marquez called Waller after he drove away.

'Soliatano's phone is disconnected and I'm just leaving his house. His wife's van is gone and he told me she wasn't driving anymore. The dog isn't barking. The shades are down and a neighbor said they left in the middle of the night.'

'It's what the neighbor said, there's a problem with the baby.'

'I checked with the local hospitals. She's not there. I think they're gone. I've got the plates and a description of her car. I'm going to ask the highway patrol to watch for it.'

'Good luck with that.'

'We can't lose track of this guy. We've got to find him.'

'So he can lie through his teeth again?'

We need him, Marquez thought. *We need him to get to Hauser.*

'Talk to you later,' he said, and hung up.

ELEVEN

That night a California Highway Patrol officer with the nickname 'Lottery Lou', having three times bought winning lottery tickets, was shopping for a new van with his wife at Hilltop Mall in Richmond. Today was the second day of a four-day Halloween sale at a dealership, and though the sales people looked weird in their costumes the prices were 'slashed' to where Lou knew they were competitive. He was ready to buy but what he couldn't do was sit around and listen to a guy dressed up as a 1920s baseball player talk about Bluetooth features and the 'capabilities' of the car.

He already knew the car was capable. He had written speeding tickets for a dozen of these vans, so he told Lisa he'd be right back. He was going around the corner to a gas station so he wouldn't have to do it later.

'You and slugger can go over how the radio works.'

'I thought we were doing this together.'

'We are.'

He drove to a Chevron station and as he did he passed a store with a van sitting alone out along the outer edge, right where the lot ended and street lights didn't quite reach. Something about it tickled at his memory though didn't quite connect. He bought gas. He drove back but not in a hurry, figuring Lisa would be haggling, though the dealerships didn't really haggle anymore and it was free money anyway. It was lottery money and all the crap about shopping for the right price was nothing more than going through the motions. She was going to get the car and get it tonight. She couldn't bear having that much money just sitting in a Wells Fargo account unspent.

He turned in and drove across the lot to the lonely green Sienna van he passed on the way to the gas station. Lottery Lou had a head for numbers. Strings of numbers and letters and license plates stuck with him. When he bought a lottery ticket he'd read the numbers to himself a couple of times and that was enough. If he heard it again he would remember, and he knew now as he studied the halfway-to-a-junkyard Sienna that these plates came over his radio earlier today.

He parked and pulled out the flashlight, looked in the windows and thought: middle-aged mixed-race male, thirty-one years old, and a white female and a dog, a terrier. There was fur on one of the back seats and he stared at the plates again and thought about Babe Ruth back at the dealership flirting with his wife as she blew up the whole negotiation by telling him they won the lottery, and decided he had time to call it in. He read off the license plate to the dispatcher and told her he was off duty, but when she confirmed the plates it made his night.

Marquez heard that story from the CHP officer who waited for him at the Hilltop Mall lot. The officer had already walked the Sienna and hadn't seen anything suspicious inside and asked Marquez before taking off if the car owner was a fugitive.

'He's not but he's got critical information and I was concerned about kidnapping.'

'What do you think now?'

'That I need to get to whoever handles the store security cameras and that's probably not until morning.'

As the officer left Marquez was scrolling his contacts for the phone number of a Richmond Police detective named Beckjoy. When he found it he left a message on his cell. A few minutes later Beckjoy called and, after listening said, 'I've got a name and a phone number for you. Are you in my cell phone, Marquez?'

'How would I know?'

'Hold on a second, let me check. Yeah, you're in here. I'll text you his number. His name is Jacobs. I don't know what his first name is but it doesn't matter. Tell him you're a fish cop and you talked to me and he can call me if he needs to. He's the type who might come down there tonight and go over the videotape with you. We had a murder out there four years ago he helped us with and I was out that way last week and saw his car when I drove by. He still works there.'

Marquez called Jacobs who listened and then said he would drive over. Then, with Marquez in a chair alongside him, they worked backwards with the videotape until they hit tape where the van wasn't there. The videotape was clear and distinct as Soliatano and the van drove into view. Emile Soliatano got out and then his wife and Jacobs said, 'Pregnant' and Marquez nodded and waited for the dog but there was no dog.

Soliatano locked the van and they started walking away and would have walked right out of view if Soliatano hadn't stopped to answer his cell phone. His wife stood close by looking uncomfortable and unhappy.

Then a black SUV pulled up and a man got out on the passenger side and reached and opened the door to the back seat. Soliatano's wife got in first and being shorter and pregnant it was awkward for her. As she slid over to make room for Emile the man who had opened the door for them glanced this way.

67

'Freeze that,' Marquez said, and Jacobs did and Marquez took a good look at the man's face and said, 'Okay, let's keep going.'

The SUV pulled away.

'Can you make me a copy of everything from when the van arrived to when they were picked up?'

'Sure, I can send you a video file.'

'Thanks.'

With enhancement they could probably get the license plate. The agency best equipped to do that was the FBI, but he knew he couldn't go there because his best guess from everything he'd just watched was that the black Tahoe was an FBI vehicle and the pair were agents. Could be another agency, but it was most likely FBI. Soliatano had called for help and the Feds came to the rescue. Was that possible and, if it was, what in the hell was going on?

TWELVE

Voight put on his coat before going out to bring Marquez back. The coat was a Men's Wearhouse number that was too big for him years ago but that fit him now, though nothing fit him this morning. He was uncomfortable with most of what they had planned. He knew he was getting ahead of himself and that was reinforced as he saw Marquez.

He shook Marquez's hand, Marquez looking

about the same—broad-shouldered, rangy, tough, but not a woodsy type and that was really about the eyes. This wasn't a uniform Fish and Game warden in a DFG vehicle driving around looking for violators. This guy was as dangerous as he was casual.

'We're going to do this in an interview room, John. Everything I do with this investigation gets taped, but don't read anything into it. You okay with that?'

'That's fine.'

'Thanks for making the trip north. You must have come up last night.'

'I drove up this morning.'

'You got an early start.'

'I did.'

Three murder files waited in the interview box, smack in the middle of the table, and Voight encouraged Marquez to open the first file. This was how he was going to roll with it, let him look through everything, a fellow law enforcement officer getting to peruse murder files, though they were not exactly complete. He had removed everything that mattered but no doubt Marquez anticipated that.

Voight explained how they were organized, his face coloring, a light sweat starting on his forehead that was probably blood pressure and expectation. He knew this needed to go just right and he had real doubts about everything he had laid out yesterday with Harknell's encouragement.

Sheriff Harknell walked into the room right on cue and was all smiles. He clapped Marquez's back and thanked him for being here. Harknell couldn't stand the Department of Fish and Game. Harknell heard they were changing their name to the Department of Fish and Wildlife soon and half an hour ago was joking about what he would call the department if he were naming it.

Harknell was proud of his part in getting Marquez here, but the stupid ass didn't realize it was really Marquez at the wheel, not him. Marquez was trading nothing. The investigation file he sent on this Rider character was a mess, initials for suspects, short notes, references to other Fish and Game investigations, something only an insider could read.

Harknell looked from Marquez to him and without warning asked, 'Did you get your walk this morning, Rich?'

'No time for it today.'

'We have to make time. It's important. Go take it right now.'

Voight was stunned.

'What are you talking about, sir? I can't go anywhere right now.'

'No, I mean it, and I'll get started with the warden. I need to get caught up on where we're at anyway and Warden Marquez needs to read and I'm sure that'll take some time.'

The way he said it insinuated that Marquez had trouble reading, but if the insult bothered Marquez at all it didn't show. Marquez looked much more curious that Harknell was sending him off on a walk and making a different statement.

Harknell pulled out a chair and sat down across from Marquez with a concerned frown, talking now as if Voight wasn't in the room, saying, 'Rich has a medical condition we're accommodating as long as he sticks with it. He's got everything you don't want—labile hypertension, pre-diabetes, and a list of other conditions he's got to take care of. We have an agreement that he's going to do that.'

Harknell turned to Voight.

'Get out of here, Rich. Go do the walk. We won't get that far while you're gone.'

'I'll do it later and it's my business, no one else's.'

'You've made it department business and you're going to walk now.'

Voight felt anger surge and the heat that came when his blood pressure jumped. He spent half the night getting ready for Marquez to look at it and didn't do it so Sheriff Hardass could sit in his chair.

'Go.'

Voight stood over his chair. He didn't sit down and the room got smaller. He had a moment of dizziness. Harknell didn't know shit about homicide investigation. Harknell's top skill was handing out paper plates at a Kiwanis pancake breakfast and leaning on donors for checks whenever he ran for re-election. He knew zero about solving a murder or getting a suspect to talk.

'Get going, Rich,' Harknell said in a stronger voice. 'The warden and I will still be here.'

The sheriff winked at Marquez.

'You and I both know Rich already stripped the files. I'm surprised there's anything left for you to read.'

Voight left the office fuming and headed out

on a walk which took him straight to his car. He drove over to the Burger King, bought coffee and then a bite to eat, a breakfast burrito, a large order of hash browns, and two sausage biscuits. This whole set-up was wrong and he knew Marquez sensed it. That's why he showed up so early.

Questioning him would run through lunch and maybe a lot longer, so it made sense to eat something now. He ate sitting in his car in the sun and then drove the route he was going to say he had walked. As he did, he turned the idea of quitting the department and suing the sheriff. Harknell was way out of bounds ordering him to go walk and it was incredible that his life had come to this, working for this pompous bastard who treated Siskiyou County as a private fiefdom. He finished the last of the coffee and biscuits and walked through the moves with Marquez one more time in his head before parking and going back in.

Marquez's stepdaughter, Maria, was key in this. She communicated on Facebook with Ellis and Steiner and somehow, he didn't know precisely how yet, the right information got passed on to Marquez. It let him build his cover and claim he was looking for a suspect the day he showed up at the town meeting and met the girls. He was supposed to be on an undercover buy but instead he was in a high-school gym with Ellis and Steiner and other people who didn't have to work for a living and could sit around and debate freeing the Klamath River by taking down dams.

Late that night the girls were attacked along a

dirt road by the Klamath River. Next day Marquez shows up after the bodies were found. They put out a 'be-on-the-lookout' call to all law enforcement for a suspect vehicle and within an hour Marquez is at the crime scene. Siskiyou County has six thousand miles of road and with something like this it takes everybody, but Marquez showing up at the scene was strange.

Voight shook the crumbs off his shirt and coat and when some of them fell on the seat between his legs he lifted himself high enough off the seat to brush a hand under and wipe it clean. That jammed the steering wheel into his gut. He didn't like the weight he had gained or the sad despair that seemed to dominate his nights and he was alone too much. He didn't like it that he didn't just tell the sheriff to go fuck himself; didn't like what he was willing to take to keep the job.

He hadn't solved the Ellis and Steiner murders or gotten anywhere on a recent homicide, three months ago when a young man was beaten, kicked and stomped to death by two men. He had good leads on that one that he hadn't gotten anywhere at all. All three had been in the bar drinking and argued and still he hadn't solved it.

Last week Harknell had asked him to take a ride with him and tell him where things were at on that one. The parents of the young man killed were people he knew. The county only had forty-four thousand people in it, but it was bigger than three US states, something the sheriff seemed to forget. It was a lot of territory to cover, though it did bother Voight that he didn't seem to have the stamina he once had or the clarity of mind.

73

He had turned into a note taker – and worse, having written something down, having both heard it or read it and written it down, he still needed to look at the notes later. That never happened when he was younger and he knew the sheriff was looking at him sideways now, thinking of making changes. A deputy, an ambitious Iraq vet who wanted his job, kissed the sheriff's ass every day.

Voight cleaned the Burger King litter out of the car and walked it over to the trash barrel before going back in. He knew he smelled like fast food, but fuck Harknell.

'What did you learn?' he asked Marquez as he pulled a chair back and sat down across from him, smiling, his mouth tight like it was being pulled open with pliers. 'Did you find the tie to your investigation?'

'No.'

'Maybe there isn't one.'

'I'm going to tell you why I'm here. The day I met Ellis and Steiner at the high school I had set up to buy from an individual whose identity I didn't know. He was supposed to meet me and do a small deal with me that would set up a bigger one, but I think he probably always knew who I was. I think this recent tip call says that might have been Rider.'

'Do you have any other evidence it was?'

'No, I've just been thinking about it.'

'No.'

'Do you have a full name or a photo of him, or any kind of likeness?'

'No.'

74

'But you're sure he exists.'

'He exists.'

'Has anyone ever questioned whether he really does exist?'

'Sure.'

'Who?'

Marquez smiled. He wasn't getting it, Voight thought.

'The captain I report to.'

'What's his name?'

He got ready to write it and Marquez watched that and said, 'Captain Waller. He oversees the SOU and I told him you'd be calling.'

'How did you know that?'

'Every question you ask is headed that way.'

'Then we'll just go there now and get to it.'

'That's fine, but before we leave this, Rider is why I'm here. I don't think you have anything to offer me or would if you did, and that goes double for you, Sheriff. I don't even have a full name on this guy calling himself Rider and it took me a long time to believe he exists because I'm like you, Rich; most of the time I have to see things to believe them. But I've heard the name too many different places and their trafficking operation is large.'

Voight let Marquez talk his wildlife going away thing and his fantastical pursuit of a ghost named Rider. It made him wonder if Marquez was delusional. He was either one hundred percent the real deal or way out there and it was good to get this on tape. Jesus Christ, the taxpayer was funding this guy.

When Marquez finished his explanation for

being here and tied it to the search for the gun, Voight made his move. He started it with a lie and though he was good at this with suspects it was still the delicate part.

'We know you questioned the same people we were talking to after the girls were attacked. It's not in the files you looked through because I took it out. I took it out along with the rest of the evidence that points toward you as a person of interest.'

Voight paused. He read Marquez's face and saw Marquez wasn't making any effort to hide what he felt. He looked disappointed and saddened though everyone in the room knew this conversation was coming and probably the real reason Marquez got an early start was he couldn't sleep.

'There was never anyone you were going to meet to do a buy. You tricked your SOU into believing it and used them for cover. The meeting didn't go down with your animal parts dealer. There was no buy and the undercover team pulled back and you went to the high school where Steiner and Ellis had been invited to sit on a panel and debate. Did you follow them when they left there? We have a witness who says you did and I've got more than that. I've been piecing things together and you can wave your arms in shock, outrage, and feigned disgust, but it won't change the facts.

'You didn't get the crime scene location from anything we put out to other law enforcement, yet you showed up at the scene within an hour of our BOLO. At some point as an investigator the facts stare you down and later you ask

76

yourself, *why didn't I see that sooner?* This is one of those times for me.'

'You're making a bad mistake, Rich.'

'Then convince me, because I see a Fish and Game officer who shows up at just the right time in an enormous county and asks to see the bodies of two young women he went out of his way to meet fourteen hours before they were killed. I've heard your explanations but you still need to convince me. I don't feel like I'm getting the whole story. Do you remember sitting in my car and talking after we looked at Ellis's body?'

'Of course.'

'She was half submerged in the water. Whoever killed her took the time to stack rocks on her chest and head to make sure she stayed under. I took you down to see her and you said it looked like a cairn, a grave marker, or that her killer may have worried that the river would rise before she was found and pull her body in. You talked like someone who had thought about it. You had a number of ideas and thoughts you wanted to communicate. You didn't mention a meeting gone bad with an animal trafficker, but you had all kinds of ideas that day about the murders. Then for a month or two after, you returned my calls. After that it got sporadic. It's all coming together, John.'

Marquez nodded as if that got through to him and Voight thought, *we're getting somewhere. He's been carrying this. It's why he went up and retrieved the gun. He can't let it rest. He's going to talk.* He softened his voice to show sympathy for the burden of guilt.

77

'Why was it so important to you to see the body, John? Why didn't you just get a long way away, fast?'

'It's the way I'm wired. It's what I said earlier. I need to see things. I told you about my step-daughter checking Facebook and finding Sarah writing about camping along the river. When Siskiyou County asked for help watching for their vehicle I called Maria and that was after your county put out a BOLO. Maria said she'd get on Facebook and see if she could learn anything there. She called me back fifteen minutes later and said based on what they had posted they probably stayed close to the river. Is this why you wanted me to come up, so you could tape this and tell me you're looking at me?'

'I am looking at you. I'm close to naming you as a person of interest if not a suspect.'

'I wouldn't do that yet. It would do me harm in the long term, and I know that's fine with the sheriff here, but it wouldn't do you any good ultimately because I'm not who you're looking for. But ask your questions, ask all of them. Go ahead.'

For two hours he asked Marquez questions and pushed him, needled him, threatened him, went and got the printed-out copy of Marquez's bullshit investigation file and Marquez walked him through the hieroglyphic notes. The notations, the abbreviations, the initials, they did tie together, but a psychopath will create an alternative reality. Still, he got the same twinge, the same questioning of himself he had earlier this morning.

'I work alone a lot,' Marquez said. 'My notes

78

are shorthand to myself and I take a lot of heat from my captain for it. He can't read them either. When you talk with Captain Waller ask him about that.'

Voight recovered his balance and pushed on. He believed Marquez was close at one point and wanted to get back there. He wanted to strike at this presumptuous fuck in the news for finding the gun, Lieutenant John Marquez, a game warden responding to a tip digging up the murder weapon just before the dam was blown and breathing new life into the murder investigation.

'I've got a timeline,' Voight said, 'and you keep popping up on it. You're like the beat cop who discovers the body of the little girl then solves the crime and gets promoted to detective.'

'And later turns out to be the killer.'

'Exactly like that. You have a penchant for being in the right place at the right time and you're in it again today, only you don't seem to realize it. If you talk to us now, everything that comes after will go better for you. Nothing is better than a voluntary confession because it says you know it was wrong and you want to make it right.'

Marquez said nothing but shifted in his chair and stared at him.

'There won't be any turning back if you do this,' Marquez said. 'The media will run with it and you'll get me suspended during the investigation and probably eased out after it's over. But I won't forget or forgive, and some whiny explanation about how the District Attorney didn't understand the evidence and you're withdrawing charges against me isn't going to cover it. I'll be in your life from then on.'

'That's very much a threat.'

'It is and I'm putting you on notice: you don't get to wreck my life and walk away. You know I've been trying to help. I went to Condit Dam because it was clear no one else was going to search. You sure as hell weren't. I called you four or five times and didn't get a call back. I called the FBI—'

'We know all this and I've looked at everything and I'm offering you a chance to come forward.'

Marquez turned to the sheriff.

'You've got the run-off, the special election next Tuesday; I know what you want.'

He turned back to Voight.

'Take what you have to your District Attorney before you do this. I'm leaving now.'

Voight watched Marquez stand and said, 'Sit down, you're not leaving. I'll get deputies if I have to.'

Marquez sat as Voight met with the sheriff. They conferenced in with the district attorney but she didn't have the balls it took. The DA sounded like Marquez and still Voight kept at it. He heard the pleading weakness in his own voice.

'Let me put him in a cell and we'll get a confession. Let me charge him and hold him.'

The DA spoke first. She said, 'Sheriff, I'm hanging up, and from what I've heard in the last hour, there's no case.' After a pause and perhaps to be generous she added, 'Yet.'

Voight heard her phone click and the line went

dead. Harknell reached and ended the call on his end. He looked at Voight. 'Release him.'

'You do it.'

'All right, I will.'

Voight felt everything hanging in the balance. He felt rage and betrayal and a wild courage to not let this happen to him anymore. He went back to his desk. The sheriff walked out with Marquez and he watched the videotape of the interview and after watching left the SCSO. He didn't know where to go now. He felt despair and the awareness he was someone he had never been before.

THIRTEEN

Sheriff Harknell put his hands on his hips and looked as if he had swallowed something that was close to making him vomit.

'No hard feelings, Warden, and you're free to leave for now. Who knows? Someday pigs might fly and we might owe you an apology.'

'Where's Voight?'

'He wanted to charge you or at the least let the media know we've got someone we're looking at. I'm more cautious. But don't get the idea this is over.'

'Then you and I need to talk some more.'

'If you want to do that, get in the car with me. I've got to run out to a ranch near Weed. Round trip will take an hour and a half. Come on, let's do it and we'll talk on the drive. Maybe Rich just made a series of mistakes and you can set me straight. And if we run out of things to say about the investigation we can talk about water rights. Everyone in your department seems to be an authority on that and I'm still learning.'

From the flat look in the sheriff's eyes, Marquez knew Harknell only saw today as a delayed arrest. He weighed that and then got in Harknell's SUV. Five miles out of Yreka, Harknell laid it bare.

'The district attorney is uncomfortable with Rich's conclusions. Conjecture was the word she used.'

'That's the right word.'

'Rich argued hard with her and he's got more on you than you know. He was offering you an opportunity earlier and you didn't take it. That's a mistake you could still reverse.'

'That you're doing this, Sheriff, I can understand, but not Voight, not coming from his homicide background.'

'You know, if you weren't a law enforcement officer you would have found your life turned upside down today. And I'll tell you another thing, the district attorney doesn't make decisions for my department. I make them. I made the decision to cut you loose, but it's temporary. The way I see it, Rich just has more work to do before we go again. He got angry but he'll get past that and continue his investigation and it won't be long before we come for you.'

'Investigation is the wrong word, Harknell. He'll need to fabricate something and even with your help that won't be easy.'

Harknell's neck tightened and an artery along the side of his forehead stood out as it pulsed.

'It's hard to build a case out of nothing even if you're wearing sheriff's boots. I believe Voight is sure he's on to something with me, but he's the type that turns things over and over in his head. He'll keep thinking and that's a problem for you. From here I think it'll be harder for you to control Voight even if you threaten to move him into a patrol car and a graveyard shift. You humiliated him today, not once but twice, and I can tell you from experience he takes things personally.'

'Handcuffing and charging you will cheer him up.'

'That'll never happen.'

'If it doesn't I don't want to see your face in this county ever again and if charges are brought I'll be there when you're arrested, and I'll be there arguing for the death penalty after a jury convicts you.'

Marquez was close to really getting into it with Harknell, yet it made no sense to. He regretted getting in the car and turned back to the windshield and the road ahead. When they got out to the ranch Harknell told him to stay in the car and Marquez got out and called the local warden he had talked to earlier today.

'Tom, I'm outside of Weed, are you anywhere close?'

'I'm way north of you.'

'Then I'll catch you next time I come through.'

The sheriff came striding back and he and the rancher argued and Marquez guessed Harknell got some of the anger out of his system. He and Voight must have been wound up and confident to try what they did today. He wouldn't have said a word to Harknell on the ride back but Harknell picked up the conversation again.

'I'll call your chief this afternoon and let him know we're looking at one of his wardens as a possible murder suspect.'

'Do it.'

He smiled at Marquez and adjusted his sunglasses.

'I'm telling you as a courtesy and I'll also tell him what I've told you, that I don't want to see you in Siskiyou County again. Of course, your department will make that decision, but I'll make clear what I've said to you. Anytime we find you here we'll bring you in and question you. In my eyes you're a suspect in two brutal murders.'

'And what will you do when you find out that you and Voight are wrong?'

'Apologize, but tell my deputies to keep an eye out for you and harass you in any way they can.'

'And what if the voters decide they're not going to finance your political ambitions and let you use the sheriff's office as a stepping stone to running for Congress?'

'I won't dignify that with an answer.'

The sheriff put his blinker on, exited into Yreka, and said, 'Your vehicle was searched while we were gone. I'll take you to the yard. If there's any damage bill us.'

'You are the guy I thought you were.'

'I am tougher than you, Marquez.'

'Keep telling yourself that.'

84

When he got his car back Marquez drove to a tire and alignment shop he remembered seeing on Fairlane Road. He described a squeak in the right front wheel that was driving him crazy and offered fifty dollars if they would put the car up on a rack and try to find it. They took him up on that and as they played with the wheel he found the GPS device he was looking for. It was held on with a magnet and clip ties. He glanced at the tire shop owner and then used a pen knife to cut the ties and pry the tracker free.

When the owner didn't find the squeak he tried to give Marquez his money back and Marquez said, 'No, keep it.'

GPS devices weren't cheap and Siskiyou County didn't have money to throw around, and though the temptation was to destroy it Marquez backtracked to where he'd seen a FedEx store. He packaged it, scrolled through his phone and found the lawyer's address he was looking for and asked at the counter what time the pickup was. The kid behind the counter pointed at a FedEx truck that had just pulled up. He paid, watched it loaded onto the truck and then called the Oakland lawyer.

'Danny, it's John Marquez, do you still owe me a favor?'

'I owe you something.'

'You'll like this. I just FedExed you a tracking device the Siskiyou County sheriff put on my car. He's way over the line doing that but I want them to get the tracker back. Just get something in return first.'

'I've dealt with him.'

'I know you have. That's why I'm sending it to you.'

Marquez stayed close to the FedEx truck, following it onto I-5 and south a few miles before taking the next off ramp. Then he drove north on his way to the Klamath River cut-off and a meeting with owners of a boutique hotel in Crescent City who thought they might have what he was looking for.

FOURTEEN

The Methuselah Tavern was a two-story building four blocks off the Redwood Highway in Crescent City. It wasn't hard to find at night; in fact, it was easy. It was the only business on the block with lights on. Rain slanting in off the ocean was caught by a white neon sign. The town's population was 7,643 if you counted the inmates of Pelican Bay Prison and smaller if you didn't, but it looked like they did okay at the Methuselah.

Marquez counted eleven people eating dinner and it was pleasant and warm inside. Logs burned in a fireplace in the dining area and the bar had windows that looked out and in daylight probably caught a glimpse of the ocean.

The concept was a modern tavern with a clean stocked bar and a restaurant serving organic food with a seasonal menu. On the second floor were a handful of rooms if you wanted to stay. He read a restaurant review framed and hanging on a wall near the bar restroom and then met the owners, a married couple named Geoff and Lila Philbrick, Geoff in black jeans and a sweater greeting guests and Lila, his wife, and the one who had called, was working in the kitchen.

Geoff introduced him to Lila who wiped her hands on her apron before shaking his hand. Her face was worn, her eyes friendly. Geoff was a harder read. His dark hair was combed back and he sported a thin mustache and goatee that made him look like a descendant of a Spanish conquistador who had shipwrecked along the coast of California hundreds of years ago. In truth he was from New York City and Lila from up on the Hudson. It was money that she inherited which rebuilt the former hardware store in 2001. Marquez learned this from Geoff after they took a table and waited for Lila to join them.

'We've got a room if you want to stay with us tonight.'

'I may take you up on that, but I'm really here to talk with you and Lila and learn what I can about this former bartender and his girlfriend.'

'I still can't figure out how you got our name.'

'I got it from a law enforcement friend who retired up here and wants me to keep his name out of the conversation. He told me about two people and I called and I guess Lila got my message.'

'I didn't and she never mentioned it to me. Does your friend eat here?'

'I don't know where he eats.'

'Is he in law enforcement?'

'He is.'

Geoff kept glancing toward the kitchen and his wife as if he was unable to say anything more about the possible lead until she got here.

'Are you hungry, Lieutenant?'

'I am.'

'We bought a king salmon off one of the fishing boats this morning.'

'I'll have that.'

'Roasted potatoes or rice pilaf?'

'Potatoes.'

'Something to drink?'

'A beer. Something local.'

As Philbrick left to put the order in Marquez leaned back against the wall. He listened as gusts drove rain against the windows and thought about Voight's almost electric anticipation of taking him down and the confidence of the sheriff that he could keep him out of the county. He took in the owner here again as Geoff returned with a beer and a story about the local microbrewery where it was made. He drank as Philbrick recounted buying this place and almost going broke their first year. That was the year Jim Colson was hired along with Lisa Sorzak.

'That's the name of the bartender and the waitress that worked here?'

'That's his name but Lisa doesn't go by that name anymore. I don't know the new one is but Lila does. Lila keeps track of her.'

'Why?'

'Because she's that way.'

This was starting to feel odd but the beer tasted good and he listened as Geoff drifted back to how they started the tavern It was clear that he and Lila were looking for more traffic, but would they ever see that this high on the north coast in this rugged country? It was a journey just to get here.

'What were you before you got into the tavern business?'

'A musician and Lila trained as a chef. What were you told about us?'

'Nothing about you and Lila, other than you've got a great place here and that if somebody worked for you, you'd probably remember them.'

That last was something Marquez tagged on, but Philbrick was good with it. He nodded. He was still nervous about whatever the connection was and asked more. All Marquez could tell him was that he was reaching out to every contact and had been for a while as he tried to find a man he believed once lived in the area.

'If he doesn't live here anymore, he may still come through here. I only know the one-word name he uses, and there's nothing that says he's the bartender that used to work for you. I'm chasing every lead I get.'

'Let me go see what's taking Lila so long. What's the name you know him by?'

'Let me hear what Lila has to say first. He may have had a girlfriend who was seven or eight years younger. Does Lisa Sorzak fit that description?'

Geoff frowned and stood up. Marquez watched him stop at the fireplace and add a piece of wood before continuing back to the bar and the kitchen. He took another sip of beer and allowed himself to hope. Then his thoughts drifted back to Voight and his own surprise and shock. He pushed that aside as Lila and Geoff walked toward him. Lila slid into a chair close to him. She smelled like grilled pork.

'We had a bartender,' she said, 'who worked three and four days a week for the first couple of years we were open—'

'Was that Jim Colson?'

'So Geoff already told you.'

'He told me you hired a Jim Colson and a Lisa Sorzak when you were getting started.'

Marquez caught Lila's glance at her husband and then she started in on Colson.

'He was secretive but hard working and people liked him as a bartender because he let them talk and never talked about himself. Sorzak was dishonest and cunning and used people in every way she could. She had Colson wrapped around her finger.'

Geoff reacted like he had just sat on something sharp. 'Lila, it's been ten years, and you're making her sound terrible. Come on, they were both fine and we were inexperienced. Jim was fine. He was a good guy. Everyone liked him but we couldn't employ him full time.'

Lila turned on him and said, 'I can't believe you just said she was fine.'

She shook her head and looked like she was getting ready to leave.

'Was his last named spelled C-O-L-S-O-N?' Marquez asked Lila, but it was Geoff who answered.

'That's right, or I think it is. I'll check. He

liked to be called James not Jim. He was James with everyone and she changed her name. Lila, didn't you tell me she changed her name?'

'Lisa was a bitch,' Lila said, and Geoff repeated, 'James was fine. He was a good guy.'

'He must have filled out an application and I'm interested in her too if they were close.'

Lila stared at her husband and then nodded at Marquez.

'I'll make you a copy. I keep the records. In fact, I'll go find it now and if I don't give it to you tonight I will in the morning. I understand you're staying with us. I know you're leaving early but I'm up early as well.'

Marquez thought a moment and said, 'I will stay the night.'

'I'll give you a copy of their employment applications and—'

Geoff cut her off. 'We're not allowed to do that.'

'Well, we're going to this time and if anyone asks you can tell them *I* gave them to you, not Geoff. Colson had this way of writing in very neat block letters. I used to think he had trained as an architect or something, but he told me once it was from writing reports though he would never tell me what kind of reports, which is weird to me but fine with my husband. He never listed any former addresses on his application and put down a Crescent City motel as his current address.'

Geoff scoffed. 'You don't remember that.'

'I remember even more about her.' She stared at her husband. 'Not as much as you, of course.'

Geoff shook his head, said softly, 'The lieutenant isn't here about her.'

She ignored him and continued with Marquez.

'He listed other bars he had worked at on the application and when I called he had worked at one of them and they were fine with him except that he told them he was moving to Miami and had a job waiting. That's like a million miles from here, right? But he had some explanation for that. He also worked in Seattle at a place called Tock's and I left messages but no one ever called back. The other bar was in Phoenix and had burned down and was closed and he claimed he didn't know that. I never got a single reference, but Geoff had a good feeling, especially about her, so we hired them. We were pretty naive in those days.'

Geoff was about to repeat that Jim Colson was a good guy, but she held up her hand and stopped him.

'Where did Colson say he was from?'

'Never said and joked that he was from everywhere but it always sounded to me like Texas. I had a friend from the Texas/Arkansas border and Colson had a little bit of that but less accent. But he did have a California driver's license. I always thought he came from somewhere in the south, not Georgia or Alabama, not that kind of slow talking, but from somewhere down there.'

'Do you have any photos of either of them?'

'We took a lot of photos in the months right after we opened. I'm sure he's in several but I'd have to go through them.'

She stared hard at Geoff.

'Those boxes are in the closet in the office. Why don't you get them down and I'll go through them later? I've got to get back to the kitchen now.'

There was an awkward moment after that where Geoff wasn't sure whether he was going to stay or follow his wife and get the boxes. He decided to do that and left Marquez with his beer. When he returned he brought Marquez's dinner and sat and talked as he ate. Then he went to get the boxes out of the closet, adding before he left: 'James Colson was a good guy and maybe he didn't talk about his past because there wasn't that much there for him.'

'What about Lisa Sorzak?'

Geoff didn't answer. An hour later Marquez had Jim Colson's employment application and a photo of Colson leaning over the bar to talk with a young woman who looked like she was in her mid-twenties.

Geoff smiled as he handed Marquez the photo. 'Here they are, though I doubt James is who you're looking for. No matter what Lila says he was a good guy. If there's anything more I'll get it to you in the morning.'

'I'm leaving early. If I can get it tonight that would be better.'

'I'll look and if there's anything I'll slide it under your door late tonight or give it to you in the morning. I'll see you then for sure.'

But he didn't and Marquez left in the morning with the photo and the copies of the employment applications. He placed the photo on the passenger seat and had time to look at it as he drove up the river canyon. He would remember both faces.

FIFTEEN

In 2007 when California Fish and Game attempted to eradicate the northern pike colonies in Plumas County's Lake Davis, Marquez was still head of the Special Operations Unit. He was in Portola after a judge gave the go-ahead to dump powdered rotenone and trichloroethylene into the lake. On a fall morning, despite emotional candlelight vigils in the days before and protestors chained to buoys, it got done.

The risk of northern pike escaping was just too great. If enough escaped into the Feather River the whole Sacramento River system was open to a predator capable of eradicating all of the native keystone species. And it was hard to downplay northern pike. One study Marquez read estimated that the number of duck eaten yearly by northern pike in Michigan was a million and a half.

They were a fighting fish and quick on bait or anything that moved. Once hooked, they fought hard and Marquez believed that over drinks or over several drinks a couple of sport fishermen hatched the idea of starting a colony in a California lake.

Maybe they envisioned a protected reserve where they could battle a two-foot pike on the line. Maybe they didn't think about the possible consequences or maybe they thought it would all work out fine eventually and the pike would coexist with salmon and trout. Or more likely they didn't worry about the consequences, and either way, it didn't start with Lake Davis. It started in 1988 at Frenchman Reservoir when pike were discovered and nothing done about them for three years. In that time as debate and bureaucracy slowed a decision on what to do, a couple of fishing buddies probably caught and moved enough to jump-start the Lake Davis colony.

That was the way Marquez guessed it happened. When he heard any pike story in those days he wrote the date, time, and place in the green log book that traveled with him in the years he was patrol lieutenant of the SOU. He went back through those log books after the first call from Hauser three weeks ago and retrieved phone numbers and the names of fishermen he had enlisted then and phoned now as he left Siskiyou County and drove south. One of those fishermen, Tony Galruda, picked up on the second ring.

'Tony, it's John Marquez.'

'Hey, where you been? I see these other wardens but I don't ever see you anymore.'

'I'm still around. I'm just harder to find. Remember that pike you claimed you caught in the delta?'

'I did catch one. I took a picture and sent it to you.'

'You could have taken that anywhere.'

Galruda laughed but knew why he was calling. He'd heard. Anyone who fished the Sacramento had heard and Marquez was asking for help,

95

asking him to call people, post on the boards, network. Talk to all of his fishing buddies.

'So it's real.'

'Very real; we're looking for three hidden hatcheries and they could be anywhere. They could be in a warehouse or even the backyard of a secluded house. They could be in Oakland in an industrial building or out on a leased farm or even in a rental house with plastic tanks in the bedrooms.'

'I need your help getting the word out.'

'Yeah, okay, I'll get on the phone. Talking is all I'm good for now anyway.'

Galruda was a retired welder, a widower who cut into his loneliness by fishing as much as he could. He knew all of the side roads and the hidden campsites. He knew the American, Feather, Sacramento, and the Mokelumne rivers as well as countless lakes. He towed an old skiff on a rickety trailer that jumped with every pothole and he carried more gear than a survivalist.

'I'm looking for anything unusual.'

'Like what?'

'Like a story of someone buying two hundred pounds of fish pellets or scouting out a section of river where you don't usually see people. Call me with anything you hear about that seems odd to you.'

Next Marquez called an angler who had once reported pike at Lake Oroville and another at Lake Almanor. He worked the list for an hour and a half and was charging his cell when Captain Waller called and, typical Waller, there was no hello, no greeting, nothing. Someone once asked

96

about that in an SOU meeting and Waller's answer was, 'When your screen lights up with my phone number consider that me saying hello.'

'What's going on in Siskiyou? Why are they looking at you so closely, John?'

'I don't really know yet. Voight and I have a bad history but that doesn't cover it. He's good at what he does yet he's talked himself into me as a suspect.'

'Well, you need to come in. We need to talk. The chief is asking.'

'What have you heard?'

'That there's too much coincidence. Also, a reporter has called and asked for information on you. Do you have a problem with the sheriff as well as Voight?'

'I do now. I never had much contact with him before this but he's right in there in Voight's investigation. I took a ride with him and he told me no matter how the investigation goes I'd better not to show my face in Siskiyou County, said he'd have his guys watch for me.' Marquez paused and added, 'For about twenty minutes yesterday Voight was looking for a confession.'

'Based on what?'

'I'll go through it with you when I come in.'

'Make that tomorrow.'

Marquez drew a slow breath. It felt as if he was being asked to come in and prove himself.

'Voight tried to bluff me into a confession and held up going any farther because he doesn't have any hard evidence. Then Harknell asked me to take a ride with him. While we were out a GPS tracker got tagged onto my car. I think they've got a source talking to them and that person fed them some story that convinced them I'm their guy.'

If Waller heard that he gave no sign.

'Where were you last night?'

'In Crescent City chasing a lead on Rider.'

'Get anything?'

'Maybe.'

'That's a long drive for a maybe.'

'It wouldn't be the first time.'

Now Waller went quiet, and Waller had no problem with long silences on a phone. He was a bright guy and not easy to fool. He could end up chief someday. He had what it took. After what must have been thirty seconds of silence, Marquez heard him clear his throat.

'You broadsided me with this.'

'Yeah, you're right, I've known about it. But I didn't know Voight and the sheriff were this serious, and I didn't see Voight ever focusing on me. I'm floored by it. I can't get my head around it.'

Waller was quiet again, then he punched through, he got it.

'Rider and the woman got you to the White Salmon. Is it possible Rider is feeding information to the sheriff or Voight? Is that what you're wondering?'

'It is.'

There was another long silence as Waller thought about that then asked, 'How good is Voight?'

'He's good but the sheriff is on him and Voight needs a win.'

'Let's say it really is this Rider pushing them. If that's true he's not trying to avoid you. He's coming after you and us. Where are you headed tonight?'

'To the Sacramento safehouse.'

'How far away are you?'

'Two hours.'

'I'll see you there and we'll go somewhere and talk.'

SIXTEEN

Late that night Marquez sat on lawn furniture in the chill air of the backyard at the safehouse talking on his cell with Katherine. Undercover work and the policies of secrecy surrounding can betray a marriage, and for years he avoided talking about ongoing SOU investigations with her. He obeyed department policy and let her live with uncertainty, long silences, the empty nights and weeks when he was gone. It all took its toll.

Then, as he resigned as patrol lieutenant heading the SOU and was no longer responsible for the team and moving into a sometimes more dangerous role, something snapped in him and he left the department rules in a desk drawer and wrote his own. He and Katherine had each other. That's what they had. He told Katherine now as best he could how it felt.

'I feel shock, surprise, anger, everything, Kath.

I never saw it coming and now I've got to start pushing back.'

In the California Department of Fish and Game Marquez was legendary for taking the battle to the enemy. That was long his style and maybe that would never change, but working alone as he often did now he was more careful how he picked his battles. Katherine didn't know Voight but she did know him and he walked her through what he saw happening next.

'It's going to get rough. Voight will come after Maria.'

'How can he do that?'

'She was a friend of both Terry Ellis and Sarah Steiner.'

'So were a lot of people.'

'Maria is how I learned about them and Voight knows Maria is the tie between me and Terry and Sarah. He's known that for a while and I think he's got some new theory about it. He'll want to question Maria again.'

'How do you know that?'

'From the questions they asked me.'

'She can say no.'

'She can but he won't quit. He'll make the case that she can help him solve the murders of her friends.'

'He'll spin anything she says. You shouldn't help him do that.'

'I can't stop him from questioning Maria and sooner or later he has to talk with her.'

'But she doesn't have to talk to him.'

'Voight took it to the edge when we met. To me that says he believes he has information I don't know about. He and the sheriff got as far as trying to get me to confess. They held me for hours and got the district attorney involved. She is why they backed off. Harknell followed up with a call to the chief and to Captain Waller. He knows naming me as a suspect could end my career. At a minimum I'd be off until it was resolved.'

'Is this investigator Voight doing this because of bad blood between you?'

'I don't think so. The sheriff can't stand Fish and Game and maybe he'd push it farther without evidence but I don't think Voight will. That's why I think he's trying to verify something he got from a tip or someone who came forward.'

'Call Maria and let her know what's coming.'

'I'll call her now.'

Maria's voice was bright, light-hearted, and teasing as she asked, 'Dad, what's up?'

He told her and she was quiet then indignant and asked for Voight's phone number, insistent that she was going to set him straight.

'Here's his phone number but I would let him call you first.'

'I'm going to deal with this, Dad.'

Early the next morning Marquez switched vehicles again and left Sacramento driving north on 99 thinking about his conversation with Waller last night. Waller's view was thoughtful and unemotionally frank. If Marquez was named a person of interest the media would circulate his photo and his viability as an undercover operative would end, or in a best case be compromised enough to bring him into the office and find a new role.

That was a place they both knew he would never go, so the assessment was stark and in truth it was worse than Waller said. If Voight didn't solve the murders yet named him as a person of interest, then until he did solve them Marquez's name would hang like a question mark. He would become the guy the police were sure did the killings but didn't have enough evidence to arrest.

Among the law enforcement across the country there was some small fraction of cops who were killers. Inside that tiny fraction were a few who killed and then taunted the detectives by insinuating themselves into an investigation. That was the implication here and it was hard to deal with and not dwell on. It made it hard to concentrate on what he needed to do today.

He drove north of Sacramento and into the area where Emile Soliatano claimed the illegal hatchery was. It was also the location of a legitimate hatchery that ENTR built as part of their project to restore native species. That's where Marquez was headed. As Hauser had pointed out, the Department of Fish and Game was among ENTR's partners. The hatchery manager was waiting for him to arrive and he was close now, eleven miles out.

He took the cut-off and was looking at the foothills of the Sierras, the foothills in hazy light this morning and the Sierras beyond hidden by clouds. When he made the next turn he was within four miles of the hatchery that ENTR ran as a non-profit research station and that, according to Hauser, gave cover to the pike project.

Twenty minutes later he was through a painted metal swing gate and driving a narrow paved road through pasture land brown with the fall. The ENTR website described it as a former sheep ranch purchased in a bank sale and given a new life.

The manager was a biologist named Reid, an easy-going guy glad for the break in his routine and oblivious to the cold wind, wearing a worn camouflage coat over a gray T-shirt. His jeans were stained and he smelled a lot like the fish he was raising.

'Where do you want to start? I don't do many tours.'

'Anywhere you want to; I'd like to know why ENTR chose this spot and what you look for in a hatchery location.'

'Did you look at the website?'

'I did.'

'So you know we have three in California and two in Oregon and Washington. We're going to do a third in Washington, and one in both Idaho and Nevada. They want to do even more but I don't know much about the plans, I'm just a farmer growing fish. Just a minute,' he said, and looked surprised as he answered his phone.

Marquez overhead, 'Yeah, he's here now,' and a surprised, 'What? You're here. Okay, sure, we'll wait.'

'This is different,' he said as he hung up. 'That was someone who is part of internal security for the company. She's at the gate and coming in now. She wants to walk with us. Do you mind telling me what's going on here? I've worked for the company eight years and have never met anyone from internal security.'

They both watched the car drive up and Barbara Jones get out. She was a striking woman, some mix of races, mid thirties, and intending to take charge of this tour. She shook his hand, asked for a card, patted Reid on the back, asking, 'How's the fishing?'

She turned to Marquez.

'Is this your territory? I didn't see your name with any territory on the Fish and Game website. In fact, I couldn't find your name anywhere. Would you mind showing me some ID?'

He did and she apologized and said the company was skittish after the pike incident on the Sacramento River.

'It's not getting much media coverage but we understand the significance of it, Lieutenant, and we know the fish were raised somewhere. Is that why you're here?'

'Indirectly. I'm a lieutenant specialist attached to the Special Operations Unit, which is our undercover unit.'

'And probably why I couldn't find your name.'

'As you guessed, we're trying to figure out where the pike fingerlings came from. I haven't worked around hatcheries and this one is close enough to headquarters that I thought I'd come take a look and talk to someone who knows how to grow fish.'

'You've got plenty of people in your department who can do that. Your Fisheries Branch is on S Street. You could walk there from your headquarters and Stafford Lehr is there. Who in the state knows more than him?'

'I left Sacramento early before that office opened and I'm headed north so this seemed like a good idea. Where did you drive from? You've got an earpiece in your right ear, you look tech savvy. Why didn't you call our headquarters and tell them you're looking for me? I would have called you and saved you a drive.'

'I appreciate that.'

'I can see that.'

He and Jones looked at each other; she smiled and Marquez said, 'I'm not investigating, I'm touring. I'm here to learn.'

'I'll walk with you both. I could use a tour too.'

As they did, she talked about the broader goals of ENTR and the modern design of the facility with its museum and interactive displays to teach visitors about the California river ecosystems and the keystone fish raised here. An arched roof design with open-air sides and a fiberglass roof let light in to the pools. Reid pointed out brood stock, explained the hatchery and nursery systems, how the fish were fed, the live food supply and water recycling system that cleansed the water.

'We fertilize the fields and lease twenty acres to a local farmer who grows vegetables.'

There was a solar array and storage batteries that went with it and Reid got enthused explaining that the buildings were almost fully automated and that the company has invested heavily in solar storage batteries. Jones stood to the side and texted as Reid talked.

'The price of batteries is coming down and we're at the front end of that,' he said. 'We're also funding the development of an inverter that will finally make it affordable to be off-grid.'

Jones reached and touched Reid's arm; impatience showed.

'The lieutenant can get this off the website. He doesn't need us for that. He's looking for any evidence that we could have taken part in what happened. Isn't that right, Lieutenant?'

'It's pretty much what I said earlier.'

'Sure, and I heard there were at least a thousand pike fry and that's scary to us too. That would make this facility with its modern solar array and all its gadgets a waste of time and Mr Reid here would be looking for a new job or maybe we would help stock lakes where the pike hadn't got to yet. We have a lot at stake too, Lieutenant. Our reputation is our capital. Without our reputation, there would be no investment money, so we're on hyper alert. What else can you tell me about Fish and Game's investigation?'

'That it just got started.'

'Are you part of it?'

'Everyone in the department is and plenty of them know a lot more about hatcheries than me.'

'So they don't need to come out here and tour.'

'I suppose not—and like you said earlier, there's also ENTR's website. It's stunning by the way, quite a website.'

She laughed. She smiled and gestured at the fish grow-out tanks.

'Some of this is funded with federal money.

DOE is interested in energy efficient aquaculture. I'll send you a link.'

'Please do.'

She turned to Reid. 'The lieutenant and I need to talk privately now.'

That was fine with Reid. His early enthusiasm had waned. Marquez shook his hand, thanked him, and watched him walk away.

'I'm going to be very upfront and honest with you, Lieutenant. I believe we're both looking for the same result, but let me tell you where I'm coming from. The unit I work in spends seventy percent of its time keeping our information secure from cyber theft and prying competitors. The other thirty percent goes to damage control and sometimes that's an employee or a contractor working for us.'

'How many of you are there in the unit?'

'Five and it's nowhere near enough. We need more techs sitting in front of computers,' Jones said.

'That's not you.'

'Right, that's not me. I'm like you. I'm out investigating. I do my homework and try to go and figure out what's happening or what's happened. I know you ran the Special Operations Unit for a decade and still work closely with them and that you're not here to learn how fish grow. I'm guessing you already know how they grow. I'm aware that one of our former contractors who is now an employee has contacted Fish and Game allegedly with information that ENTR is engaged in something illicit, something having to do with seeding rivers with invasive species.'

'When did you become aware of that?'

'That's a smart question to ask but I don't have the answer this morning. Let me check into that for you and let me bring you up to speed on Matt Hauser. The first thing you need to know is he thinks that without his help global warming wouldn't have been discovered. In some ways that's all you need to know, but I'm told his analysis of future microclimate trend-lines is brilliant work and so the company has put up with his ego until now.'

'What's changed?'

'Well, for one thing we know he embezzled eight point two million dollars and I won't go into the mechanics of how he was able to do that, but let's just say he was overseeing three research projects and had the authority to move money. The missing money was discovered right away but by then it was bouncing around the world in smaller amounts. Basically, he transferred it offshore three and a half weeks ago and then started moving it around. That's FBI territory but Hauser has been one of our key guys and the publicity would spook investors, so we're trying to get it back quietly first. Has he mentioned any of this to you?'

Marquez held Jones' gaze and didn't answer.

'We know he has called you. We know when he first called you. He may be a brilliant scientist but he's lousy at covering his tracks.'

'Does that mean you know where the money is?'

'Not yet, but we're getting there. All communications are recorded and stored and employees sign a significant non-disclosure agreement. It's not the type of agreement you want to fuck with. If you have privacy issues, you go work somewhere else.'

'So cut to the chase.'

'We think his call to Fish and Game was to try to use you as he negotiates a severance package.'

'A what?'

'He stole money and wants to hold the company's reputation hostage as he negotiates keeping part of it. There's more to it that I can't go into right now that involves his pride and an affair and his humiliation. It's complicated.'

'He wants to keep some portion of embezzled money?'

'I know it sounds crazy, but yes, and the company will pay to keep this quiet.'

'He must have known it would be quickly discovered missing. What has he said?'

'He hasn't said because we haven't confronted him. He knows that's imminent so we're playing a kind of game here and I'm bringing you into the circle.'

'When was this money embezzled?'

'About a month ago and he contacted you with the pike story about a week later. I know the day and the time he called you.'

'He didn't make up the pike project.'

'So where did the pike come from that were in the pickup?'

'I don't know. All I can tell you is he embezzled eight point two million and that I can prove it. Is there a secret hatchery project inside ENTR? Ask yourself why would there be? Look at all we have to lose. It would destroy the credibility of a company worth two billion dollars and employing one hundred fifty people, and with the potential to get a lot bigger. He's trying to blackmail or to negotiate with us, call it whichever you want.'

'So prove it to me.'

Jones looked a little rueful and tugged her hair back behind her right ear.

'They aren't going to let me do that yet. We're trying to keep it very quiet. You have to understand that investors put money into the projects and it'll get reported in the next week. That's the law and right now we're in a stage of confirming the evidence. When it gets reported, he'll get charged. At which point his lawyer will call a press conference to say his client is working with Fish and Game to save all of the western rivers from the evil company ENTR. I know what you're up against and it's scary, but that's what *I'm* up against. I want to work with you.'

'I'm listening but I need to learn a lot more first.'

'Wow, and after what I just shared with you.'

'That's where we're at this morning.'

She shook her head and Marquez got her cell number and gave her his. Then he took in her face again, strong and confident. She was certain she would convince him.

'He stole money and we're going to get it back.'

'Call me when you've got proof you can show me.'

'I will.'

They walked around the rest of the hatchery

and then she walked him to his pickup and Reid poked his head out again and said, 'Be careful as you drive out. We've got turkeys; they're everywhere now and make a mess if you hit one.'

When Marquez looked in his rear-view mirror Jones held her left hand up to her ear in a gesture to say, *we'll be talking*, and Reid was right about the turkeys. A flock crossed the road at a curve on his way out. He believed her about the money. It was too much of a wild card to just throw out there. He believed her but Hauser of course would have a completely different explanation.

SEVENTEEN

That afternoon Marquez flew north out of Sacramento with a Fish and Game pilot named Barry Wheeler. Wheeler was like the pro baseball player whose father had started pitching fastballs at him at age two. Wheeler flew with his dad as soon as he could walk and piloted a crop duster before he was sixteen. He skimmed the earth dusting endless acres of vegetables and cotton in the Imperial Valley, his plane rising only to loop high enough to avoid the telephone and power lines along the roads at the edge of the fields before turning back for another pass.

Wheeler was comfortable close to the ground and as long as he was, so was Marquez, who liked Wheeler's tight focus, But Wheeler wasn't arguing for flying low. He liked ten thousand feet and pulling his props back and cutting to nineteen hundred rpm to stay stealthy. The MX-15 mounted on the nose could comfortably read the terrain from there. If they dropped to five thousand feet, it could read a license plate.

The quadrant of terrain northeast of Sacramento that Soliatano identified was just ahead. Off to the right was the northern crest of the Sierras, off to the left, the Sacramento River. Wheeler turned to him now.

'For the camera to get everything between the two roads we'll need to make three passes.'

He argued for staying high but at some point Marquez wanted to get low. They flew the roads in a rectangle large enough to cover what Soliatano and Hauser told him, and that took them past the ENTR hatchery he saw this morning. Looking down, he got a good look at the connecting roads you could use from that hatchery.

The plane bumped around as they flew back toward the Sierras and then returned lower for a last pass, crossing over straw-colored hills dotted with oak with folds dark green with trees and the glimmer of creeks running again after the early rain. They swept over cabins and houses and ranch buildings and over road again and then just above a crest of hills and down to no more than three thousand feet over the brown fields. Wheeler circled and Marquez's seat creaked and the belt pulled tight as the plane banked hard.

'Another pass?'

'No, I'm good.'

'I want to fuel up in Chico. If you're hungry they've got food.'

They landed and Marquez bought two sandwiches, a Coke for Wheeler, and a black coffee for himself as Wheeler casually oversaw the fueling of the plane. Wheeler left as little as he could to chance. He was a competent aircraft mechanic and held a commercial and multi-engine certificate. His path to doing what he was doing now took him out across the country and through a half dozen flying jobs before making his way back home and here. Marquez watched Wheeler look over the plane and then checked his messages. He listened to one from Matt Hauser.

'This is my new phone number. It's one of those phones you don't keep. I bought a half dozen of those today. Things are getting very serious and I need to talk with you immediately. I'm on my way to the Department of Fish and Game in Sacramento. Call me as soon as you get this.'

Hauser had left the message less than twenty minutes ago. Marquez returned his call and as he waited for it to connect he realized Hauser didn't really know what he did. Hauser must think he worked from nine to five each day at headquarters on the Thirteenth Floor of the Water Resource Building. The call connected and Hauser answered, saying, 'I'm here and I need to meet with the head of your department. Things are escalating way above your level, Lieutenant.'

'I'm an hour and a half away.'

'Why? Where are you?'

'If you're worried go up to DFG headquarters

and tell them you're there to wait for me. Or go be a tourist. Go to the capital building. There are police and cameras and no one is going to bother you there. I'll call you when I'm ten minutes away. That's all it will take you to walk back over.'

Wheeler carried his sandwich and Coke to the plane and ate his sandwich after they were in the air and lined up on the Sacramento River.

'How do you want to do this?'

'I'd like to get a good look at both banks of the river. I'm looking at access, at where you could drop pike in the river if you were coming out of this illegal hatchery we're looking for.'

Wheeler brought the plane down and on the river sunlight sparkled and the trees along the banks flashed by.

'I couldn't do your job,' Wheeler said, 'but I sure love mine.'

Which is why I like to fly with you, Marquez thought, and they followed the river south and Wheeler didn't ask or say anything until he picked the spot where he left the river.

'Are you going to meet the guy you were talking to?'

'Yeah, at the office right now.'

'And he's helping us?'

'I'm not sure about that yet but I am sure he knows more than he's saying.'

'So you're staying on the dance floor.'

'That's about right, I'm staying on the dance floor and I'm going to learn more about him this afternoon.'

114

EIGHTEEN

Hauser was standing in a corner of the lobby of the Water Resources Building with his back to a wall and scanning faces until he picked up on Marquez coming toward him. Marquez led him to the elevator and up to the thirteenth floor. Now they were in a small conference room sitting across from each other, an agitated Hauser demanding to meet with the head of Fish and Game.

'What's changed, Matt?'

'They're following me and they'll destroy my reputation and career if I'm not protected. I made the decision to approach you and I'm going to frustrate you today. After three weeks of trying to get me to come across, I'm ready to talk, but I have too much on the line to negotiate my future with anyone other than your chief.'

'You've said.'

'I'm sure it's not the first time someone has gone over your head.'

Hauser reached in his pocket and pulled out a red and black plastic SanDisk memory stick. He put it down on the table in front of him and picked up again, holding it tight between his thumb and forefinger.

'What's in here ties ENTR to the pike project. Get your chief in here and I'll call my lawyer and we'll reach an agreement.'

'Show me what you've got and then I'll find out when the chief is available. I know at the moment he's out of state at a conference in Virginia, but even if he were three doors down the hall I wouldn't get him involved without proof. You want protection, then take me through what's on the memory stick.'

Hauser frowned and stared down at the table for a long twenty seconds.

'Good God, Lieutenant, we're talking about the destruction of the keystone native species and great harm to the fishing industry, tourism, and the quality of life in the state. This is a seminal event. This is eco-sabotage. Get the Governor involved! Do what it takes to make me believe you'll protect me! If your chief is out of town, then call him! Aren't you able to do that? I want to explain this to him.'

Marquez left the room for ten minutes. He talked with Waller and then returned to the conference room with his laptop, turned it on, took a chair next to Hauser with the screen facing them and said, 'Show me what you've got.'

Hauser picked up the memory stick and felt for the slot along the right side of the computer, but rather than slide the memory stick in he pulled his hand back and started talking.

'ENTR has called a meeting with me tomorrow. They haven't said what it's about other than to say it relates to the management of the projects I'm in charge of and there are four of them. Emergency meetings happen but usually there's a detailed explanation. There was nothing. It's a summons and that says to me they know I've been in conversation with Fish and Game. I need to go into that meeting with your department behind me. It's critical that I know today I'm not alone standing up to them. Otherwise, you're going to lose me.'

'Show me.'

'I have pieces. You have to put them together. It's a lot easier to move water around if you're not hamstrung by lawsuits and regulations favoring fish species. But if the fish in question are already effectively extinct due to an invasive species that can't be controlled then the reach of the lawsuits is diminished. We're talking about forced natural selection and millions of years of evolution erased in a seven-to-nine-year period. After the native species are no longer viable, then hard truths have to be faced. The salmon and trout are gone and water is needed elsewhere.'

'Give me the name of the biologist who is your source.'

'I made a promise not to reveal his name but I'll give it to you if we have a signed agreement. It has to have the Governor's signature and your chief's.'

They stared at each other and Marquez asked, 'What's changed since I last saw you? What made you drive here, Matt?'

'They're framing me.'

'Who is?'

'ENTR. They moved money around and made it look like I embezzled over eight million dollars from project accounts I manage. My lawyer says we'll have to hire forensic accountants but it's going to be a multi-year fight. I don't know how they moved the money or where it is, but they're threatening to bring in the FBI and turn me into a criminal and they're asking for the same things you are. They want my source.'

'Do you know Barbara Jones?'

'A woman by that name from internal security has left me several messages in the past two days, but no, I don't know her.' Hauser closed his eyes. 'Who is this captain of the Special Operations Unit you report to?'

'Captain Waller.'

'Do you think I could get a few minutes with him?'

'I can ask him.'

'I'd like to talk with him alone if I can.'

'I'll get him. Before I go, do you want to show me what's on the memory stick?'

'Not yet.'

Marquez folded his laptop shut and took it with him. He left Hauser sitting at the table doing a very good job of looking betrayed and miserable. In terms of being tracked and having his phones tapped and spyware inserted into his computers, Hauser was probably right. Eight million dollars was enough for the internal security to hire private investigators who wouldn't shy from bending the law if necessary.

He found Captain Waller and as they walked back Waller asked, 'What's the bottom line? What do you want me to tell him?'

'Tell him no deal until he delivers. Tell him he hasn't given us anything yet and that he lied about Emile Soliatano. Ask him where Soliatano is.'

'What about the embezzled money charges?'

'Tell him it's not our problem, but we'll protect him in every way we can if he delivers the illegal hatcheries. If he does that we've got his back. If he stalls on that, we've got a problem and I need to find another source.'

'Is that what's going to happen?'

'I really don't know yet, but it's not working out how he planned.'

'Is he scared?'

'He is. I don't know what he really knows or what he's done, but something got to him. He is afraid of what's coming and I don't think he's faking any of that. It's coming and he knows he's out of time.'

NINETEEN

Hauser was a bright guy but vain and superior and even if the embezzlement scheme was about to come down around his head he would stall. He would stall and the risk was more pike would get dumped in the rivers while Hauser schemed to protect himself. Marquez thought about it and then scrolled through the address book in his phone and called a number he hadn't in a long time.

'It's John Marquez.'

'Marquez, I'll be damned. I was thinking about you this morning. Remember that afternoon we met in that little town on the eastern side of the

Sierras? What was it called? Lee something or another—'

'Vining.'

'That's right, Lee Vining, and we walked out and talked looking over Mono Lake with those gulls overhead and the crazy rock formations in the lake and me trying to talk you into letting us make you a Task Force Officer and getting you deputized with the U.S. Marshal's office. I didn't think you'd do it. You were pretty down on yourself about one of your team getting killed.'

'Why were you thinking about me today?'

'I don't really know why; going back over my career in my head I guess, what mattered, what didn't. I've only got a couple more years here at headquarters. What's on your mind?'

'I need your help. I'm trying to find a guy named Emile Soliatano.'

Marquez told him the story, a pike problem that turned catastrophic, and Emile Soliatano masquerading as the dead man's brother, and who later with his wife abandoned the family van and got into a black Chevy Tahoe in a parking lot at Hilltop Mall in the Bay Area.

'Send me the videotape.'

'I just did.'

Desault played the video twice as he talked with Marquez then said, 'Interesting. Let me run this by our techs and I'll call you back.'

He called later that afternoon.

'This didn't have anything to do with the Bureau and we don't have an Emile Soliatano in our system and I didn't find him in the national database. You probably already know he owns a house in Vallejo but you might not know he paid off a lien the IRS has had on him for ten years for seventy-five thousand with a check for thirty-two grand last month.'

'I didn't know about the lien.'

'I also got a tech to look at the video. They're all busy so this was just a quick look, but she agrees someone was trying to make it appear as if he was getting picked up by Federal agents.'

'Why bother to stage that?'

'I have no idea why. You'd have to tell me. Maybe someone is trying to fool you.'

Marquez thought about that. 'It's probably not me they were thinking about but someone else looking for Soliatano, somebody who wouldn't have access to some ageing agent riding out his last years at FBI headquarters. What you left out in that Lee Vining memory is that you were in your car asleep when I got there.'

Desault chuckled. 'Yeah, I was beat. I was so tired.'

'But the coffee place was right there.'

'Yeah, but the sun felt better than coffee sounded. We did a good thing with that operation, John.'

'We did.'

'How does this Soliatano tie into the pike problem?'

'I'm still sorting that out, but I know he connects to a climatologist who works for a firm called ENTR that may link to the pike scheme. We've tied Soliatano to this climatologist, Hauser, and it could be Hauser is trying to back ENTR away from searching for Soliatano. I know how that sounds and I agree none of it makes much sense, but it's all that fits for me right now.'

'Okay, well, I'll call you if we come up with anything more; and I'll call you next time I'm out in the Bay Area.'

'Do, and we'll get a drink and reminisce about the old days.'

Desault laughed and hung up. Marquez doubted the drink would happen but he looked forward to it anyway; it was good to hear Desault's voice and know he was there and that he could reach out to him and get help. He had no proof but the call only reinforced the gut feeling that Hauser knew where Soliatano was.

TWENTY

Terry Ellis was tall and lean and built like the runner she was. Marquez saw that when he met her the day before she and Sarah Steiner were killed, and he knew from Maria that Ellis made a mark at Oregon State running the 1,500 meters. Maria described her as smart, funny, and tough. She believed that Ellis ran that night to save both herself and Sarah, that the terror of the assault did not cause her to abandon her friend. Rather, she realized that if she could get free she could outrun the attackers and get help. The miles of winding dirt track back out to the first houses would not have intimidated her, or at least this was how Maria dealt with it.

Marquez had never said anything to dissuade her but he was sure the terror Steiner and Ellis felt was overwhelming. He knew Voight would get graphic with Maria and give her details that made vivid being jerked out of the back of a camper and hitting the road hard while still in a sleeping bag. Even in the sanitized files Voight let him look through that was there, a wounded and dying Steiner left behind, the killer's footprints chasing Ellis down to the river.

Some of the comments Maria read online painted Ellis as a coward who abandoned her friend and ran. Those had deeply disturbed Maria and Voight would pick up on that. He would work it.

At the Klamath River meeting where Marquez had met them, Sarah Steiner did most of the talking. She had thick dark wavy hair and Ellis was a straight-haired blonde, her hair parted down the middle, and yet somehow they came across as sisters. Maria told him they were close enough to be that and tonight as he talked with Maria he heard how strong that belief was still. Ellis heard her friend scream as a knife cut through the sleeping bag and into her. She heard her stabbed as she struggled to get out of her own bag and Voight would want Maria to visualize that. Voight would show her photos that Marquez wished Maria didn't have to see. He knew they would stay with her forever.

'Dad?'

'I'm here.'

'You went quiet.'

'I'm thinking about Rich Voight interviewing you.'

'He wants me to come to Yreka to their office. He'll pay for me to fly up and they'll put me in a motel for the night. I asked if we could Skype, but he wants to do it in person. Is that normal?'

'In person is best.'

'He has this list of people he wants to ask me about, names he got off their Facebook pages. And he was asking questions about you and me, how close we are and what you were like when I was growing up. Even when I called you my father he kept saying stepfather, you know, like repeating it on purpose.'

'Well, you knew he was going to ask about me.'

'I know but it's weird. It was like he was trying to be my friend while he asked these really personal questions about you and mom. I told him about when you and mom separated. I wish I hadn't and I don't know why I did.'

'It's all okay. We did separate. We separated and got back together. What he is doing is trying to find a connection with you. That's part of the job.'

'But he's not on your side, Dad. He asked me why you wanted to meet Sarah and Terry and why you went to the thing at the high school. I'm pretty upset about it. It's like he thinks you're hiding something. What's wrong with you meeting Terry and Sarah? Why is he making such a big deal about that?'

'Right now he's looking at me as a possible suspect.'

'How can he do that?'

Marquez realized he hadn't told Maria that's

what was happening. He assumed she knew and that it disturbed him too much to talk about it.

'I was with him and the Siskiyou County sheriff a few days ago. Voight's suspicion comes from me going out of my way to meet Sarah and Terry the day before they died and showing up right after their bodies were found. Sometimes a murderer will turn into a spectator at the scene. They get a thrill out of it and Voight is playing with that idea.'

'Playing with? He's investigating you, Dad!'

Three SOU wardens had been with Marquez. Voight knew that operation was legit and his real question was why did Marquez stay along the Klamath River after his suspect blew off the meeting and the rest of the SOU pulled out? The answer was he stayed because he wanted to see how the local crowd treated Ellis and Steiner. The pair had become targets of hate and he was going to step in if there was an incident. A local newspaper derided their right to speak at the debate as allowing outside environmental activists who knew nothing about the area to squander the time of potato farmers who drove in for the meeting. 'Go the fuck home,' was spray painted on the right side of the pickup they had borrowed from Terry Ellis' brother, Jack, black spray paint over the faded red paint of the truck.

Marquez saw that before he walked into the high-school gym. Ellis and Steiner had parked where the truck with the painted message couldn't be missed. But when they left that afternoon they drove back into California and a distance down the Klamath River Highway. So maybe they were pulling back. Maybe the incident frightened them—or somebody did.

But Marquez didn't think so. What he had gathered was that Ellis and Steiner were aware of the disdain and anger focused on them, yet still traveled in a bubble of well wishers, some of them online and a handful of them in the towns they visited. In the farming areas along the river there was plenty of distrust of outside environmentalists, though that didn't start in 2009 when Ellis and Steiner came through. The great die-off of salmon along the Klamath River was years before in 2002 and after another push had already begun to remove dams along the Klamath.

Anger and fear of change imposed by the ultimate of unknowing outsiders—federal bureaucrats—inflamed the farming communities, and restoring the Klamath wasn't as simple as removing dams. Rivers need estuary systems and much of that land had been agricultural property for generations. Then there was the tight Presidential election of 2008 where the vote was close in Oregon. The views of the Oregon Potato Commission versus those of environmental groups led to then Vice President Cheney and the Republican political operative Karl Rove proposing bypassing the Endangered Species Act in order to provide water to farmers.

But that was over with before Ellis and Steiner showed up in 2009 and Cheney and Rove were long gone. The water problems of the Klamath remained, of course, and the frustration, anger, and fear that big government would make the wrong decisions were still there when Terry and

Sarah came through. It was why Marquez had made a point of checking on Maria's friends. It had worried him to see their pickup tagged with spray paint. He wanted to hear them talk and know that they were aware of how intense the water issue was along the river.

According to Maria, Terry and Sarah's plan was to travel the 263-mile length of the Klamath to talk to people and blog in favor of dam removal. That was a long stretch of country, running from rainforest country in California to dry eastern desert in Oregon. They moved slowly up the Klamath, two days near Orleans, three at an organic farm, then onward with the beeswax candles, dried steelhead, and salves they had bought. They rented kayaks and bicycles and went to parties at night at least twice. It was, after all, also a summer road trip.

They crossed into Oregon, did the event at the high school where they got to speak, and perhaps it was the hostility that caused them to retreat as many miles back down the river as they did. Voight's files charted their progress up the river and the retracement the night they were killed. He chased witnesses. He backtracked. The files showed his frustration.

Marquez met up with Maria two hours later in San Francisco not far from where she worked. Then they did what they had done for years when there was something difficult to talk about. They walked into an afternoon soft with fall light and under a clean blue sky with only a streak of feathered cirrus on the horizon. At the foot of Mission they crossed the Embarcadero and walked along the waterfront, talking through many of the same things they talked through on the phone earlier.

Maria stopped for a moment to make her point.

'I have a photo on my Facebook page of the three of us that I reload every three months or so. I still do that even if they're not ever coming back. It matters to me and I want to know who killed them and I wish I could kill the person who did it. I wouldn't have any problem pulling the trigger.'

'Yes, you would.'

'No, I really wouldn't.'

They started walking again and he moved the conversation on.

'Can you remember anytime anywhere you were with Terry and Sarah and my name came up?'

'No, but I'm sure I mentioned you. Why are you asking?'

'Same as Inspector Voight, I'm just looking for any connection.'

'You're not the same as him at all.'

'He's doing what he thinks he has to, Maria.'

'No, he isn't. He's an asshole and there's no big aha moment he's going to have talking to me. I never told you or Mom this, but Terry and Sarah wanted me to do the Klamath trip with them. We were going to make more of a road trip out of it. It wasn't going to be all about the dams. They wanted to have fun. They were really good people and totally normal. There was no reason to kill them and it's not like they were raped before they were killed. This wasn't some sex killer. It was about what they were doing and Voight doesn't know anything. If he knew anything he wouldn't be questioning you.'

Her eyes clouded and she turned away. She brushed the corner of her eye with her right hand and shook her head.

'How close did you come to going with them, Maria?'

'Super close but then I talked to my boss and he said I'd have to take a leave of absence and they would have to get another intern. There wouldn't have been any job to come back to, so I didn't do it. And there was Terry's brother's pickup with the camper shell. It was perfect for two people but not for three. I would have had to drive my car.'

Marquez listened and guessed she did come close. She didn't like where she was working. The pay was very low and her boss had been very cool toward her since coming on to her and getting rebuffed. That was over a year ago and her mom had encouraged her to quit immediately, which was probably why she didn't.

'I'm okay, Dad, let's keep walking. Are they sure the gun you found is the one that killed them?'

'Yes.'

They went there now and talked about guns and ballistics and this was the Maria he was counting on. She wanted to understand in every way how Voight could look at him as a possible suspect.

'The connection might be me, not you, Dad.'

'How do you get there?'

'I have friends who knew her a lot better and one of them you know. Remember Kevin and Ridley?'

'Sure.'

'Kevin was up there and might have met up with them during the trip but nowhere near where they were killed, maybe a lot farther south. Still, he might have given them some people to call when they got farther up. He has friends in that area.'

'What kind of friends?'

'Dope growers.'

Marquez nodded. It didn't surprise him but nothing did anymore.

'I always thought it was about somebody angry that dams might get taken out, but there were other people they hung out with along the way and those names aren't on Facebook. They got invited to some places they couldn't post about and if they went to a party with Kevin he wouldn't have wanted their names on Facebook.'

'Did he tell you he was there?'

'No, I ditched those guys. By then, we weren't talking anymore. But I can call him. I'll call him before I talk to Voight but I don't really expect anything from Kevin.'

'Voight knows they went to parties as they worked their way up the river but do call Kevin. If Voight hasn't already talked with him he'll want to now.'

'I want the murders solved, but I don't want to help this Voight.'

'Yes, you do. If he gets a good lead he'll go somewhere with it and he's not going to frame me. I won't let that happen and you've got to remember Voight has the murder weapon now. He didn't have anything before that. Now he's got a place to work from.'

'Yeah, but you—'

'I won't let it happen.'

TWENTY-ONE

'This is Lila Philbrick.'

Marquez knew when he left Crescent City that if it was one of the Philbrick's it would be Lila who called. His pulse quickened because she wasn't just responding to a call from him.

'Hey, Lila, did you find something?'

'I found a photo with Jim Colson in it. His face isn't all that clear but it's him, and I'm also sending you one of Lisa Sorzak. There's a lot about her that Geoff didn't tell you.'

'Like what?'

'Like she was everyone's girlfriend, including my husband, and that's why it got so tense when you were here. I haven't talked about any of this in a long time and I'm supposed to be over it, but it still makes me want to punch Geoff in the face.'

She laughed.

'Not really, I'm over it and I was kind of a mess in those years too and it's a miracle we didn't go bankrupt. Geoff likes to pretend it never happened or that he can't remember. That's why he got so foggy on the names. He does that little boy act.'

131

'What did Lisa Sorzak do for you?'

'Bartended, cooked, waited tables, slept with my husband, a little bit of everything. When we fired her she found a job in Ukiah at a bar and got fired there for dealing drugs to the staff. How much do you want to know?'

'Everything.'

'Okay, well here goes. When I caught my husband in one of the bedrooms upstairs with her she was on top, he had a gag in his mouth, and his wrists and ankles were tied to the bedposts. This was an old Victorian-style bed. We really didn't know what we were about when we opened this business. It took all of my inheritance to figure that out, but anyway, she was on top and looked at me and got off him, got dressed and said, 'He's all yours. Have fun.' I fired her ten minutes later and I left Geoff tied to the bed until the next morning.

'When he gave that little whiny, "it's been ten years, Lila," that's what he was talking about. Sorzak was a manipulative secretive bitch and I didn't say that because we're not supposed to talk about ex-employees, but I don't think I have to worry about anything with you.'

'You don't.'

'She was also a painter and she thought she was a poet and I hope she thinks that still because her poetry sucks and it's never going anywhere. She was a pretty good painter though. I had Geoff burn the paintings she gave us. One was a very good watercolor landscape looking north from Crescent City that a customer offered to buy for five hundred dollars. It was a very good painting but also one that Geoff liked a lot and it was therapeutic to watch him burn it along with a bra she intentionally left behind. Her poetry is as self-centered as she is, so by the time you read two or three lines you want to stick your finger down your throat.'

'You've still got a special place for her in your heart.'

'Yeah, I do, and I've kept track of her.'

'Where she is now?'

'She left Ukiah and with money she saved from selling drugs or stole from her employers she bought a bar in Weaverville. She has something else going on that's probably illegal down near the Mad River. If you find her, ask her where the money to buy the Weaverville bar came from. I'd love to know.'

'What's the name of it?'

'It's got some really stupid hokey name. I'll think of it in a minute. Our bar would come up short sometimes – I mean, missing money, not a lot but some – and we were so naive and trusting we believed her and never did anything about it. She had a really good way of controlling the men around here, including Jim Colson. Geoff and I were doing lines of coke every day and drinking too much and she and Colson just made themselves at home. I remember walking back around midnight on a rainy winter day when we had no customers and hadn't for hours. She was on her back on a bar table and Colson was fucking her and get this, I apologized. That's how messed up things were around here.

'At some point she got tired of Colson. He was

older than her by eight or nine years and mysterious and strange but she had a real sexual appetite. It was one of the few things she didn't fake. She picked men like a farmer picks tomatoes. When she wanted another she just reached for it and Colson couldn't keep up with that. What I think happened with her and Colson is she figured out how she could control him and when she did that she lost interest. But they were also bad people, her especially, and something was wrong with him. He had a creepy quality.

'But I'll give Lisa this, men were drawn to her. She got us our first regular customers.'

She laughed again, this time deeper and Marquez smiled.

'I never thought of it this way, but maybe she brought in the business that saved us. There were a few of them that hung around and drank and a new one would show up after that one left. I'm sorry if I sound vindictive but she was bad news. But even if I don't sound like it, I'm over it. You've got to forgive, right?'

She laughed at that.

'I remember the name of the Weaverville bar now. It's a perfect name for a bar owned by her. It's called the Come On In.'

'And you think she still owns it?'

'She does and she can't be doing well enough not to be there. If you want to find her, go there and wait.'

'Lila?'

'Yeah?'

'I appreciate your call but how do you know all this?'

'It's because I'm still working on the forgiving part, and it's not about her sleeping with Geoff. Men are easy. It's the way she stole and kept talking to me like she really cared about what happened to the tavern. It's the way she burned us. She was like a low-grade infection, the kind where you know something is wrong with you but you're not sure what it is yet, and I was so stupid. I hate looking back and knowing I was so stupid and naive and we went through all that money. If we never did the inn we could have lived the rest of our lives on that money. And she stole from us. That still makes me angry. She was stealing from us and sleeping with my husband and we were all having staff meals together and were best of friends.'

Lila wanted to talk more and needed to and Marquez listened and got a little more about where to look along the Mad River, though what she knew about that was pretty sketchy. The Weaverville bar he could find easily.

Lila made an odd promise now, that she would talk to Geoff about Lisa, and she didn't come out and say it, but sent the signal she thought Geoff knew more about Sorzak's whereabouts. Marquez got a description of Sorzak, chickenpox scar on her right bicep, long legs, beautiful legs, blue eyes, brown hair, two small moles on her right cheekbone.

'I'll scan these photos and email them to you, but it's not really what she looks like that sticks with you; it's the way she is. You'll get it if you find her and since you're a man you'll like her.'

'Okay, and what about Colson?'

135

'Haven't heard a thing; maybe he went back home, wherever that is. He was never completely here anyway. I don't care what Geoff says, something happened to James Colson before we ever met him.'

'Who would you call if you were going to try to find him?'

'You haven't had any luck with tax records, driver's license, and all of that?'

'We're working on it.'

'I don't know who I would call. I'll ask Geoff.'

Marquez thanked her for the help and Lila sent the photos soon after and in her email added one more thing about her. Sorzak didn't use her last name anymore. She signed her poetry Lisa X and somewhere she found – or as Lila said, slept with – a judge who let her change her last name to X. That last didn't turn out to be true but it did help Marquez find her.

TWENTY-TWO

Later that afternoon a distraught Hauser called.

'They just fired me.'

'You knew that was coming.'

'Two security guards were waiting when I got back to the office from a lunch meeting. They gave me fifteen minutes to put my personal things in a cardboard box. My computers were already gone and they're not even company property. I bought those. They took my company ID and

136

keys before they would let me out of the office and told me that if I'm seen anywhere near the premises they'll call the police and the company will get a court order if needed.'

'Where are you now?'

'In my home office reading a lawsuit that a process server just handed me at our front door. I thought it was my wife Paula getting home but it wasn't her. I've never seen a process server before. I didn't even know what he was talking about and for a moment I thought he was here to rob me.'

'ENTR is suing you?'

'Yes, and it wouldn't have happened if your department had helped me. Even from here I can't access any of my documents. I don't know how a defense is going to be put together. Everything is in the cloud and I can't access anything and none of my passwords work, none of my back-door routes work. I can't get a hold of my wife. I've left her messages and she hasn't called back. She should be home by now. I think they called her and told her, and I don't think she's coming home. I think this is it. I'm going to lose everything and I blame you. I blame your department.'

'I'm going to come to your house and talk with you. I'll be there in about an hour.'

'It's too late for talk, Lieutenant.'

'Maybe not.'

'You needed to help me when I asked for it. There's nothing left to talk about.'

Now Marquez was sitting in Hauser's study and Hauser still hadn't heard from his wife. That was his biggest worry and it was about the marriage, not that something might have happened to her. He looked pale and feverish as if what had happened made him physically sick. His forehead beaded with tiny drops of sweat.

Marquez had called ENTR on the way here. It was after business hours and he didn't expect anyone to pick up the phone, but a woman did and she was very interested to know who he was after he asked for Matt Hauser. She told him Mr Hauser was no longer with the firm and that any work Mr Hauser was doing would now be handled by others. She pressed to know who he was. She wasn't getting it from caller ID.

'Where did he go?'

'He resigned.'

'He was fired?'

'No sir, he resigned.'

Hauser flipped the lawsuit across the desk in his study as if Marquez had some role in it.

'Read it, Lieutenant, it's everything I warned you about.'

The lawsuit alleged fraud, embezzlement, destruction and theft of intellectual property, willful and injurious disregard of company protocols, sixteen violations of the employment agreement, and damages in addition to the 8.2 million dollars in embezzled funds and sought unspecified damages that could total in excess of one billion dollars if the company's reputation was severely damaged by the alleged theft.

'Are you making the claim that they framed you in the transfer of the eight point two million and that it wasn't you who transferred the money?'

'I've never stolen anything in my life.'

138

'You didn't transfer the missing money?'

'The money disappeared after I learned about the pike project. I knew it was gone and I've been trying to figure out where it went.'

'Did you inform the company?'

'I should have but I didn't because a routine audit was coming up.'

Marquez waited for more and when it didn't come, said, 'That doesn't make any sense.'

Hauser didn't respond and looked down at the lawsuit. He rested his hand on it and when he spoke his voice was slowed as if it took great concentration to have this conversation.

'My lawyer believes if the money is returned and the pike issue resolved then everything else can be negotiated away. He wants me to immediately cease contact with the Department of Fish and Game. But I don't think it matters anymore. Paula is going to leave me and my life will be ruined by ENTR. I can no longer get into the files I need and I'm not going to be a source of information to you anymore.'

'Why would your wife leave you?'

'She'll choose them over me. They'll talk to her. They're probably talking to her right now.'

His face fell. He shook his head.

'I can't think clearly. I'm worried and scared and wondering why I ever warned you about the existence of the hatcheries.'

'If Enrique Jordan wasn't killed trying to dump pike in the Sacramento I still wouldn't have any proof, Matt. And I need the hatchery locations. I need your biologist friend.'

'Then go do your job and leave me alone. If

you had backed me up, they would have held off coming after me. Now they're going to destroy my reputation and make me look like a thief and a liar.'

'They may do that, but there may also be a way we can still work together.'

'I think you blew that chance.'

'Just listen. When the pickup rolled and Jordan was trapped he didn't make any phone calls, but someone used his phone to call 911. The caller didn't stay on the line long but gave enough of a description for the first responders to find the accident location. They found a badly injured and unconscious Enrique Jordan. The found his wallet and other personal effects but no cell phone. I didn't find one either and I looked pretty hard and trying to locate it with GPS failed. I think the phone either got taken apart and stayed with the man who made the call or it went into the river after the call got made.'

Hauser's cell rang and without a word he turned it so Marquez saw the caller ID on the screen. It read Paula Hauser.

'I don't know where you're going with this, but I've got to talk to her right now. You're welcome to wait outside.'

The wait was almost two hours but Marquez was like that. When Hauser came out of his study he looked shocked and defeated and offended that Marquez was still there.

'She's not coming home, Lieutenant. Are you happy? You helped make that happen. She wants me to move out. She wants me to find another place to live by tomorrow night.'

'Keep talking to her.'

'I've been talking to her for five years. I've walked on eggshells because I haven't wanted to lose her and all that time she was looking for a way to leave. Are you married?'

'You asked me that once before.'

'Does your wife love you? That's all I've wanted, for her to love me. But you can't make someone do that. That's how it has felt the last several years, as if I'm trying to talk her into loving me. They got to her. They told her I embezzled money and she believes them. She wouldn't listen to me as I tried to explain.'

'Listen to me. You might still have a way with us. I talked to my captain and also to the chief on the drive here. So here's the offer: you tell us Emile Soliatano's role and give us him and we'll start working to shield you from ENTR if he gets us to the hatchery where Jordan got his pike.'

'Who is Emile Soliatano?'

'He's the guy who made the mistake of going to the hospital and pretending to be Enrique Jordan's brother. He was convincing enough and they didn't have another next of kin so they rolled with it and he got the word from the trauma surgeons that Emile didn't make it. Once he knew, he was on the phone and out of the hospital and in his car on his way to you. The only problem is we were following him. I was there. I saw you and Emile meet and it wasn't very hard after that to figure out you weren't quite who you said you were, and you can tell me that you were forced into that or whatever story you come up with, but don't bother. We're past that. We are at the

141

point where you have to make a decision that we can verify tonight. Where is Soliatano?'

'I don't know where he is. He found a place for his wife and him. I supplied the money.'

'Why?'

'I needed him. He was in a position to know.'

Marquez nodded and it was possibly true. It was basically what Soliatano had said.

'How did you find him in the first place?'

As he asked, Marquez knew it had to be the biologist and the biologist was on the inside of the pike project not the outside. He listened as Hauser spun something about how he got the Soliatano connection and another piece came together for Marquez. He wondered why he didn't see it sooner. They stared at each other and Marquez said, 'Call him.'

'He has a new phone and we're not talking anymore. I don't know his new phone number.'

'Too bad you don't; that was our one chance.'

Marquez stood.

'Good luck with everything, Matt. I'll let myself out.'

Marquez got as far as the sidewalk before Hauser spilled out of the house and hurried down the steps, calling to him, 'Lieutenant, wait.'

TWENTY-THREE

'Are you going to ask me about my dad every other breath? Is that the only reason I'm here?'

'Maria, I have to ask you about everything that might have anything to do with this investigation, but let's get off to the right start. I want what you want. I want to find the killer of your friends and bring them to justice. It's that straightforward. That's all I want.'

Maria felt tired and a little hazy from the long drive and the early start this morning, but that feeling was gone now and she was ready to deal with this Voight dude. Voight's eyes were warm but his face was heavy and his eyes drowning in flesh. She was going to give him two hours and then drive back. She wasn't staying the night or missing work tomorrow. This guy was like on a mission to nail her dad and it was disgusting.

'I do have questions about your stepfather. I won't deny that and I'm sure he has told you. Hasn't he?'

'He's the only father I've had so I call him Dad. Is that okay with you?'

'Of course.'

'I only have about two hours and when I leave here I'm driving home.'

'We have a motel room rented for you.'

'Unrent it.'

'You may be a very critical link in this, Maria.'

'Then you waited a long time to talk to me. Where do you want to start?'

'Tell me about Terry and Sarah, where you met them, what kind of friendship you had, how close you were to them. How much did you know about this road trip and their activism?'

'You asked me the same questions last time we talked.'

143

'Some of the questions will be the same and, as you know, I'm taping this so I have it to refer back to. I have notes from our last conversation but I'd rather have your words. I probably look like an old, fat middle-aged guy but I was a homicide detective at LAPD for a lot of years. I didn't come off a sheep farm up here and drive around as a deputy until I got promoted. I know something about homicide investigation.'

'Okay, but you sure don't know much about my dad and it's even worse if you do, because if you do know him and you're doing this anyway then you're evil. Why did you leave LA to come here?'

'I'll tell you sometime. Today I'm the one asking the questions.'

'Then ask something you haven't already asked five times.'

'Okay, I will, and let's start over. Talk about Terry and Sarah in any way you want. I'm looking for what I missed.'

Maria's stance toward this interview softened as she talked. She knew Sarah best and could picture her easily: green eyes, dark wavy hair parted down the middle and to her shoulders, some freckles, her smile and sense of humor. She missed Sarah's sense of humor and her way of getting at things. She missed that a lot and she hadn't known Terry like that. Terry was more to herself, not quieter, but more contained. It wasn't completely natural the two of them made the trip together and she told the detective it was more about both having family up here, especially Terry's brother, Jack, the river guide. Jack pushed

144

Terry to get involved. Sarah was already involved.

'Involved in the movement to take out the dams on the Klamath?'

'Yes, and other dams in California, San Clemente, the one on Malibu Creek, and on the American and other places.'

Voight acted interested but he could care less about the dams. He said he had interviewed Terry's brother several times. Did she know Jack Ellis? Maria shook her head. She didn't. She had two guy friends who knew him pretty well and they were in the Bay Area and one of them went out with Terry for a little while. Voight seemed really interested in that, though Kevin supposedly talked to Voight a couple of years ago.

'That was your friend Kevin that you called me about?'

'Yes, and you've talked to him before, right?'

'I have to check, Maria. We got a long list of names from Facebook.'

'Kevin Witmer knows Jack Ellis too.'

'How big is Kevin's dope business?'

That surprised her. He must know a lot more than he let on. Maybe it was like Dad said; this guy has issues but is the real deal as an investigator. He showed her his list of names now and wanted her to look it over and put a mark next to anyone she thought he should talk to. Some of the names had numbers alongside them, like some old school thing. She asked about that.

'I'm not sure I remember why I wrote those numbers.'

'I thought detectives were all supposed to be really good liars.'

145

'Do you think I'm lying?'

'You are lying.'

Voight liked that for some reason and his eyes watered in the corners as he smiled.

'You're tough, Maria.'

'So answer the question.'

'It's the number of times each of them posted.'

'A lot of people don't post but they're still on Facebook. Those two guys I was just talking about don't do Facebook but Kevin was a good friend of Terry's, or maybe not, but they hung out and he wanted to know her better.'

'As in go out with her?'

'Yeah, or that's what I heard, but she wasn't very interested in him and I don't know much about Kevin's dope business. I know he's doing it.'

'I'm not interested in busting him. I'm after who killed Terry Ellis and Sarah Steiner.'

'Then why are you doing this bullshit thing with my dad?'

'I'm doing what I have to. How did you follow them as they made this trip along the Klamath?'

'I called them and there was Facebook. They were posting photos and Sarah wrote about the meeting and stuff. Facebook is mostly about photos and if someone was trying to follow them up the Klamath by checking Facebook it could be a good way to do it. They were doing like a journal, but you already know that. We talked and texted. Instagram wasn't happening yet. I called Sarah a few times but the connection sucked so it was mostly the photos and text. You probably already have my emails to Sarah.'

He did and it kind of annoyed her the way he

didn't just come out and say he did. It was friggin' annoying.

'When is the last time you saw your friend Kevin Witmer?'

'Not in a while. We stopped hanging out a while ago, but I left a message for him a couple of days ago.'

'Is that because you think he might know something?'

'My dad is wondering more than I am.'

'Your dad asked you to make contact with Kevin Witmer again?'

'After he and I talked, yeah, he did, but Kevin isn't going to tell me anything. I'm not really friends with him anymore and it's not like he would have said if he knew anything.'

'How do you know that?'

'I don't know him.'

'You said he was hitting on Terry. Could he have become very angry if Terry ignored his advances?'

She looked at him coolly. 'You're pretty desperate.'

'Let's go get some lunch.'

At lunch he ordered a double cheeseburger with bacon and fries and asked how much she knew about her dad's work.

'Like what?'

'Oh, what he does and where he goes and what the purpose was.'

'You know he's like a TFO with the FBI and a deputy US Marshal, right?'

He didn't know that and he really didn't know shit about what her dad did, or else he was lying and he already told her that lying was part of his job. But she didn't think he was lying this time. He really didn't know that much about her dad's job and tried to hide that by taking a massive bite out of the burger.

But that's what he wanted to talk about and what Dad was working on now she wasn't that clear about. It was an international animal trafficking operation he was trying to break. It was different than a poaching ring and he said the animal business was more commoditized now. She told Voight that and he asked about a guy named Rider. She shook her head.

'I don't live at home anymore and we talk about other things when we see each other. I know he works alone a lot. My mom thinks too much, and thinks that it's dangerous. Sometimes he's only with the FBI.'

'He gets to write his own ticket.'

'I don't know about that. Do you get to write your own ticket?'

He looked at her like that was the last thing he got to do.

'Was he working on something in Siskiyou County before Sarah and Terry were killed?'

'He wouldn't have been there otherwise.'

'Try to remember.'

'Why don't you ask him?'

'Well, I know he was in Oregon the day the girls were part of the debate in the high-school gym and that like them he was all the way down the Klamath and back in California that night. He showed up at the crime scene less than an hour after we issued something called a BOLO.'

'I know what a BOLO is and it was Sarah and Terry, so of course he tried to help. You really don't know him, do you?'

She watched him pick up six or so fries and then drop two of them before biting the others in half. His eating habits were weird. It was like he was nervous all the time.

'I wouldn't be doing my job if I didn't look at everybody who showed up at the scene. It doesn't matter if they're law enforcement; I still have to look at them.'

'Seriously, why are you so focused on Dad?'

'I've got other information I can't talk about.'

That sort of creeped her out and she didn't feel like eating anymore. She didn't believe him but it still made her feel weird.

'Did he ever get really angry with your mom when you were growing up?'

'Not as angry as me.'

Voight smiled and had ketchup on his upper lip.

'Do you think he sees women differently?'

'What does that mean?'

'Does he have more difficulty dealing with women?'

'My dad is like the best.'

'Then he's got to come up with some answers.'

'He does or you do?'

He didn't answer and she sat on that a second and then repeated: 'Dad has to come up with some answers? Is that because you don't have anyone else?'

She lifted her purse and pulled thirty dollars out of her wallet. 'This is for lunch.'

149

'We're buying.'

'I just did and I don't really believe you have other information.'

'I'm not asking you to believe.'

'Okay, what is the other information?'

'I can't tell you yet.'

'That's exactly what I expected you to say. See you later.'

TWENTY-FOUR

On Hauser's forehead was a bright-red mark from leaning forward in the pew with his forehead pressed against the knuckles of his right hand. He looked haggard and defeated and offered a damp hand before sliding over on the oak pew to make room. Marquez would never have figured him for religious or church going, but maybe the reason for being here was in what he said next.

'We were married here twenty-two years ago. We have two kids in college, one at Amherst and one at LSU. Both got into UC campuses and could have stayed in state and saved us a lot of money, but that would have put them within their mother's reach, and they wanted to get away from her. There have been times when I've thought the same way, yet I'm having a very hard time dealing with her leaving me.

'Paula filed for legal separation. She says it's the only way to protect our money from the lawsuit, but I know it's just the first step. She's going to ask for a divorce.'

He turned and stared at Marquez.

'In the end she's just another lawyer.'

An elderly parishioner three rows up turned and looked at them then got up slowly and left, the church door allowing bright sunlight in before it closed and returned them to softer shadows. The Holy Virgin Cathedral, Joy of All Who Sorrow was out on Geary Street. Marquez had turned around and recrossed the Golden Gate Bridge when he got Hauser's call.

Hauser sighed now, his voice quieter as if he'd reached some resolve last night.

'I'm going to give you Emile's new phone number but I have to ask something in return. Barbara Jones and the little security group don't know I was paying him for information and I don't want them to know. They don't know anything about him or maybe they know everything, but they don't know where he is. At least we did that right. I am so over my head. I so wish I'd never gotten involved. The salmon are gone anyway. The snowpack will decline and they won't make it. All of these native species will be gone. What you're doing won't matter on any scale. Humanity treats animals like a product that's there to harvest and sell. Poachers will get drones and there won't be a herd of anything left in Africa.'

'You could be right, but I'm going to keep at it anyway.'

That seemed to interest Hauser. He turned and studied Marquez before continuing.

'Enrique got told he was stocking a breed of trout that had to go into the rivers at night so they could get adjusted and weren't immediate prey for other fish. He was told that the stocking was illegal but important for the rivers and the penalties were very small. The very good pay offset that worry.'

'Did you pay off Soliatano's IRS lien?'

'You have a way of surprising me sometimes, Lieutenant, but perhaps my ego blinds me. I did pay it off after he delivered what I needed, and honestly I thought I was being clever.'

'How many pike have gone into California rivers?'

'Thousands and you would be wasting your time if they hadn't had a problem with a virus. They found that out about a month ago after monitoring several of the spots and seeing the early fish plants die off. Same thing happened with the hatchery fish they still had. The virus destroyed their motor control. There's a conflicted biologist who made that happen, but he won't be doing it again. He's scared now.'

'Your biologist friend?'

He didn't answer that and pointed toward the cross.

'Maybe there is a God. When Enrique's truck flipped over he was carrying the first of the new plants and now they're waiting until everything is under control again before they release more.'

'Your mysterious biologist friend could make all the difference, but you guard the gate. You won't let us talk to him.'

'I made a promise to him.'

Hauser turned to look at him again.

'ENTR's lawsuit against me is now public knowledge. They'll follow with a statement tomorrow or the next day and then they'll really go after me. They probably sat Paula down and gave her a choice and she chose them. Part of the deal will be she helps them discredit me so that no one in the scientific community will ever take me seriously again. You might think I'm exaggerating but climatologists are paranoid for good reasons. The deniers can't refute the science so they're after the scientists.

'It's not unlike the Catholic Church and Galileo. He said look through my telescope and you'll see these bodies are moving. He proved the earth was moving and in return was tried for heresy and lived out his last years under house arrest. It's the same with our science. The deniers can't handle the truth so they look for email conspiracies and fabricated evidence. And in reality, they're just frightened of the truth.'

'Where's Emile Soliatano?'

Hauser reached in his coat. He pulled a folded piece of paper and handed it over.

'The address is on there.'

Marquez opened it up, asked, 'What about a phone number?'

'I have one but I'm not going to give it to you yet. Emile and his wife are there and he has worked with me for one reason only—money. Don't forget that when you try to get him to talk. I know you drove around with him—'

'I get it.'

'He'll be shocked I gave him up but you

should be able to get him to talk. He's had twenty thousand dollars of my money in addition to the lien being paid off. That's more than enough. He can live without any more money from me.'

'You put out twenty grand of your own to find out how pike were getting moved to the rivers?'

'I did.'

'Was that the only reason?'

'How honest do I need to be in a church?'

He gave an odd, sad smile and said, 'You really don't have much time, Lieutenant. They drained the tanks and the concrete runways and they're breeding and growing with new stock. What I've done will slow them down but not for long.'

'What did you do to slow them down?'

'I called Fish and Game. I called you and tipped you to the pike project and could have given you the whole thing if you had worked with me.'

They sat a while longer in silence then talked more about his marriage. They didn't talk about the missing eight million dollars or ENTR's lawsuit, though Marquez intended to before leaving and after another ten minutes brought it up. Barbara Jones had sent him copies of wire transfers and the statements of two European bank officials and forwarded three emails from an FBI agent whose career was built around finding embezzled money.

'You've made a mark as a scientist but you're not much of a thief yet. You moved the money. You knew they would find it with the monthly audit and they did. Now what? What's the plan?'

'I have never lied to you and I would never do

154

what you're describing. Why would I risk going to prison?'

'ENTR forwarded copies of wire transfers and told me this morning the FBI has identified the Brazilian banker you paid off and has tracked half of the money to Luxemburg and then Zurich, exactly half of the money, and I'm guessing you figured to offer ENTR a split with terms. On your end maybe you don't go public with the pike project and your proof and in return their investors never learn that one of the top scientists went rogue. You leave your wife. You go to Europe and secure the money and then make a new life.'

'Do you know what the zeitgeist is, Lieutenant? Do you know why we have all of these dystopia movies and novels right now? It's because people sense what's coming. The world is going to come apart with climate change. Societies are going to collapse. Don't imagine that nations will go quietly. Are China and India going to share the rivers if there's not enough for both? We'll see wars as we enter a period of climate pendulum swings when the earth tries to balance what can no longer be balanced. After that it'll be really very simple. It'll get fucking hot. Is it so wrong to want to live more before that happens?'

'They've got you, Matt. They've called your game. I'd return the money now if I were you.'

Marquez rested a hand on Hauser's shoulder and then stood. He left him there in the empty church, alone and hunched forward in the pew.

TWENTY-FIVE

It surprised him that Soliatano chose a beach town, but why not here? Marquez knocked on the door of a small, well-maintained house with a good ocean view. Stinson Beach was probably as good a place as any to sit and wait, although if his wife went into labor they had a pretty long drive to a hospital. But maybe Soliatano had a plan for that as well.

With his knock the door rattled and he heard footsteps, but they were too light for Emile. When the door opened he met Soliatano's wife and she seemed a gentle person and unaccustomed to lying. She made a run at it and then gave up and said Emile was at the beach.

'Doing what?'

'Trying to learn to surf. He's always wanted to be a surfer.'

'I'll find him. Do you have a name for the baby?'

'Camille.'

'Pretty name.'

'Thank you. Are you going to arrest him?'

'That's up to him.'

She stared past him and seemed unsure what to do and a dog trotted down the hall and pushed its nose out the door. Marquez reached and stroked the dog's head and then drove down to the beach.

The surf was low and flat and he watched Soliatano try to ride the small waves and finally give up and paddle in. The afternoon was cold, the sky gray, and the beach largely empty. Soliatano picked up a towel and when he picked up his phone Marquez started toward him. Soliatano recognized him as he got close and not knowing what else to do he smiled as if greeting an old friend.

'I'm sorry I took off. Hauser freaked out and this is what he paid me to do.'

'You made a deal with me and you didn't keep up your end.'

'I had to put my family first.'

'Is that what you're doing learning to surf?'

'I'm getting a new career figured out. I'm done with that factory.'

'Good for you, but here's some bad news. You're not going to get any more money from Hauser. He's going to be arrested and charged with embezzlement and he's being sued by his former company. It might have all worked if Enrique hadn't gotten killed.'

'I'm really down about Enrique. That's why I'm out here thinking things through.'

'I can see your grief.'

'You don't fucking believe anything.'

'At least you didn't get hurt, not even a scratch when the truck rolled. It did a number on the pickup and it killed Enrique and I don't know why I didn't figure it out sooner. I mean, look at you. You're surfing.'

'I don't get hurt easily, man.'

'Yeah, but that doesn't quite cover it.'

'Doesn't cover what?'

'I'm getting to it. There are some other things first. I found out Hauser paid your IRS lien. That's bigger money than you told me, much bigger. If it's true, and it seems to be true, I guessed you lied about that too.'

Marquez let that rest a moment and watched a roller break and lap into the shore.

'I paid, not him.'

'I just came from talking to him. He's sitting in a church pew trying to figure out what to do next. It's a fucked-up situation, Emile, totally fucked up, but I still need something you can trade. I need the hatchery location.'

'Only Enrique knew.'

'I don't think so.'

Emile picked up his board and the towel but didn't quite get around to leaving.

'Here's what I figured out. You got out of the truck because you've got a kid coming and the situation wasn't the best. The track you guys wanted to back down to get close to the river was in poor condition. It was muddy and steep, but you had no choice but to put the fish in the river. We found GPS tags on the tails of a dozen of the fingerlings, so the hatchery had a way to monitor the drops. So anyway, there you are and there's a dirt track and it's steep and muddy and dark, an all round lousy place to back a loaded pickup down.

'And that's when you stopped driving. You got out to direct Enrique as he tried to back the truck down. You saw the risk and I know you didn't think the truck would roll, but you didn't want

158

to be the one at the wheel. He took the wheel and you stood outside with a flashlight.

'Now, maybe you brought Enrique along to keep you company and do the dirty work that as driver you'd otherwise have to do yourself. Who wants to ferry a jillion buckets of fish down to a river? I'm guessing your cousin did the muscle work and then the two of you tipped over the cooler and dumped out the rest. But that only worked if you got close to the water, so you bent the rules a little about where to offload the fingerlings.'

'He was the driver.'

'No, he wasn't; don't blow up your one chance here. How much did you pay him?'

Soliatano's gaze went back to the ocean and Marquez didn't really sit in judgment of him. The deal with Hauser got him out from under the IRS lien that probably would have taken forever to pay off, and no doubt Hauser sold himself as a white knight ultimately saving the salmon and trout. Getting out of the truck and letting the inexperienced Enrique Jordan take the wheel, well, that was cowardice, but we all have faults and he did have a kid coming.

'I paid him a couple hundred bucks.'

'Where is the hatchery?'

'I don't know.'

'You can lie but you can't disappear without a fugitive warrant this time and sooner or later your wife gives birth.'

'I never went to the hatchery.'

Marquez took a chance now.

'Hauser just told me you've been there.'

Now they had their longest silence.

'How do I know how it will end for me and my wife?'

'It ends if you come clean and I find the hatchery.'

'I can't go to jail.'

'Let's hear it.'

'Brookfield Road off Ninety-nine and right toward the mountains and it's something like ten miles. I've never been there. They bring the pickup to me. One guy drives it and they wait for me to leave.'

'The pickup already has the coolers and the fish in it?'

'Yeah, they don't want anyone to know where the hatchery is and that was cool with me. But it's not that far from where we meet. I know from the way they talked about having just loaded the fish and how to take care of them. One guy is named Barry. I think he's in charge.'

'I need the spot on Brookfield Road where they meet you.'

'There's a map at the house.'

'Let's go get it.'

TWENTY-SIX

Late in the afternoon Marquez crawled slowly east in heavy commuter traffic on his way back to the Sacramento safehouse. He wanted to be north on 99 before dawn and working with a tech as he searched for the hatchery. He called Captain Waller and asked for Nick Chen to get cleared to help him tomorrow. Chen and Marquez teamed up often, Chen on his computer at headquarters and Marquez out in the field.

A spotter plane would go up if they found anything tomorrow as Marquez worked from what he got from Soliatano. He felt like they had to find it tomorrow and Soliatano was the break they had needed. Finding the first hatchery might lead to the other two. Or that was his hope—that and hoping there were only three.

As he hung up with Waller a gray dusk settled over the Central Valley and a call came from Hauser. After three weeks of Hauser's calls Marquez had grown used to the late-night harangues designed to burn time and serve as diversions from whatever tease about the pike project he started the call with. But after leaving him in the church, he didn't expect a call today.

'There's nothing more I have that will help you but you need to know what you're up against. Five years ago they funded a major study on the Asiatic carp migration working its way to the Great Lakes. That was a significant study. So was one they did with snakehead in the Potomac. There's good science in both and it has helped everyone, but they have two faces. They're using what they learned from the Great Lakes study with the pike introduction. They do that with everything.

'They make money by studying current problems and then making forecasts and starting businesses that anticipate future problems. I was hired to model climate change in the western

United States from 2015 to 2025 because they're looking at future water usage. Trying to save a fish like smelt in the delta will be so yesterday and quaint no one will understand why it ever mattered.'

'Where are you, Matt?'

'In my car.'

'Near your house?'

'A couple of miles away but I can't go there and I don't know where to go. I stayed in the church until the priest came out and talked to me. I agreed with Paula that until things are figured out she's in the house and I find a place to live. I stayed in a hotel last night and I lay in the bed there as I talked to her and she told me she doesn't want to live with a thief. I'm a scientist. I was a possible Nobel candidate and that's what she said to me, that she doesn't want to be married to a thief.'

'I think your lawyer's idea is the right one. Ask ENTR not to press charges if you return the money. Start negotiating.'

'It's not just pike they plan to introduce into western rivers. They're testing different species of carp too.'

Marquez started to ask about that but stopped and let it be. He edged forward in traffic, still listening but thinking about tomorrow and Brookline Road.

'Almost all the salmon sold now is farmed and grown in pens and ENTR is getting into that business.'

'You told me about Chile, Thailand, and Indonesia.'

'I did?'

'Yes.'

'When?'

'Several times you've told me ENTR expects to beat the disease and musculature problems penned salmon are susceptible to.'

'Did I tell you about the species selection team?'

'No.'

'The species selection team evaluates my models and makes predictive guesses about which species are likely to thrive and dominate. Their focus is on the river systems. They've predicted pike and carp as predator survivors in many rivers and lakes that now have other native species. They don't know it but their work got used for the pike project. Are you still there?'

'I'm here, Matt. I'm listening.'

'The future is about fighting for resources and food. Have you looked at my climate models?'

'I've looked at what you sent me.'

'After the Arctic ice goes part of North America enters a permanent drought. That's where I focused. Overall, the warmer it gets the less snow-pack. The less snowpack, the more plant and animal species change, the more fires, less water storage in the dry states, and it's a cascade from there. You have one thing changing, then ten, then a thousand, and a Bible-thumping dystopian on his knees praying for the end times may be certain this is God's plan, but the people you're up against look at it differently. They see winners and losers.

'They see losers not adapting and becoming

successively weakened by heat spells, crop fail-ures, lack of water, and businesses moving in and everything coming down to who controls the resources. The government will control the water but the people with the money will control the government and a lot of money is going to be made in rebuilding water distribution systems. Politicians are just part of the pay structure. They're a business expense. Do you understand what I'm saying?'

'Where are you going with this?'

'The illegal pike hatcheries are going to be near legitimate hatcheries such as those we have in partnership with your department. They ran a two-year pilot to assess the viability of elimin-ating salmon as a keystone fish in western rivers before they moved forward with the salmon farm investments and they used the science from earlier studies and from the Species Selection Team before setting up the pike hatcheries. They expect an acceleration as the climate change cascade begins. You understand what is meant by that, don't you?'

Hauser didn't wait for an answer and Marquez's focus now was on a van that had stayed well behind him most of the drive and exited ten miles ago in Dixon but was behind him again, which might mean they were just trying to get an edge on the traffic by running up the frontage road off to his right. He decided to be more cautious getting to the Sacramento safehouse.

'People imagine that we can reverse climate change at the eleventh hour, but that won't be the case.'

'How soon can you return the money?'

'What?'

'I'm asking how easily you can return the money. If you return it and you give us the biologist's name we can work something out.'

Marquez knew what would happen next. He heard the phone click as Hauser hung up and called Captain Waller and let him know he was coming into Sacramento.

'Come here first, John. The ENTR people are all over us. They know people in the Governor's office. The chief is on the phone with the governor right now and the Governor is telling us to back off ENTR. He wants to meet with you as soon as he's off the phone with the Governor. Who *are* these people?'

TWENTY-SEVEN

In a funny way it was Barbara Jones who got them there, calling Marquez the next morning at dawn as he drove north on 99. She sounded as if she was well past her first cup of coffee and ready to lock and load.

'Matt Hauser embezzled, stole, transferred eight million dollars to a secret account, and I don't really care why. I mean that. I could care less why he took it. I want it back and Hauser doesn't want to go to prison or defend himself against lawsuits that will go on for fifteen fucking years, so I'm calling you again. He's not listening

165

to his lawyers and this thing is on the edge of getting ugly and public. Consider this my reach out. You might be the only one who can convince him before it's too late and in return we'll triple the resources we're putting into finding these illegal hatcheries.'

'You now agree they exist.'

'Someone grew the pike you found so they must exist.' She paused before adding what didn't need to be said. 'ENTR denies any involvement.'

'Of course.'

'Here's something else for you to think about. Matt Hauser started coming apart seven to nine months ago, long before Fish and Game heard of him. People he works with started getting odd emails, some of them threatening, some delusional, like proposing ENTR spend ten million on a campaign to raise public awareness of who he is with the goal of getting him nominated for a Nobel Prize. I mean that. He wrote stuff like that. He felt that his name being in circulation, even if it was just Internet chatter, would benefit ENTR.

'But the real thing is his wife has had an open affair with one of the founding partners and Hauser has known and the stress has unraveled him. I'm telling you this because some people at the top making the decisions about how to deal with this current problem are sympathetic and would like to see Hauser avoid embezzlement charges.'

'You're full of surprises.'

'I'm like that and I'm just bringing you up to

speed because we want to continue what's been a great relationship with your department.'

'Wonderful.'

'It is and we want to keep it that way and really when you look at all the evidence against Hauser and where he's at now that his job and credibility are gone, it's a pretty good offer for him. He's got forty-eight hours to take it.'

'And I'm the messenger?'

'He calls you and he calls his wife. We can't really ask her right now. We're talking to his lawyers, but you know what that's like.'

'I'll let him know.'

'And we'll keep working the pike problem. We're very interested in finding out who's behind the fish stocking. We don't want our reputation damaged so maybe it's time to share. If you agree, let's start today.'

'I agree but I don't have anything to share right now.'

'But you're hearing me.'

'I am.'

'I've also got a little advice. You've got a reputation for pushing the boundaries. Don't do that with ENTR. You could end up needing a lawyer like Hauser.'

'You have a nice day, Barbara.'

Marquez broke the connection. Last night he and the tech, Chen, came up with a list of properties off Brookline Road and Wheeler was on standby if they needed help from the air. He figured that was their best move today: eliminate as many sites as they could and continue searching, Marquez on the road and with binoculars and on

167

the phone with Chen who looked down with the real-time Google Earth. It was a limited approach, but if Soliatano wasn't lying this time then they were already close.

Marquez was twenty-two miles from highway 99 off a rural road and on a dirt track above a stand of oaks talking to Chen on his cell when Barbara Jones' white Audi A4 sped by on the road below. He got just enough of a look at her to say, 'We may have just gotten lucky.'

Jones was white, black, and Asian—mostly white but her beauty was from the other two and the intermingling. Her skin glowed with radiant energy as the first ray of sunlight caught her face. She held a phone to her ear and then was gone, speeding into the next curve.

Marquez chased and when he caught sight of her car he hung well back. He missed where she turned off, but a mile later knew she had and backtracked, found it, and called Chen.

'I think it was just given to us. Here's an address. See what you can find out. It looks like a ranch.'

He called Wheeler and stayed clear until he was overhead to the south and reporting a car leaving on an access road to what he called a cattle ranch with grapevines. Then Chen came back with an answer.

'The property was foreclosed on a year and a half ago and bought by a partnership.'

'That could fit. What's the name?'

'Ravil Vineyards.'

'Okay, she's gone. I'm going wine tasting. Try to find out more.'

Ten minutes later he was on an asphalt road that wound through low hills and former pasture land that held only rye grass and thistle now. As he approached the buildings he slowed and saw two carpenters putting new batt and board siding on the face of a building. Near them was a pickup. He didn't see any other vehicles.

The carpenters took him in and from their looks he guessed she had asked them to keep an eye out. He got out, putting on his coat as he walked up to them, a cold wind blowing from behind him and in the distance Mt. Lassen with new snow.

'Hey, I'm late and looking for my boss. Did you see a white Audi roll through here with a super-hot babe at the wheel?'

'Dude, you just missed her.'

'How long ago?'

'Fifteen minutes.'

'Fuck.' Marquez pulled his phone and made sure they saw it. 'I'll call her. See you. Thanks.'

He turned the car around and they were still watching and he didn't take any photos, but he could tell he was good with them. They weren't going to call her and he had seen enough to know his next move. He called Chen.

'There's a lot of new construction. Give me some directions to the county building department and call ahead and see if there's a building inspector or someone I can talk to. There are two carpenters out there working. I'll come up with something for the inspector.'

It took him forty minutes to find the building department and half an hour to convince a

169

building inspector who had done his morning rounds and was planning to eat lunch at his desk and be in the office the rest of the afternoon to make the drive back with him. The inspector knew the story: 140-acre family ranch, quarreling kids who inherited it and no one to work it, then an investment banker who knew nothing about growing grapes who bought just before everything crashed in 2008. Now there was a new set of fools who thought they were going to make money with aquaculture. The inspector turned.

'Why does Fish and Game have a problem with aquaculture?'

'We don't.'

'So does that mean they're doing something else?'

'It does but I can't say much.'

'How sure are you?'

'Pretty sure and there are a couple of carpenters working there that I don't want to get another look at me.'

'I can chase them off. There's not supposed to be any more work out here until they renew the permit, but you want a look inside.'

'Yeah.'

'Then that's up to them but I bet I can get them to let me inside.'

Marquez took in the inspector again. He saw a middle-aged guy ten pounds overweight wearing jeans with an oversized belt buckle and boots, and a tucked-in button-down shirt. He looked like he knew who he was and could pull off whatever was needed.

The inspector got one of the carpenters to

unlock and let him into the concrete building built back into a hill. The lights came on inside and Marquez saw how big it was and all about wine storage when it was built. He watched the inspector and the carpenter walk back out, the carpenter going to shut the door and the inspector hesitating and the carpenter nodding.

The door stayed open and the inspector slowly walked down with the carpenter and across to where the second man was still at work on the siding. When they were far enough away and the carpenters facing the inspector, Marquez walked in. He smelled fish and found round concrete raceways still dark and damp. He checked the equipment, took photos, and emailed those to Chen. He reached into a tank after finding fish scales and gathered samples and got back to the car before the building inspector started back his way.

As they drove out, the inspector asked, 'Did you get what you need?'

'I did and thank you.'

'I'm big on trout fishing. We go up to the Feather River from here and I'm not one of those who waits around for the stocking dates. I like to work for it.'

Marquez understood what he was saying. DFG posted the dates on the department websites when a lake would get stocked with fish. Those stockings included trout big enough to take and a certain amount of fisherman watched the stocking dates and showed up same day or the day after. It wasn't hard to catch regulation size fish that had spent their lives being fed in a tank.

'The people I'm looking for aren't growing trout.'

'What are they growing?'

Play it close or talk to this inspector who was also a fisherman? He went with his gut.

'Northern pike.'

'That's no good.'

'Not good in any way.'

'It looked like they knew you were coming and cleared everything out.'

'It does.'

It did and could mean the pike project was more evolved and the situation worse than he thought, but more likely Barbara Jones was here today to make sure everything was out and shut-down and if that was true she knew what she was looking for. He thought about that a moment. He liked her and that disappointed him.

With the building inspector's help Marquez gathered a lot more information before leaving. He got the name, Stream Systems Aquaculture, and later in the afternoon wrote a search warrant application to get back into the building, though he wasn't sure he wanted to tip his hand with Jones yet. He did get scales and one small dead fish and that would get looked at this afternoon at the Fisheries Branch. He was still debating going back into the building today when Katherine called.

'John, Maria is hurt and I don't know how badly. I'm on my way to the hospital.'

'What happened?'

'She fell!'

'Fell where?'

172

'I don't know where. She was skateboarding. That stupid sport! She may have a concussion and broken ribs. She was trying to find someone that inspector up in Yreka wants to talk to, someone she knows. I'll call you from the hospital. Where are you?'

'In Sacramento but I'll leave now. Call me when you know anything.'

'She shouldn't have been looking for anybody. Why can't you keep Voight away from her?'

'Call me.'

TWENTY-EIGHT

When Marquez got home the front door was unlocked and lights were on throughout the house. He guessed Katherine left in a frightened hurry. He had talked with her twice on the way home and learned that Maria had a good-sized bump on her head but no concussion. Her right clavicle and two ribs were broken and the road rash on her right shoulder and elbow was going to hurt for a while. Katherine called now as he walked through the house.

'We're on our way home but we've stopped to pick up a pizza. I'm inside getting it and Maria is in the car. She says she's hungry but you know how she is. As soon as she gets hurt she tries to make everything normal. It isn't going to work this time, but you and I can eat the pizza and at least she's not bouncing around in the car and the pain pills should start working. They wouldn't give her any pain-killers until they were sure she didn't have a concussion. She's got a couple of Norco in her now.'

'How bad are the ribs and the collar bone?'

'The collar bone didn't separate and that's good and she says it doesn't hurt or at least not right now. The orthopedist said clavicle breaks hurt some people a lot and some not at all. Two ribs are cracked and they definitely hurt her. The orthopedist said six weeks on the clavicle or collar bone and less on her ribs. Remember the tattoo on her right shoulder? It's gone.'

'Okay, tell me again what happened.'

'She was skateboarding down a steep hill with Kevin and Ridley and a car ran a stop sign below them and she collided with Ridley and fell when they were all trying to avoid the car. Remember, these were the two guys she was never going to hang out with ever again. The Siskiyou inspector talked her into calling them and Kevin decided it would be fun to loan Maria a longboard she had never ridden and then ride some steep hills together.'

'Like they used to.'

'Exactly, except that Maria hasn't ridden in years and they knew that. By the way they couldn't stick around at the hospital because they had to get to a party. Hey, John, the pizza is ready. We'll see you at home.'

Marquez opened a beer and sat out on the back deck looking out through the darkness toward the ocean and thinking about the conversation with Barbara Jones. When he heard a car out front and car doors open and shut he stood. He saw the sling and Maria limping but with her stoic face on, a look Katherine claimed she got from him.

'What's up, Dad?'

'I'm having a beer and thinking about some new friends I've met. I just got home. How are you feeling?'

'Crummy. My shoulder hurts and my elbow and the rest is a drag, but it was my fault. I screwed up. The board is a total carver and I kind of freaked because a car ran a stop sign and blew my turn. I haven't been on a board in awhile.'

'I thought you were done with boarding.'

'I wanted to get Kevin to talk to me and he was pretty stand-offish. I kind of dropped these guys a few years ago and he hasn't forgotten.'

Marquez couldn't touch her head or put an arm around her. He put a hand lightly on her back.

'Dad, don't do that, it hurts my ribs and my collar bone. 'I'm going to take a shower.'

Maria showered and didn't feel like eating when she got out. She leaned back on pillows on the couch with a blanket over her legs and studied him before asking, 'You've broken ribs, what should I do?'

'Not much you can do. Try not to cough, sleep on the other side, take hot showers, and breathe as deep as you can stand, a little deeper every day, but mostly wait it out and try not to whine too much.'

'I'm going to whine.'

'Aspirin works for me.'

She thought about that a moment. 'This all sucks.'

'It does.'

'It's because of Voight.'

'Getting on the board is because of Voight?'

'Kind of.'

'I wouldn't go there.'

She nodded then looked away and didn't have any of the pizza or salad but sipped on a glass of red wine to mess with her mom who didn't want her to have any because of the pain killers, and Marquez and Katherine ate most of the pizza and salad. Marquez talked about Voight and asked about Kevin and Ridley and Maria touched her wounds and glanced at him like she had something to say but wasn't ready yet.

Her mom listened quietly and Marquez knew that Katherine's view of Kevin and Ridley was that neither was ever going anywhere in life. They were both several years older than Maria and raised in well-to-do homes with a lot of opportunity but hadn't yet done much with it, but mostly she never trusted what their interest in Maria was.

Marquez remembered the friendship of the threesome differently. It was strongest when Maria was a senior in high school. There was chemistry and a bond. Maria was killer at sports and Kevin and Ridley had liked it that she was quiet about that yet competitive. Both of the guys were natural athletes. They didn't fit into organized high school sports but they were the pair

176

who would snowboard down the steep chute and off a cliff or catch the big waves in January.

What Ridley and Kevin got in return was hanging with a cool girl who was on her way to becoming a woman. Maria grew more graceful but remained the same kind of tough and semi-fearless. Then something happened between the three of them but he and Katherine never got the full story. Maria pretty much dropped them. He had asked about it once and her answer was, 'They're too uninvolved. It's like they're always standing at the edge of the party.'

But there was something more and he thought it had to do with Kevin and guessed it was probably Kevin who had talked her onto an unfamiliar longboard today. It was Kevin who took the bigger risks and who might be dealing dope on a much larger scale than the joints he sold in high school. Kevin had a thing he threw off that said he didn't care what happened. He took chances he didn't have to. When he was fifteen or sixteen another boy surfing with him drowned and it wasn't Kevin's fault but parents learned to keep their kids away from him.

Later than night Maria made a half-hearted throw at saying she was going to drive herself back to the house she shared with five others in San Francisco. She asked him to drive her to her car which was at Kevin's place and Katherine stepped in.

'You're not driving anywhere. Your dad and I will go get your car and bring it back here and you need to lie down.'

It settled that way and what they learned when they picked up her car was that Kevin was living by himself in a house that was probably worth two and a half million. He came out after they reached the turnaround at the top of the driveway: probably Maria had called him. He seemed to know they were coming.

Katherine looked at Marquez and said, 'Guess he didn't go to the party after all. How about if you talk with him and I leave? I think it'll be better all the way around that way. I'll get in Maria's car and go.'

Kevin was in shorts and sandals and an Oregon shirt with a big green O on it.

'Hey, Lieutenant, how's the wildlife doing? How's Maria?'

'You saw her get hurt. How close a call was it?'

'It could have been worse. I thought the dude in the Lexus was going to nail her but she made a killer turn.'

'Did he run the stop sign?'

'Totally.'

'Did he see her go down?'

'He hit his brakes and I saw him watching, but then he jammed.'

'But he knew?'

'Yeah, he knew.'

Kevin smiled for no particular reason, maybe just for the way people can be. His hair was shoulder length now and his face drier and with some lines. They looked at each other, Marquez just a little taller and both with the broad shoulders of a swimmer.

178

'Did Maria talk with you about Terry Ellis and Sarah Steiner's road trip?'

'She talked, but, you know, they're dead. They're gone.'

'Did you know them?'

'I knew Terry.'

'What about Sarah?'

'I met her a couple of times.'

He paused. He looked from Marquez to his open front door as if somebody was waiting there for him, then turned back.

'Terry was pretty hot and Sarah was fun. It's a bummer what happened to them.'

He pointed a finger at Marquez.

'Maria said the detective dude thinks you killed them.'

'I doubt he thinks that.'

'Yeah? Maria said you're pretty worried about it.'

'Well, Voight is a question mark. I don't know where he's going with it. You knew Terry well and you spent time up in the area where they were going. Did you set them up with people to meet?'

'I might have but like I told Maria I don't remember, so I'm not going to remember for you standing in my driveway either. Terry was from up there. She knew all kinds of people. Her brother is a river rat.'

'Know him?'

He shrugged. 'Sure, I know him but Terry had her own friends up there. If they went to parties she knew who to call. She knew people through her brother. He blew off college and moved there

179

and she was on the rivers with him in the summers.'

Kevin touched the O on his shirt. 'Jack Ellis went to Oregon for a couple of years.'

'What's he doing when he's not on the river guiding?'

'No clue, dude, you gotta ask him.'

Kevin stared and then smiled as if he'd just thought of something funny.

'Maybe you can partner with the detective dude Voight and help him solve the case. Maybe ask him if he wants your help. I mean, we used to say nothing scares Maria's dad and we always thought Maria was like you. Like that board today, I knew she would ride.'

'You knew?'

'Yeah, and that's a dangerous badass road.'

'Did you know she would crash?'

'I knew she might have trouble and it would be nasty if she fell.'

'You were okay with that?'

'She got on the board, dude.'

'So her choice?'

'Always is.'

'And riding is much more fun than dealing with her questions.'

'Dude.'

'Yeah?'

Kevin squared off in front of him and stood in closer.

'Voight talked to me way back when, and he's called again. He left a message yesterday. He's a dipshit working down his old list and I haven't called him back yet, but I will and maybe I'll

180

remember seeing you more places and hitting on Terry or Sarah, and take it even farther back and come up with some memories of Maria's stepdad hitting on her other friends. Shit that will really get Voight going, vague stuff that I make up as I go and that's a warning to you. Do not fuck with me.

'You sent your daughter here and she started asking bullshit questions and now you're asking what I think about her getting hurt. Shit, I don't think anything about it. To me she's already dead. She blew me off. She blew Ridley off. She was done with us a while ago and coming around with long-time-no-see bullshit doesn't change that.

'So, yeah, if she crashed today and she was in a coma or if the crash took her out, I still would have said, "Hey, Mrs Lieutenant, your kid is inside in the hospital and sorry about all that work you did raising her, but I've gotta go to a party right now."'

Marquez moved to his car and opened the driver's door.

'Oh, so you're leaving, it's getting too heavy for you and you're not going to say anymore.'

Marquez looked over the top of the car roof.

'There'll be time, Kevin. I'll be back one way or the other.'

'Do not fuck with me.'

'I've heard that before too. I don't know how many times but a lot.'

Kevin was still standing there watching as he drove away.

TWENTY-NINE

Very early in the morning as Marquez made coffee he heard a noise in the darkness out on the rear deck and found Maria with a blanket wrapped around her and her legs up on the bench, her back to the house wall. It looked like she'd slept in her clothes.

'It hurts a lot and I couldn't sleep and I keep thinking about Kevin and Ridley.'

'Do you want to talk about them? I'm making coffee.'

'Let's talk out here. I don't want to wake up Mom.'

That used to mean she didn't want her mom to overhear. He made coffee and Maria warmed herself inside, and then they moved back out, Maria with a blanket around her shoulders and the broken collar bone painful this morning. He watched how she shifted the blanket so it didn't put any weight on the sling.

'Do you remember that Kevin went to the University of Oregon for a couple of years and then dropped out?'

'When I saw him last night he had an Oregon shirt that he said he got from Terry Ellis' brother, Jack.'

'Jack Ellis never graduated from high school.'

'So why would he lie?'

'Because he's a dork and he's messing with

182

you since I asked him questions he didn't like. Kevin was at Oregon for a year and a half so he could sell dope and make connections to sell more. Supposedly he was making three grand a week selling marijuana. He was like one of those dope stores. He sold smoke and chews and brownies and everything. Then he moved south to be closer to his farms.'

'How big is his dope business now?'

'I don't know but he inherited money when his mom died and he funded growers. He has partners. He's sort of like vertically integrated and his business getting bigger was pretty much why I said goodbye to Kevin and Ridley.'

'Kevin said last night it would have been okay if the car had hit you.'

'Typical him, but he doesn't really mean it.'

'I think he did last night.'

'I can't deal with that this morning, Dad.'

'He said you left. You blew him and Ridley off and there's no going back.'

'So like he wanted me to get hurt?'

'He doesn't want to be questioned about Sarah and Terry.'

'Yeah, but he didn't kill them and neither did Ridley. Kev and Rid and I knew a lot of the same people once. Facebook was still happening then and plenty of people followed their trip. Sarah was posting every day and just before they left Kevin posted on Terry's wall that he knew some good people up there. What he meant was he knew where to get primo weed, but it was also so Sarah or Terry would call him. Sarah wanted to see a grow field before she started law school and she was interested in organic farms, mush-room foragers, bee keepers, and some of the trippy back-to-the-land types. Kevin had some friends for them to call and he probably helped them because he wanted to sleep with Terry.'

'Did you ask him about that yesterday?'

'Yeah, and I also asked him after they were killed. His answer yesterday was "let's go ride and then we'll talk after." But I already knew Sarah wanted to see grow fields just to see what they look like. She always wanted to see stuff so she would know what it was really about and she thought once she became a lawyer it wouldn't be cool to walk through a forest to look at a grow field. But Voight knows that. He talked with me about it.'

'What's Ridley's story?'

'He's just a stoner working for Kevin. He prob-ably drives dope from Humboldt down to here as his day job, but I'm not down with those guys anymore. I don't really know and I don't think anything they do is cool and they know that. I have an idea for Voight though. He should put up a photo of the gun you found on Instagram. Somebody might recognize it. Should I suggest it?'

'Sure, why not.'

Maria pulled out her phone and showed him a text: 'Dude, let's get together.'

'That's what I got from Kevin yesterday morning. He wanted to meet me. It's not like he's writing *forget it, I don't ever want to see you again.*'

Marquez held the phone a moment, read the text then handed it back. It was an invite from

Kevin and friendly enough—not the guy he saw last night.

'I'm going to leave before Mom wakes up. Tell her I'll call her.'

He walked Maria out to her car and watched her back up with her good arm. She lowered her window to tell him one last thing.

'I have a really freaky feeling they got in touch with one of Kevin's connections and maybe they got shown something that later someone decided they shouldn't have seen and their getting killed didn't have anything to do with taking down dams.'

She put in her ear piece and worked her phone with one hand as she slow-rolled out the gravel drive. She was talking as she turned onto Ridge Road. She was hurt but she was going to be okay. He doubted whether Kevin Witmer or Ridley knew something that might help solve the murders. But that Kevin was hiding something he did not doubt and he knew he would continue that conversation, but not today.

THIRTY

That afternoon as Marquez neared Yreka, Judge Sally Mantegna called with a torrent of pointed questions about the search warrant application Marquez had sent her. That he had tricked his way inside a building by colluding with a building inspector didn't work for her at all.

'You searched the building, found fish scales,

remains of fins, at least one small whole fish and then took them to your Fisheries Branch on S Street and they confirmed what you found is northern pike. You have already searched the building and found evidence and you now want an ex post facto search warrant that validates what you've done. Am I correct? I just want an answer, I don't want an explanation.'

'That's not how I would put it.'

'I'm sure it isn't.'

Marquez heard paper rustling as he exited into Yreka.

'Is this the same individual in the news this afternoon after being arrested and charged with embezzling more than eight million dollars?'

'I hadn't heard about the arrest.'

'Are you saying that I know more about him than you do? Is his name Mathew Hauser?'

'It is.'

'Then it's the same man you refer to here as your "credible source", which frankly I find incredible. I don't see how I can approve this.'

'There's a lot at stake here.'

'There's always a lot at stake. I hear it all the time.'

'This is an effort to introduce an invasive species that will wipe out the native salmon, trout, smelt, and most other fish species in our rivers.'

'You allege they're trying to plant and your source was charged with a felony today. You need to get me more.'

'That's not easy to do.'

'Come back to me when you've got it.'

She hung up and Marquez parked across from

186

the Siskiyou County Sheriff's Office after checking the lot for the sheriff's white SUV. Sheriff Harknell was in his office and didn't make him wait at all. He pointed at a chair and said, 'Close the door.'

Harknell was a tall, lean-faced man, with hard-eyed confidence. His predecessor died when a tractor trailer rig crossed I-5 six months into his elected term. That led to his appointment and a special election that led to yet another run-off next Tuesday. That had to be what was on his mind when he asked Marquez to come see him.

'I'm surprised you showed.'

'My chief asked me to. He said you were expecting me today.'

'That was just make-happy bullshit as he and I talked on the phone. I agreed that I was a little steamed up when I told you to stay out of the county. I'm not supposed to say something like that but I really didn't expect you to show up. Maybe it's like you showing up after the girls were killed. It's the thrill.'

'Well, I stopped and I've talked to you about as much as I want. I'll leave now.'

'Don't go just yet, Warden. I do have some things to say to you. I want you to know what will happen if you cross me again. With or without Voight's approval, I'll go forward and your name will go out to the media as a person of interest due to your proximity to the scene of the crime and as yet unspecified other reasons that our very seasoned investigator Richard Voight can't disclose without compromising his investigation.

187

'We'll put out your photo and let the press know we've recommended that the Department of Fish and Game suspend you or at a minimum give you a leave of absence or whatever it is they do in your department. That way you can go sit at home while your career dies quietly and we expand our investigation. When we distribute your photo we'll ask for the public's help and always there's someone who has seen a potential suspect in a compromising situation. We'll give that person a good airing.'

'You do that and you'll be seeing a lot more of me.'

'Be careful what you say in here. You're in my county. What you need to know is that your outrage means absolutely nothing to me. You mean nothing to me and I don't have a problem destroying what you call a career, or you for that matter. I didn't mean a single conciliatory thing I said to your chief yesterday afternoon and at some point I expect to stand in front of TV cameras and say we've arrested you, but the takeaway here is don't ignore my warning to stay out of Siskiyou County. Now get out of my office.'

Harknell pulled a gun out of a drawer and laid it on his desk. He did not point the gun toward Marquez or say anything. Marquez looked at Harknell's face, not the gun, and asked, 'Why is your gun out?'

'It's there in case you attack me, which in this case is taking a single step toward me.'

'I'm not going to attack you and I'm leaving.'

It occurred to him as he stood that Voight wasn't

188

in lockstep with the sheriff, and that there was something wrong with Harknell that was more than megalomania. When Marquez turned back at the door the gun was back in the drawer and the sheriff was standing with his hands on his hips and a hint of a smile on his face.

Marquez called Voight from the car and left a message for him. 'Maybe I've been wrong about all this. Call me.'

THIRTY-ONE

The Come On In Bar was near the center of Weaverville but not along the highway running through town. It was on an upslope wooded lot several blocks back from the main road and with a gravel and asphalt lot below for parking. You parked and walked up a short flight of steps to the front door of a long wood-sided building that probably didn't begin life as a bar.

Little light leaked out of it tonight. The sign out front was burned out or turned off. He smelled grilled burgers in the smoke drifting down the street and there were a few cars in the lot.

When he stepped inside he saw four people at the far end of the bar and a young man at a table off immediately to his right sitting with his cell phone and a drink. The bartender was slump shouldered but looked powerful, his big head mostly bald, his glance at Marquez unfriendly. Three patrons at the far end of the bar took more

189

interest in him as he slid onto a stool and waited for the bartender to drift over.

The bartender wasn't in any hurry to do that but Marquez wasn't in a hurry either. He took in two watercolor paintings on the back wall, both river landscapes. A floodlight lit an outside deck in the back that had a good view of the trees overhanging it. He glanced at the one woman among the three at the far end and decided she wasn't Lisa Sorzak. He checked out the rest of the dank uninviting bar and finally the bartender moved his way.

Marquez ordered a beer and when he asked about food the bartender said, 'The kitchen just closed. You'll have to go somewhere else.'

'I'm not from here. Where would you go?'

'I wouldn't. Do you still want the beer?'

'What about peanuts or potato chips, do you have anything like that?'

'No. Anything else?'

'Yes. I'm looking for Lisa Sorzak.'

The bartender nodded toward the three at the end of the bar, the woman with a few drinks in her and the two men trying to hold her attention.

'Her name is Donna Carson. She's all we have for women tonight.'

After the bartender got his beer, Marquez asked, 'Isn't Lisa usually here?'

'Why are you looking for her?'

'A friend suggested I talk to her.'

'How does your friend know her?'

Marquez took a sip of beer and the woman at the far end called, 'Harry, I need a refill.'

The bartender leaned over and asked Marquez, 'Are you alone?'

'Yes.'

'Don't go anywhere.'

Marquez watched him slosh orange juice from a half-gallon plastic container into a glass with ice and glance at the woman before adding very little rum. Then he came back this way.

'I asked why you're looking for Lisa.'

'Like I said, a friend said to look her up. He said she was a good person and that I'd like her. Look, I just got divorced and I'm on the road and I'm going places where maybe I can start again.'

'Well, you picked a good bar for losers, but there's no Lisa here.'

He walked away and Marquez watched him pull out a cell phone. With his back turned he made a call, and Marquez moved over to the table where the young guy was still texting but had overheard the conversation. He pulled a chair out and sat down.

'Ever hear of someone named Lisa X?'

'Sure.'

'Do you know her?'

'Everyone knows her. She owns the bar even if she's never here.'

'Is Lisa X also Lisa Sorzak?'

'I think so.'

Marquez went back to his stool. He took a long drink of beer and the bartender gradually worked his way back and said quietly, 'You feel like a cop to me.'

'No kidding.'

'Bottom line is you're not welcome here and I have the right to refuse to serve if I believe someone is already intoxicated. I think you are.' He turned and pointed at the threesome. 'They will all testify that you started a fight with the bartender.'

'Really, all of them, I'm impressed, but if I leave now, I'll just have to come back tomorrow. What time do you open?'

None of this was going to get him anywhere and he knew it. When another in the party of three called for a drink, the bartender left, though he had already disengaged. He was older, experienced, and backed away from the confrontation he initially sparked. But when Marquez spoke again the bartender could still hear him.

'Hey, do you know a guy named Rider?'

The bartender froze but didn't turn and the men at the end were looking his way now. Marquez left the bar and moved to the young guy's table again and this time it made the kid uncomfortable. He knew it would.

'I need to find Lisa X. Why is everybody in here so spooked about Lisa if this is her bar?'

'What's she done that you're looking for her?'

'She hasn't done anything I know of but she's a friend of someone I'm looking for.'

'What's the name of the friend?'

'He calls himself Rider.'

Marquez could see that didn't mean anything to the kid. He gave him a chance to turn Rider's name in his head and then asked, 'Do you know Lisa?'

'Sure, I know her from here. I come in every night but she hasn't been in lately.'

'Ever hear of a man who calls himself Rider?'

'No.'

'How can I find her?''

The kid didn't answer. Maybe he was debating it. Marquez finished his beer and decided the men at the bar weren't a problem and the bartender was just waiting him out. Marquez walked down the bar toward him and said, 'Tell Lisa that John Marquez was here looking for Jim Colson.'

'I don't know what the fuck you're talking about.'

'You don't have to know, just give her the message. She'll know what I mean. Thanks for the beer and the good time.'

He walked back to the young guy's table and finished his beer there. The young man was texting again and talked to Marquez without taking his eyes from his phone.

'She's got a cabin farther down the Trinity. It's past Big Bar and you've got to know where to cross the river and pick up the trail. I don't know if it's her cabin but supposedly that's where she is. You know he's going to tell her you were here. You know that.'

'Sure.'

'He's not going to like me talking to you either, so I didn't say anything.'

'I'm good with that and I'm not after her. I'm after someone she knows.'

'She goes to that cabin for like a month at a time.'

'Got it—thanks.'

Marquez left the empty beer glass on the bar and walked out.

THIRTY-TWO

Marquez stayed that night in Weaverville and met up the next morning with one of the Trinity wardens, Brent Logan. Logan opened his laptop on the hood of his DFG truck and showed him trailheads and a map of cabins and homes along the Trinity River. He touched the screen.

'If the cabin you're looking for is out here, you'll need to hike in or I can loan you a boat. There's an old forest ranger I'll call this morning. He knows everything built along the Trinity.'

From Weaverville Marquez drove south to Sacramento and three hours later he was at headquarters at a table eating lunch with four of the Special Operations Unit, including the current head of the team, patrol lieutenant Adrian Muller.

Muller did three Iraq tours and saw combat that affected him more than he liked to admit. He could get agitated and impatient and there was some of that today but Marquez couldn't blame him. An informant was on his way here to meet Marquez and it was a meeting no one on the SOU team had seen coming. Muller had only known himself since this morning.

'Faesy is going to call any minute. He's got a US passport and claims his father had dual citizenship in the US and Mexico and that he grew up both places. He won't say much about mom

194

or dad, but he says his dad worked with you, John.'

'His father worked with me?'

'That's what he's claiming. What were you doing with his dad?'

That got a few laughs at the table and Muller moved on.

'We've watched him move animal parts and drugs in his food truck. He parks and sets up for business and they come to the truck, buy food, and either take a delivery from him or give him one to drop off. It works for everybody. They get lunch out of it and paper bags get passed back and forth. It's pretty good cover as long as the deliveries aren't too big. On the drug end it's probably as good as a kid delivering on a bike.'

'Where is he picking up?'

'A mix of places including just this side of the border and lately in a beach parking lot, or he meets a truck coming out of Long Beach Harbor farther down the highway.'

'What's his full name?'

'William Faesy.'

'I thought he was Mexican.'

'He's like you, he's a mix. The Faesy name is from a stepfather.'

'And the food truck is his business? That's what he does every day?'

'There's no every day with this guy, but yeah, that's what he does. He doesn't always deliver with the food truck. He'll switch to a rental truck, U-Haul, that kind of thing, if the delivery is bigger.'

'And you're saying he's getting a mix of animal products.'

'Yes.'

'Why haven't I heard about this?'

'Because I've kept it inside the immediate team.'

Muller expected to be challenged on that and was ready.

'Keep going on Faesy. I'm not questioning why you haven't told me this before now.'

'You don't share everything either, John.'

Marquez took a bite of sandwich and said, 'You're right, let's keep going.'

Muller sat on that a moment then continued. 'The food truck works well for him. It's mobile and flexible. He'll do a hand-off right out in the open or at a rest station off the freeway or turnout or vista overlook, places like that.'

'What does Faesy think you have on him?'

'A lot of videotape of buys, but we're bluffing. We've one good one and it wasn't from a food truck deal. We've got an exchange of money and him loading turtles, tortoises, tropical birds, and venomous snakes into a U-Haul with the help of another man. He drove that load all the way to Seattle.'

'We've seen plenty of drug deals too, but we haven't given LAPD or anyone else a heads-up. Those are pills and cocaine and he's got a girl-friend in Ojai who sometimes nips a little from the coke shipments. She often rides with him. We don't know if she's involved but that's one of the questions for him today.

'He's also in San Francisco regularly and some-times it's a food event, a pop-up deal. He's into selling and making his food and we think the animal trafficking pays for travel and juices his food business with cash. His food is decent. The chicken taco is his best thing.'

'If he's got the truck I'll get one today.'

Two wardens laughed.

'We'll need to script it with you, John.'

'What do you mean?'

'We've been able to name places he's picked up or delivered and he thinks he's totally fucked, but like I said we only have footage of one U-Haul deal that was mostly tropical birds.'

'What about the people he's delivered to?'

'We've got some okay tape there. Would your Rider walk up to a food truck?'

'I doubt it.'

Marquez listened as he finished his sandwich. Muller made sure he understood that this was an ongoing SOU field investigation and beyond this meeting today he didn't need any help. He viewed Marquez's working as a lieutenant specialist attached to the SOU as a choice Marquez made. He once told Marquez he would have quit Fish and Game if the same thing had happened to him. That Marquez was also an FBI task force officer and deputized as a US Marshal was just smoke from Muller's point of view.

'Okay, so back to his father who he claims knew me.'

'It came out of nowhere and I promised him I'd get you here for this meeting.'

Marquez nodded. He looked around at the group and said softly, 'Well, he's like a son to me. It'll be good to see him again.'

More laughs but they were as surprised as Marquez that Faesy had played this card.

Now the call from Faesy came and Muller and one of his team went down to meet him in the lobby and bring him up, and Marquez thought, why not a food truck? They were everywhere now, big enough, and pretty good cover if as Muller said the deliveries weren't too big or too far away.

The elevator dinged and he heard Muller talking to Faesy as they walked him down the hall. The first thing Marquez picked up on was Faesy had some Japanese blood and there was a resemblance. He got that right away and shook Faesy's hand.

'You knew my father but he got killed and my mother married my stepfather. I took my step-dad's name after he adopted me.'

'Where did you grow up?'

'Escondido.'

'Are your parents still there?'

'No, they're both dead. But my mom said you were with my real dad when he was killed. He gave her a piece of paper you wrote your phone numbers on.'

'And she kept it all that time?'

'He told her that if anything bad ever happened to call you and you would help.'

'That's a long time to keep a piece of paper.'

'She found out ten years ago that you worked here.'

Looking at him Marquez saw it. The resemblance was unmistakable. With some people the second you see them you know exactly whose

198

kid they are; the resemblance sent him back to his DEA days and the drive through the Juarez with Billy Takado's body.

'Do you still have the piece of paper with the phone numbers?'

He started to pull his wallet out. 'Do you want to see it?'

'Do you remember your dad?'

'Honestly, hardly anything, only that he wore sandals and these flowered shirts.'

Hawaiian shirts and always sandals, Marquez thought, as Faesy unfolded a piece of yellowed paper and handed it to him before answering.

'His name was William Takado. My mother said everyone called him Billy.'

Marquez was looking at his name and the phone numbers written on the paper, numbers he had written when he worked for the DEA. He looked at the paper and remembered and still it didn't feel right. Something was wrong here. The paper was right. The phone numbers were right and this probably was Billy Takado's son, but something was wrong.

'I have an ordinary name. How did your mother find me?'

'I don't know. She knew people.'

'Ten years ago?'

'I don't know if it is exactly that long ago, but something like that.'

Marquez glanced at Muller and knew this could get Muller upset, but he did it anyway.

'I didn't work here ten years ago, so what's up? Who put you up to this? You're getting in deep here and you're already in a bad spot.'

'Come on, man, my mother gave that to me. She said I could trust you.'

'It's you we're talking about.'

Marquez heard a chair scrape and a sigh. No one was sure where he was going with this and they needed Faesy. He was their key and they didn't want Marquez screwing it up.

'Do you go by Billy like your dad?'

'Bill.'

'Bill Faesy?'

'Yes.'

'Who got you into what you're doing now?'

'Come on, man, my mom saved that and gave it to me. It couldn't be more real. I'm telling the truth.'

Marquez tapped the piece of paper with the phone numbers.

'Someone screwed up telling you I was working here ten years ago. I wrote these phone numbers down and I believe your mom kept the paper, but whoever you told the story to and sent you here with it screwed up the ten year part. You got the timing wrong.'

Muller coughed. He was increasingly uncomfortable with this, for Muller knew Marquez had been here ten years ago and was wondering why lie to Faesy, why mess with him? Marquez nodded toward Muller.

'He's in charge. His team caught you and they're the ones you have to work with; I'm just a gatekeeper. My job here is to validate you. Do you know what I'm saying?'

'I get I have to prove it to you, but I'm telling the truth.'

'Yeah, you have to prove it to me and if you don't, you're screwed. I've seen what they've got on you. You'll go to prison and for me, that's okay, so you're not getting past me without telling me who put you up to this.'

'I've told you everything. Maybe she got the wrong number of years, but what's the big deal? You still work here. You recognize the phone numbers and remember writing them. I could tell on your face that you remember. My mother said I look like my dad. Do I? Do you see him, man?'

'I see him.'

'So what's up?'

'Your mom didn't find out I work here.'

Faesy looked away. He shook his head and then looked at Muller.

'That's all I have, the piece of paper, what my mom told me.'

'Then I can't vouch for you.'

Marquez stood up. He apologized to the SOU wardens and left the room with Muller following. He walked down the hallway talking with an unhappy Muller.

'Where are you coming from with that, John? This guy is our key to the door. We need him. What's wrong with his story?'

'It doesn't feel right.'

'Doesn't *feel* right? Really, our investigation is riding on your gut feeling?'

'Let him sit and then let me go in alone.'

Muller was fine with that but an hour later got impatient and wanted back in the room with Marquez and Faesy. Marquez argued against it.

'If you go in there with me he's going to turn

to you for help. He knows you want to work with him.'

'I don't want you blowing up our operation.'

'I'm not going to blow it up.'

'And no more of the gatekeeper shit. I'm not losing this guy.'

Marquez sat across from Faesy and saw the bull ring in the Juarez, saw Billy Takado.

'I want to talk to you, Bill. I don't want to threaten you and they're offering you a good way out. They want to work with you. You know that, right?'

'They don't give a fuck about me.'

'I didn't say they did. I said they want to work with you and it's better than prison. I saw your record. You've been in jail on some minor stuff, but you haven't done time in prison. You don't want to go to prison and I can't okay you without knowing how you got to me.'

'I told you.'

'Do you want to shake hands and leave it there? I'll do that right now and leave the room if you want. But if I stand up, it's over. We're done and I'm gone.'

Faesy pulled his brown leather wallet out and held it in front of him.

'I've carried that paper a long time, man.'

'I know you have and you told the story to someone who recognized my name and knew how to put it together. I need to know who that was.'

Faesy sat a long several minutes. He sighed. He looked down at the table then up at Marquez and said, 'They're after you.'

202

'Who's after me?'

'A dude called Rider is looking for you.'

'Have you met him?'

'No, he sent a chick to tell me what to say. How does he know you?'

'I've been chasing him and he figured out who I am. I'm going to need to get an artist to sketch the woman who came to meet you. I'll need you to describe what she looked like.'

'I can't, man, she came at night when I was cleaning my truck. She came up behind me and stuck a gun in my back. I thought I was getting robbed but what went down is she told me what I was going to do. She heard about the paper. She wanted to see the paper.'

'Who did she hear about it from?'

'I don't know. I think it was this guy I delivered to. I showed him the paper and maybe he told somebody. I don't know, but I know she put the gun right on my head and made me get my wallet out. That was before your dudes busted me. She wanted me to come here and say what I said today.'

'Before Lieutenant Muller talked to you?'

'Yeah.'

'And then you decided to use it a different way.'

Faesy didn't need to answer. That's what had happened and now he needed to avoid the woman with the gun who told him she would kill him if he didn't follow through. She wanted him to say he knew about jaguar skins and condor feathers and rare turtles and birds being sold and where to buy them.

'She wants to set a trap and fuck you up, man.'

'Okay, we'll figure that out and we may need your help. Wait here, I'll go find Lieutenant Muller and we'll get this going.'

THIRTY-THREE

The signed search warrant for the defunct Ravil Winery came through when he was still at headquarters with the SOU. He sat down at a desk, laid his phone down, and thought about it before calling two biologists from the Fisheries Branch who were standing by. He figured to serve the warrant to the caretaker and search the buildings with the biologists. He walked down to where Muller's team was holed up and told Muller they would have to do the rest by phone.

Marquez made it to his pickup and was north on 99 before a call came from Barbara Jones. The call didn't surprise him but as he answered he was still debating what he was going to tell her.

'Sounds like you're driving,' she said.

'I'm on my way to the Ravil winery building. Two of our biologists are meeting me there.'

'So am I.'

'How did you know we got the warrant approved?'

'It's a wired world and I work for some sharp people. I'll unlock for you so don't knock any doors down. When you finish at Ravil I'll lead you to the second pike hatchery site. We found that one this morning after combing through your friend Hauser's computers.

'Can you tie it to him?'

'Not necessarily, but you're backing a complete fraud in Mathew Hauser. He's going to go down for embezzlement.'

'Where is this second hatchery?'

'It's in the Sacramento area but I'm not going to give you an address yet. I want to manage this my way. You'll follow me. I'll take you there and I don't want some DFG press release about how you've discovered an illegal hatchery. What ENTR wants is a thank you for finding it.'

'Can you send me the file or files you found that located it?'

'Are you listening to me? Your unemployed climatologist friend had multiple computers, six of them, and it took a while. He's a bright guy but he's not a hacker. He had it well hidden. By the way, I added up what ENTR has paid him in nine and a half years of employment. It totals what I'd make in twenty years.'

'How long before you get to the winery?'

'You don't want to hear me talk about Hauser anymore? Okay, I won't rub it in. You can get there your own way. See you there.'

At the winery Marquez did a slow walk through but left it to the biologists to scour the concrete runways and tanks where the fish were bred and raised. He took a return call from a friend at the Alaska Department of Fish and Game while he was still inside the building.

'Calling you back, John, and yes, we have a

205

real problem with illegally stocked northern pike in lakes in the south central area. We don't even stock those lakes anymore. We used to stock with char, rainbow, graylings, landlocked salmon, and other fish, but with northern pike already there nothing lasts long enough for the fishermen to get to it. We were just feeding the pike. What kind of problem have you got?'

'We're trying to figure that out right now. We've got someone setting up pike hatcheries so they can stock our rivers.'

'That's bad news. Find the pike and kill them as fast as you can. There's nothing they won't eat. They've got a tiny brain and razor sharp teeth, which is a lot like my boss now that I think about it. Call me back if I can help.'

Barbara Jones arrived now with an older white-haired man in a dark blue suit who didn't introduce himself. He stared at Marquez as if he were some sort of curiosity and wandered through the building with the look of a man killing time until his limo arrived.

Marquez pulled Jones away and walked with her.

'Who's the guy with you?'

'One of the managing partners – don't worry about him. Everyone is concerned about bad publicity and fallout that could affect raising venture capital. We create business models around the science—'

'Save it, I've heard it all from Hauser. You like frank talk, so I'm going to give you some and this is just between you and me. You're young. You're bright. We're about to go see this second hatchery and then you're going to try to prove to me that Hauser set all this up on his own. I think that guy over there in the suit is encouraging you to focus on making everything tie back to Hauser.'

'I find that insulting.'

'I think you should follow your own instincts.'

'You just got burned by an embezzler and you're giving me advice?'

'That guy in the suit over there doesn't care about your investigation. He only cares about how it affects the company.'

'And how the fuck would you know that?'

'He's here to keep an eye on your investigation and help steer it. You know it, and I know it.'

'I don't know anything about that and he isn't steering me at all. Are you done here at the winery? Do you want to follow us to the next pike site or do you want to insult me and the company some more?'

'We'll follow you.'

Marquez and the hatchery biologists followed and Muller's undercover team picked them up on the drive back to Sacramento. The SOU also picked up on another car trailing them and then trailed that man who as it turned out was first to go to the warehouse. The warehouse was in a cluster of tired-looking buildings with a new sign that read Delgado Creek Industrial Park.

The water recycling unit was compact and portable. The thousand-gallon tanks held several hundred fish each. Many were nearing six inches and at a point where they needed to be released. Overhead were long skylights that let in a milky light. Marquez studied the simplicity of design, the water supply, pellet food dispenser, the high-end water recycler, and it impressed him. The tanks were fiberglass, probably loaded on a flatbed and backed in through the rolling door.

He took it in and it filled him with a sense of loss, a feeling that they were always going to be fighting the next thing, and walked outside trying to lose that. When he walked back in the man in the dark blue suit wanted to talk to him. Marquez watched him put on a puzzled face.

'We thought you'd be happy.'

'Don't I look it?'

'No.'

'I'm awfully sorry. But you must be happy to help out like this.'

'We're very disturbed that someone who has worked for us for so long could be suspected of an act this terrible. I can't tell you how troubling it is. As you know, we've partnered with Fish and Game on a number of things. We're very much on the same side. We've even consulted with you on your new logo and name that rolls out in 2013.'

'What are we going to be called?'

'The Department of Fish and Wildlife, and we're very proud to be partners with you.'

He introduced himself as Ned Cowler and Marquez left questioning the hatchery biologists as they took samples from each tank. A debate carried on into the late afternoon about whether to kill the fish with rotenone or just pump the water out, but Marquez didn't hear the conclusion. He and Muller searched the rest of the building instead, moving quietly through sad little offices in the back and upstairs to storage above.

They found footprints in the dust but not the man who had gone in ahead of anyone else and not shown himself since. They found where he lay down on a dusty stack of lumber and where his elbows rested as he lay on his belly. Muller turned to him.

'Was he up here with a rifle?'

Marquez shook his head. That's not what he was seeing.

'I think he filmed your team and me and went out the back door. He probably got picked up by somebody, but sooner or later they'll come back for the car he arrived in.'

'ENTR filmed us?'

'Yeah, to find out who the members of the under-cover team are. They already have me and I think they got tipped or anticipated the SOU would show up as I was led to the next winery. One of their security people also seemed to know the search warrant for the second winery was approved.'

'Okay, when this guy comes back for his vehicle we'll be waiting and wherever he goes we'll go with him. I'll call you. This is starting to get to me, John. I feel like we're being used.'

'We are.'

THIRTY-FOUR

The driver returned to the warehouse hatchery after midnight. He was dropped by a taxi two blocks away, walked in, and drove out of the industrial park with his lights off. The SOU trailed him to the Sacramento Hyatt and didn't get his name but did get the floor and the room he was in. They were waiting for him to move again early the next morning when Marquez took a call from the Trinity warden, Logan.

'I may have found her cabin. It's about half scuttlebutt whether it's hers or not, but I know where the trail is, or what passes for a trail. It's down the south fork and you've got to know where to cross the river.'

Marquez listened and said, 'I know where that is.'

'But that's just the start and it's not easy to see the cabin from the water. There's a beach and it's tiny but if you want to borrow a boat the offer still stands. The cabin has been around for a hundred years, or that's what my friend told me.'

'And if I walk?'

'It's three miles, more or less, from the other side of the bridge and some of it is pretty damned steep. What are you driving?'

'A late-model green Tacoma pickup with a short bed.'

'How long will it take you to get to the bridge?'

'Four hours.'

'I'll meet you there and we'll find a different place to leave your truck. There's river access farther upstream. Maybe we'll park it there and I'll run you back to where the trail starts. If you've got questions call me before I leave Weaverville. There's no cell reception where you're going. Are you sure you don't want to borrow a boat?'

Marquez talked with Muller twice on the drive north. Muller told him that shortly after nine this morning the man who had checked into the Hyatt last night left Sacramento and headed west in an Avis rental car. He wasn't listed as an employee for ENTR but could be headed for their offices in Palo Alto.

Less than half an hour after meeting up with Logan, Marquez was climbing through trees on the south bank of the Trinity River. The trail rose onto a rocky bench and threaded along the top of a steep bluff above the river. Below, the water was dark green and running hard with last night's rain. The sky was cloudy, gray, and cold. More rain was forecast for the late afternoon and wind gusted hard through the high branches of the trees as the trail crossed a forested area and ended abruptly in a small meadow.

Even if he didn't find the trail again, he had the river and Logan told him a narrow switch-backing trail led up from the beach below the cabin. He could work downstream and would find that. He also carried a Garmin that tracked his progress with GPS, but it was another hour and a half before he found it. He spotted the gray weathered wood siding and a stone chimney of a small cabin built between two trees high on a steep face above the river.

If she was there – and from what he'd been told he guessed she was – then she had a good view of him as he made the climb from the small beach at the base of the rocks below the cabin. That trail climbed to a shoulder and then worked up the backside. It took him straight to the cabin and he liked the spot. It looked out on a curve in the river and you couldn't see any of the highway or anything man-made. He knocked on the door.

After knocking again he started looking for her outside but wondered if he had wasted his time hiking here. Then he picked up on movement or felt something down in the trees to his left and watched as a tall dark-haired woman with an authoritative gun in her right hand climbed into view. She looked in his direction and he watched her movements for several minutes before stepping out in front of her and identifying himself.

'You don't need the gun for me. If you're Lisa, I'm here to talk to you.'

'And if I'm not?'

'I'll leave.'

She gripped the gun with both hands now and aimed at his torso.

'Show me a badge.'

'Right.'

Marquez retrieved his small backpack and she moved higher and repositioned herself, comfortable in her stance, familiar with a gun. She had him face her as he unzipped a pocket and pulled out his badge. After studying it, she lowered the gun and said, 'The legend himself.' She tossed his badge back to him.

'I had two guys up here a couple of days ago and they scared me. I don't know what they had in mind but it wasn't anything legal. Maybe they heard about this cabin and me here alone and thought they could have some fun, or maybe they were just looking for something to steal. My imagination tends to run when I'm out here alone. Why do you want to talk to me?'

'I want to talk with you about someone you used to know when you worked at the Methuselah Tavern. Well, you still know him, but I want to start there.'

'I still know him?'

'I think you do.'

'You've got to be kidding.'

'I'm not.'

'The Methuselah was a lifetime ago and we were all drinking too much and doing drugs in those days. I slept with the husband of one of the owners for a year though Lila was fine with it before she decided to catch us. She didn't do that until her boyfriend lost interest in her because she was such a cokehead. And she was the married one, not me.'

'I'm looking for Jim Colson.'

'They fired Jim and I the same day and we went separate ways, no matter what Lila says. I hardly ever hear from him.'

'So maybe now I should thank you for your trouble and apologize for bothering you and leave.'

She smiled at that.

'Don't leave yet. You don't have to do that. Let's go inside where it's warmer. It's going to rain again this afternoon. We can build a fire and talk. I'm not going to say I haven't heard from him at all or that I can fool you.'

Marquez put her in her early thirties with crow's feet at the corner of her eyes that said some of those years were hard. She looked fit and walked

213

up the steep slope with the gun in her right like she was used to it. She stripped the gun of bullets after they were inside. She did that and looked at him as she laid the gun on the fireplace mantel.

'So you don't worry.'

'What were you going to do if you shot me?' he asked.

'Roll you into the river and throw the gun after it and then try to clean up before they came with dogs looking for you. The river would take you some distance. You'd get found downstream after someone driving 299 spotted you and they would come here because I'm sure you told someone you were coming here. The dogs would pick up scent but I'd be gone and wouldn't be seen for a long while.

'My grandfather did that once with a man who came here armed and claiming he was owed money.'

She pointed.

'Grandpa shot him right there where those old wooden chairs are and rolled him off the edge. The man was a thief and no one cared that he disappeared; shooting him was something my grandfather didn't share for fifteen years. He didn't like himself for having done it and I think he told me because he was afraid of a violent streak in me.'

'Is there one?'

'I don't know.'

'Well, that's a nice family story.'

'It's one of my favorites.'

Marquez took a look around, a one-room cabin with a cot, a table, and two chairs. She probably learned to shoot and fish from her grandfather. She made tea and stoked the fire and they sat in front of it, Marquez holding the warm mug of tea in his big hands, Lisa talking calmly though the room didn't feel that way. It felt small. He felt a nervous quicksilver energy coming off her now as if she was balancing a red-hot wire inside.

'If I knew where to look for Jim and told you, would you leave now?'

'We need to go farther than that. I'd like to know about your relationship with him and I also recognize your voice.'

'I don't have a relationship with him. Sometimes he finds me. Usually, that's when he needs something. I don't think we've met before. How sure are you that you recognize my voice?'

'Pretty sure.'

'Fascinating.'

Marquez took a sip of the tea and it tasted like wood chips. He put the mug down on the stone hearth.

'I know the tea sucks. It's a plant that grows around here and we need something stronger for this conversation. It's too early for whiskey. I'll get two beers and if we get philosophical later I'll get out the whiskey. You went to all this trouble to find me so I'm guessing you don't have to leave immediately.'

She stoked the fire again, leaning over with her back toward him and her shirt sliding up the smooth skin of her back and higher still as she leaned over a cooler and pulled two bottles of beer, water dripping from each onto the stone floor.

215

'There's no refrigeration so it's going to be on the warm side. If you want to cool it, put it outside. The beer foamed as he opened it. She moved her chair closer to his.

'Would your testifying that you recognize my voice stand up in court?'

'No chance.'

'That's what I figure too, but there it is, you recognize it. I didn't want him back in my life, I can promise you that and it's the real reason I'm out here. I didn't like making that phone call to you or goading you or even thinking he knew where that gun was. Did it turn out to be the gun used to kill them?'

'You'd have to ask Rich Voight at the Sheriff's Office in Yreka that question.'

She smiled. She touched his wrist.

'You're not a great liar but you're a pretty good one. I know that because I'm a little like you. He was in my kitchen when I woke up that morning. I don't even know how he got in and it scared the shit out of me to walk in and find him there. I go into my kitchen and he's sitting in a chair with a Starbucks coffee in one hand and one on the table for me, smiling like crazy, like it was such a wonderful surprise. I hadn't seen him in five years, though he called every so often.'

'Why?'

'To say hello, to make sure something in his world was still tied down.'

'You made the call to me for him. Why didn't you call back when you were alone? Why didn't you come forward?'

'The short answer is I didn't want to get involved. The longer answer involves wondering how he knew where to dig for a gun. When I started thinking about that I decided it was time to come up here for a while.'

Marquez nodded. He took another sip of beer and waited. She'd already said enough to put herself in an interview room with Voight and she had to know it was going to lead to many more questions.

'Do you know why I'm looking for him?'

'Yes, and I don't know how he got into the animal thing, but he's way into it.'

'Do you call him Rider?'

'I'll never use that name but I know it the same as you.'

'How much do you know about his trafficking?'

'I know he does it and he's bragged to me about the money he's made.'

'How much money?'

'Enough to retire and never worry.'

'Have you ever thought about calling us?'

She took a long drink of her beer and put the can down and came out of her chair to roll two smoldering logs so they burst into flame again. Kneeling and facing the fire with her back to him she started talking.

'Of course, I've thought about doing that, but I don't really trust cops. They promise you they won't use your name and then they do and Jim would figure it out and I wouldn't be able to give you anything to arrest him with. I don't even know where he lives, so eventually he would come for me. He can be very cruel when he wants to be.'

'Why not tell me where to look for him and give me your phone number and a way to start a conversation with you.'

'You must really want to get him. Let's find out how much.'

She moved her chair closer to his and undid the top button of her shirt.

'It's hot by the fire. You want him and he's looking over his shoulder for you, yet talks like he wants you to keep looking for him, which I wouldn't do if I were you. I really wouldn't. There's a lot of money in the business he has and he can hire people to do what he needs done.'

'I'm building a case.'

She leaned against him slowly and breathed in his ear, 'That's so cop.'

'I need your help.'

'Then what are you willing to do?'

She pulled back from him and when he didn't answer, took her shoes off and slipped out of her pants and underwear and pulled off two shirts and a bra then stood with her back to the fire, her long legs and lovely hips facing him.

'You're married, aren't you, Lieutenant?'

'Yes.'

'Love her?'

'Yes.'

She had a beautiful body.

'What if I said I want you here and now in front of this fire? I want your clothes off and when we're done I'll give you a way to find him. That's my offer. You're right on the edge of getting him and I'm sure your wife will understand. I'm sure she's very supportive. What do you think?'

THIRTY-FIVE

A light rain started before Marquez left the cabin. The rock of the chimney was wet and dark and droplets pattered into the duff beneath the trees as he came off the steep slope and picked up the trail out. Low fog lay over the river and strands moved through the trees. If he hadn't been close to the river and still near enough to her cabin he wouldn't have seen the boat.

He saw two men, twin outboards, an aluminum-hulled boat working its way slowly along this bank as if searching for where to put in. He heard the engines rev before losing sight of it in fog and decided to get a better look. He moved back toward the small beach below the cabin and heard the aluminum hull grate over rocks and sand as the boat landed. When two men climbed out, Marquez climbed quickly back up to the cabin and rapped on the door.

'I'm back. Two guys are getting out of a boat at your beach right now. At least one has an assault rifle. Let's get you out of here.'

She had opened the door with her grandfather's gun in her hand and now asked him, 'What are you carrying?'

'A Glock .40 and it doesn't matter. We're not

looking for a shoot-out. I'll deal with these guys later.'

'I thought you never ran away from anything, but that's twice today and I only just met you.'

'Stow it. Let's go.'

She threw water on the fire and pushed the hearth screen tight around it, turned off an electric lantern, slipped a pack over one shoulder and snapped a Master lock over an iron hoop and clasp at the front door. Without another word she went off the steep back slope fast, the only sound her pack and her coat rustling ahead of him. That told him more about her. They moved down through the trees off the backside of the bluff and circled around under the men who were now climbing the steep switchbacks to the cabin. Marquez and Sorzak were close enough to hear them talking though they couldn't make out the words.

But Marquez didn't need to. Both carried assault rifles. One had a backpack. He motioned her to get down lower and closer to him, then whispered, 'We'll let them get closer to the cabin before we go to their boat.'

The men climbed and when fog hid them Marquez and Sorzak hurried down the trail to the beach. At the beach they heard a hollow pounding above them and then a burst of gunfire as Marquez boarded the boat. He turned to her.

'They just broke into your cabin. What are they looking for?'

'Me.'

'What else?'

'I have no fucking idea but I'm angry.'

Now there was a deep whooshing concussive roar and a rush of flame and glass tinkling as the cabin windows exploded onto the surrounding rocks. They saw flames and what smelled to Marquez like high-octane fuel.

'Fuck! They just torched my cabin.'

'Push the bow around. We're leaving.' She moved the bow and climbed on as he touched the ignition wires together. The engines kicked over and caught. With the fire he didn't think the men would hear, but they must have already started back toward the boat because one yelled. Then they started shooting, shots zipping into the water, but nothing came close and Marquez drove the boat into fog. As he did, she reached to take the wheel.

'I grew up on the river. I know the river. I'll steer.'

'Are you sure?'

'Don't be a dumb-ass.'

She took the wheel and there were more shots but they were around the first bend and couldn't even see the fire anymore and the pair couldn't see them.

'Why do you think they were here, Lisa?'

'To rape and kill me and lose the evidence by burning the cabin. I don't know why they're here and they just took out something I loved. I don't feel much like talking about it right now.'

It was slow and a little iffy in the fog but she seemed to know the river and inside twenty minutes they were at a boat access point and tied off. There were four boat trailers and a narrow dirt road leading up to the highway. After they tied off Lisa went from one boat trailer to the next.

'I know that one and that one. He lives here and the other man is from over in Weaverville and has a cabin like me or like I had.'

Marquez listened then said, 'I'm going to hike up to the road and see if I can get cell reception there.'

The phone worked and he got through to the local warden, Logan, who reported the fire and started toward them. Marquez walked back down and found Lisa.

'Show me the vehicles you don't recognize.'

She did that and told him she wouldn't need a ride anywhere. She had a friend she could call.

'You can't leave yet, Lisa, you're the victim here. You need to make a statement.'

'I don't have anything to say except I want to kill them.'

'You're not leaving yet.'

Marquez disabled the boat so if the men showed up it wouldn't start. Then he and Lisa got out of the rain and waited under trees. He could feel how anxious she was to get away and didn't read it as fear of the men showing up. He tried to talk to her.

'You're alive. You could have been in the cabin.'

She moved away from him when he said that and sat on a fallen log staring out at the river fog. He gave her a few minutes then sat down alongside her.

'They were looking for something.'

'Me.'

'And what else? They searched inside before burning the cabin.'

'Leave it alone today, okay?'

'I heard them before they went in.'

'There was nothing in there. You were inside. You know that.'

'Where is Colson from?'

'From hell, and why are you asking about him?'

'Lila Philbrick said he sounded like he came out of the south. She guessed he was from along the Arkansas-Texas border.'

'Lila was stoned, drunk, or high on drugs for the two and a half years I worked there. It's amazing she still remembers what her name is. She used to do a line of coke on the bar top and chase it with two double cappuccinos laced with vodka every morning. She doesn't know shit about where he was from.'

'How close were you and Jim Colson?'

'Look, my cabin just got torched and I'm not really in the mood to talk more about Colson. I already told you everything I know and I was never close to him. Yeah, we slept together and we looked out for each other for a little while, but that was a long time ago.'

She turned. 'Colson has serious fucking issues and they're not mine. He once told me that he left everything behind and I don't know about that but he definitely left his soul back wherever he came from. When he got here he didn't care about anything and he didn't believe in anything.' She paused on that and added, 'That's what we had in common.'

'What about now?'

'Now I'm cold and sitting down along a river thinking somebody tried to kill me today and I need to do something about it.'

She was quiet now but he knew she wasn't through talking about Colson.

'Jim might have been a cop somewhere. Sometimes we'd pass a cop parked on the side of the road writing a report or whatever and he'd say I know what that feels like. Or we'd see a cop eating alone in a diner and he'd make some comment. He'd talked about going someplace warmer, Hawaii, or Mexico, even though his Spanish sucked. He was always talking about getting the money he needed to go somewhere else. That's how he got into the animal thing, to make that money to go somewhere beautiful and warm where he could be anybody.'

'You must have asked him about the gun when the call got made to me.'

'I did and it was one of the answers he uses, that someone told him one night when he was bartending. You know, late at night and close to closing and he's the only bartender and no one is at the bar until this guy comes in and orders a Jim Beam or something and then tells him he killed two girls and the gun is buried in a fishing tackle box three quarters of a mile from the Condit Dam up in Washington.'

The tackle box was very much a police secret and it was the first thing she had told him that confirmed everything. She was sending him a message telling him that, but he wasn't sure what the message was yet or how to read it.

224

'I know a lot about him and I can tell you it was better before he got comfortable here. When he stopped worrying so much that he was going to get found he started to bully people. He likes making people afraid of him. He made this Mexican girl who wasn't legal and was cleaning the Methuselah bar at night give him blow jobs. He didn't care about the sex. He was getting plenty of that anyway. He just wanted to break her down and make her obey him. He'd call me over to watch.'

'And you'd watch?'

'I was curious and frightened of him. I'm more frightened now that he has money. He did a smart thing up here. He figured out how to move things quietly. He moves plenty of dope grown here in Humboldt, but you would never know that because he doesn't deal in it. The same guys that carry the animal parts move the dope.'

'He probably learned that from the Mexican cartel he works with.'

Marquez saw her flinch at that and she turned her face quickly and changed the subject just as fast.

'You got me out of the cabin and I'm going to help you, but you really missed a chance with me this afternoon. I would have made you feel so good it would have stayed with you the rest of your life.'

She pointed.

'Here come the cops.'

Lisa Sorzak made her statement to the police and didn't give her name as Lisa X. She said Sorzak and also said she had no idea why she

225

was targeted. She wondered aloud if they were actually after Marquez and added that she was still naked when Marquez returned and knocked on the door, so she just made it out in time.

The two men were arrested at gunpoint as they made their way back to the river bridge. They had no other way across but claimed they were returning from scouting fishing sites for next season and their boat was stolen when they were on foot along the shoreline.

That story changed after they were separated and were asked for more details. Marquez listened to that questioning and about an hour later it came out that one was a parole violator wanted for an armed robbery and murder in Nebraska. The other didn't have any criminal record and neither knew anything about a cabin that had been burned. Marquez was never close enough to them to identify either in a line-up so he didn't try. The Fed who stopped by after the Nebraska felon was identified summed it up.

'The asshole going back to a murder trial and prison may want to trade on what he knows later, but admitting to burning a cabin and trying to name who hired him isn't going to get him anything. If he goes down for the Nebraska murder he's looking at a life sentence already. Your best chance is the other man if you can track him after they kick him loose.'

And they had to kick him loose. He was out the next day and by then Lisa Sorzak had disappeared and Marquez got a call from Voight that took him south.

THIRTY-SIX

When her cell rang Maria debated answering. She really didn't want to talk to Voight again. She let it ring twice more and walked outside so no one at work would overhear.

'I've got just a few questions about Kevin Witmer, and they won't take long.'

'They can't.'

'We're on the same side, Maria. Give me some help here. How long have you known Witmer?'

'Since grade school but we didn't really become friends until high school. Same with Ridley and the three of us were buds for awhile, but that ended when I moved here and started this job. Part of it ending was about Kevin's dope business.'

'How long has Kevin been dealing?'

'It depends what you call dealing.'

'How long has he been seriously at it?'

'In high school he sold a little and always had some to sell and now I think he's got a lot more sources.'

'And the sources are up north?'

'Not where you are, mostly from Humboldt, maybe some from farther north, and I don't know anything except rumor. Have you talked to Ridley Daniels?'

'I've left messages. Do you know people who buy from him now?'

'No, and I'm not protecting him or anything

like that. I just don't know, but what's up with him selling dope? Do you think a dope grower might have killed them?'

That idea had circulated right after they were killed and she knew from talking to Voight he was totally tuned into that, which was why she was surprised he was on it today.

'Until a few days ago Kevin hadn't seen me in years. He's not going to talk to me about his dope business if that's what you're thinking. Besides, selling dope is still illegal.'

'Don't tell that to people around here.'

Voight cleared his throat. He was getting to the reason why he called and Maria could tell.

'Sarah and Terry may have visited someone who supplies him and then gone to a party that individual invited them to and when that happened a man at the party got very angry they were there. He may have threatened the individual who invited them. And it's not the same as what you're remembering from Facebook about their murders being related to visiting grow fields. Did either ever say anything to you about that?'

'Maybe.'

'Maybe?'

'I called Sarah and I don't remember what day it was because I called them every day. I was supposed to be on the trip, so if I didn't call them they called me. That was our way of making up for me not being there. This was a morning when they were at a place on the river where the cell reception was lousy and we didn't talk long. But she said the night before they had been to a weird party. It could have been that party.'

'That's all she said about it?'

'Yes. I think it was two days after they left Crescent City.'

'Maria, I need your help finding out if they were at a party where the person who invited them got cut on the arm with a knife.'

'It's weird this is coming up now.'

'I know it's weird and I'm trying to get to the name of who got hurt. If I can get to that person, maybe I can get to who killed them.'

'Why are you calling the one who got hurt an "individual" or a "person" but the other one, the one who might have threatened Terry and Sarah, is a man.'

'I believe it's a woman who got cut but I'm not sure yet.'

'Okay, okay, let me ask some people, but I really can't talk to Kevin or Ridley. They just tried to get me killed.'

She told him her story and how she figured out when she was in the ambulance what Kevin did to her. Voight listened without interrupting and it made her like him a little more.

'I'd appreciate anything you can do, Maria. This man may have come on to Sarah at a party before he got angry they were there. He may be the one who painted the side of their vehicle. He may have also painted road signs to mark where they were found.'

'And you're just finding that out now?'

'It's only an idea at this point and a very thin lead that Kevin Witmer might be able to help with.'

'Then why don't you tell him you'll close his

dope business and put him in prison if he doesn't come across?'

'He's smart. A DEA agent up here told me they've looked at him for years and haven't been able to get anywhere. But you might be able to. Will you at least try once more?'

She felt the fight go out of her and sadness flood in.

'I'll try.'

THIRTY-SEVEN

Marquez listened to Muller's account. The SOU followed the man from the Sacramento Hyatt to the clean new ENTR building on Cambridge Street in Palo Alto. He didn't drive straight there but neither did he strain to lose anyone tailing him. What that said to Marquez was the man believed he got in and out of the second hatchery without being seen. It said he worked for ENTR or someone within the company, so they could discard the idea that ENTR was 'one hundred percent with them.'

Or perhaps videotaping Fish and Game officers was the standard information-gathering method of a firm whose business was built around intellectual property. Marquez doubted that but the whole thing didn't anger him the way it did Muller. He believed the truth lay somewhere between Barbara Jones and Hauser. There probably was a shadow operation running in the

230

background and Barbara Jones might not know anything about it.

After the call with Muller, he called Jones and left her a message. He left another for Maria and then Muller called back.

'When do you get back to the Bay Area?'

'Later tonight.'

'We may need your help with Faesy. He's in his food truck headed up the coast. We had him set up for a delivery tomorrow in Compton and now he's on his way north. We thought he was going to his girlfriend's in Ojai but he's already past Santa Barbara and the tusks he's supposed to deliver tomorrow are with him, so it's not happening as agreed. After the meeting at headquarters I thought he was with us, but now I don't know what he's doing. He's not answering his phone and I've got to leave half the team in the south. Depending where Faesy goes, I may need you to help cover him. Are you good with that or are you too used to sleeping through the night nowadays?'

'Call me when you know.'

His phone rang again soon after he hung up with Muller and at first he thought it was Muller calling back but it was Voight.

'What were you doing holed up in a cabin with a woman?'

'Where did you hear that?'

'From your wife.' Voight laughed, and the laugh was derisive but there was also humor. 'I heard it from a deputy in Weaverville who said you apprehended an escaped convict.'

'Yeah, they hiked up to her cabin with a couple

of assault weapons and whatever accelerant they set the fire with in a backpack. Did you get my message a few days ago?'

'I got it and I want to talk. I've been thinking about you. How close are you to Yreka?'

'Are you serious about talking or is this another game?'

'I'm serious.'

He was close to Yreka but after Muller's call knew he should keep driving, keep pushing, yet this might be the moment with Voight. He was just ahead of a storm blowing in out of the Gulf of Alaska and forecast to bring the first hard cold rain of the fall. Off to his right he saw it coming and the smart thing was to stay on the road and not lose time.

'Marquez?'

'I'm here and I'm not far from you. I can stop for about an hour. How about we meet at that restaurant you like?'

Voight's car was there as he drove up and got out, his muscles stiff from the drive and sore from yesterday. He slid into the booth and listened to Voight order the same roast beef, mashed potatoes, and gravy he'd ordered when they were last here. Marquez ordered fried chicken and iced tea. He didn't get what Voight liked about the restaurant, but they definitely knew him here.

'What were you doing at a cabin up on the Trinity?'

'Tracking down the woman who made the call with the White Salmon gun tip.'

'Say that again.'

'I was looking for Lisa Sorzak and found her.

232

She gave me the name of the man who calls himself Rider. It's Jim Colson.'

Voight settled his beer back onto the table.

'Do you believe her?'

'I do, though I'm not sure yet why she's telling me. I got her name from the owners of the Methuselah Tavern in Crescent City. That's the place I told you about last time we had anything close to a talk. The owners are named Lila and Geoff Philbrick. Sorzak and Colson were the first two employees when the place opened a decade ago.'

'Colson is Rider?'

'That's what Sorzak is claiming.'

'What's wrong with her? What's your hesitation there?'

'She also goes by Lisa X and it's not really clear to me where she's coming from. She owns a bar in Weaverville and through a patron there and a Trinity warden I found her in a cabin along the Trinity. I told her to expect your call and that you're working the Ellis and Steiner murders.'

'Did she already know that?'

'She seemed to.'

Marquez opened a small notebook, turned it around on the table and Voight put on reading glasses as the waitress refilled Marquez's ice tea. She glanced down at the notebook and without offending her Voight slowly shielded the pages with his hand. He copied Lisa Sorzak's cell number and slid the notebook back and folded his glasses as Marquez texted him the number as well.

Neither of them was old school but each still

carried a notebook. It was one of the first things Marquez noticed about Voight. He was an investigator with strong habits and in his experience investigators who stuck with their habits did so because they worked.

'Rider is your animal parts smuggler and Rider is Jim Colson. He's the one who put this Lisa up to making the tip call and you and I are now looking for the same person. What does Lisa Sorzak say about this Colson?'

'That he's damaged goods and that he changed from the guy she first met who was lonely but could be fun, to someone who enjoys holding power over others. She said, and these are her words, when she met him he didn't even seem to own his name and didn't care what he was called. He was trying to live with as little identity as possible and the name Rider may have come before the animal trafficking.'

'And this Sorzak hit it off with him.'

'She said they recognized something in each other. Colson used to talk about living out their lives in Hawaii in a big house. That was his dream.'

'According to her.'

'Yeah.'

'So I'm supposed to accept her version and that you and I are after the same people.'

'I don't care what you accept or don't, especially what has to do with me. What I'm doing is passing on what I learned. Take it or leave it.'

'Slow down, Marquez, don't get so hot so fast. I know why you called me and I wouldn't be sitting here if I didn't believe there was reason for us to talk and for me to back off you. What else do you know about this Jim Colson?'

'Between Lisa Sorzak and the owners of the Methuselah, I've got a few more things. What he wrote on his employment application at the Methuselah puts him in his mid-forties and Sorzak says that's about right. She keeps repeating that she doesn't know anything about him but seems to know he was married and had a son who was eight when he left wherever he came from. The boy got sick and the disease he had caused the doctors to look for a genetic cause, so they tested mom and dad as well and it came out that the boy's real father was a neighbor down the street. Colson flipped out and left.'

'Left where?'

'Could be Texas.'

'There's got to be a lot more than one Jim Colson. Have you asked for help in Texas?'

'I did this morning.'

'Okay and this Jim Colson somehow got from bartender to trafficking in animals. I'm sure bartending is a gateway to selling animals but maybe you could explain it to me how it works. I mean, if he was selling cocaine and pills from behind the bar I'd believe that, but snake skins?'

'So you know, Rich, there's a breed of macaw that Rider deals that goes for one hundred thousand dollars a bird.'

'Bullshit.'

'No, it's true, and he's the go-to guy in the US for that particular species. He also moves venomous snakes that go for fifty grand and rare turtles and tortoises for twenty-five grand.

Elephant tusk is going for a thousand dollars a pound in Beijing. Colson is tapped into the vein and rich enough now to protect his route.'

'What do you do when you take delivery of a basket of venomous snakes?'

'You take orders from clients who have pet stores or you deal direct to collectors and you get the buy orders first. The buyers are out there and eager to pay. Colson, if he's Rider, has warehouses in the LA Basin and one or more in Vancouver. Vancouver is his distribution point for Asia.'

'And if he gets arrested for two murders that works for you.'

'He won't be. This isn't a guy who would give up a gun he used.'

'I've had cases where I was taunted.'

'And now you've got a suspect helping you with an investigation.'

'I want to make something clear, Marquez. I'm not apologizing for anything yet and you and I aren't on the same side of the table until I see a lot more.'

Marquez stared at him wondering if he was wasting his time. He read self righteousness in Voight's look and believed him. Voight wasn't apologizing for anything. He debated then continued.

'There was a raid of a warehouse in LA about a week ago. A robbery unit went looking for a truckload of flat-screen TVs that got lost on its way to a Best Buy distribution point. They didn't find the truck with the TVs but they did find a murder victim, a young Latino man who was dropped with two shots to the head. They believe he was guarding approximately a million dollars worth of illegal animal products. About three hundred thousand of that was in elephant tusk and the value on all of it may be more. I need to go there and meet with US Fish and Wildlife and it may turn out that murder ties to Rider.'

'But it's not tied to him yet?'

'No, but it was a kid guarding the stash who got executed just ahead of the police raid. He was probably taken out so he couldn't talk.'

'I'm listening, but help me out here. What makes elephant tusk worth a thousand a pound? Do they cure brain cancer and heart disease or make your dick hard?'

'None of the above, they get carved into knick-knacks, bookends, that kind of thing.'

Voight ordered another beer and started to eat again as he put it together. He looked up from his plate as he reached a conclusion.

'If you're telling me this, then you've already talked to your FBI friends.'

'I have and they're helping dig for a Jim Colson who went missing a decade or so ago.'

'Why are you telling me?'

'Even if you don't, I think you and I are on the same side.'

'Despite everything?'

'Yes, despite you letting the sheriff tell you how to investigate.'

Voight put his fork down. He leaned back in the booth, started to say something and Marquez cut him off.

'A couple of years ago, after you and I first bumped heads, I asked a friend at LAPD how good you were as a homicide detective. He told me he's seen a lot of detectives and only a handful that really have what he called the unteachable thing. He called it unteachable because you can't identify it when you interview and promote someone. He said you had it.

'So if you've got it, I know you're not looking at me and never were. You know I didn't kill Terry and Sarah. The sheriff may think I did kill them but I don't believe you do. In Harknell's world Fish and Game is something he occasionally steps in and has to scrape off his shoe and rub off his boots on the lawn grass before he can go back inside a building. I'm sure he encouraged focusing on me and has asked for updates and to be kept in the loop. That's how I hear him and you can tell me I'm full of shit.'

'You generally are.'

'Am I wrong?'

'As long as I'm lead investigator you won't become a suspect without hard evidence. It's a cold case until we learn something new that I can work with. I had hoped the gun was that.'

Voight glanced at two guys seated at the bar but no one was hearing this.

'There's a deputy he's grooming for my job. That's why he rides me about my weight and everything else. When I brief Harknell, Deputy Turner is in the room to listen and learn. He's ambitious. He's got a wife and two kids. He's a vet and the sheriff trusts that, but he's also a smart kid and he doesn't mind volunteering off duty on a Saturday morning to put up 'Harknell for Sheriff' signs.

'But it's hard to be from a rural area and learn how to manage a homicide investigation. There are only forty-five thousand people in the county and there aren't that many homicides, not yet anyway, so the job involves a lot of other things as well. Turner is already as good as or better than me at some of those and he's loyal to the sheriff, and he's a good guy, but combat doesn't teach you investigative skills and that's all that's holding Harknell back from replacing me.'

'Then let me help you in any way I can. I want to see their murders solved. I want to take Colson down if he's Rider. Let's join up here.'

He couldn't read anything in Voight's eyes so he said, 'Think about it and call me.'

When he left Voight was staring out across the room, but he did call. By then Marquez was a hundred miles farther south and the rain had started.

'All right, Marquez, I'm in. We'll try to work together, but use this number when you call me. It's my personal cell and no one other than me looks at what calls I've made. I'll try calling Lisa Sorzak tonight.'

THIRTY-EIGHT

Marquez knew a retired warden who lived in a cabin at timberline in the eastern Sierra. There was no road to the cabin and supplies were hiked in or brought in by mule. Rossini was the ex-warden's name and he stayed there from late May until the first heavy snow of the fall and then took a bus to Arizona and lived the rest of the year in a mobile home in the driveway of his sister's house in Phoenix. He didn't own a car. He told Marquez he was done driving. He had patrolled enough to never want to drive again, and had once told Marquez that the same thing would happen to him.

Marquez understood that. After the long drive home tonight and food and a shower and two in the morning sex with Katherine that left him deep asleep he did not want to move. Nor did he want to answer his phone but maybe he sensed what was coming. He slid his hand from the warmth of Katherine and answered his cell phone as he slid out of bed. He picked his clothes off the chair and walked down the hall to the front room. Lisa Sorzak's voice was warm and alert and edged with something offered as humor but wasn't.

'Are you in bed with your wife?'

'I'm home.'

'I called the investigator.'

'You called Voight.'

'That's right, and it wasn't very satisfying. It was like talking to a door knob. I'm calling you because Jim wants to meet with you. He wants to make a deal but you have to go to him alone.'

Marquez dressed slowly and listened as he moved into the kitchen and made coffee. The intensity of her voice, its low controlled urgency disturbed him.

'When did you talk to Colson?'

'Tonight and I told him you found me in the cabin and that you were there when it burned. I hope you don't mind this, but I said you knew that he sent the two goons.'

Marquez didn't know that. He knew she might have left in the boat if he hadn't gotten back down off the slope in time. He didn't know anything about where the men came from except that they were hired guns, a Nebraska con who skipped out on parole and a local named Tom White. They were paid five thousand each up front and promised another five grand after she was confirmed dead. They didn't know who hired them. It was done through phone calls and a third party whose name they hadn't yet given up.

'He laughed when I told him the cabin was gone.'

'Did you hike back up there?'

'Yesterday. It burned to the ground and trees around it will die. He said now I have no place to hide. If you go on his terms you need to be very careful.'

'Why does he want to meet?'

'He says he wants out of the business. That's all I know.' She paused before adding, 'You don't have to meet him and I wouldn't if I were you.'

'Set it up.'

'He may try to kill you.'

'Do it anyway.'

'Keep your phone close.' She broke the connection a moment later.

THIRTY-NINE

Late that morning Faesy parked his food truck and walked a half-mile to an underground parking garage in San Francisco's Sunset District. Fifteen minutes later as he drove a ten-foot U-Haul van out of the garage Marquez got a call from Muller.

'He's headed your way in a U-Haul and we're on him. It looks like he plans to cross the Golden Gate Bridge.'

'Okay, I'm rolling.'

Marquez stayed on the phone with Muller as he left the house and drove down off Mount Tamalpais to the freeway. Muller's voice crackled in and out.

'If he crosses the Golden Gate he's probably going north and we'll fall back and let you lead for fifty miles if you're okay with that. Last time we followed him as far as the California/Oregon border and then let him go. I couldn't get cleared to go farther. Hang on, he just ran a red and almost took out a cyclist. I'm not sure what he's doing here.'

'Where is he?'

'He's dropped off and down to Crissy Field and watching his side mirrors. He may know we're here but he doesn't seem to know the rolling door on the end of the truck isn't latched. It's bouncing up and down every time he hits a rut. It's almost bouncing high enough for me to get a look inside.'

Marquez reached the freeway and got on southbound toward San Francisco. As he did, Muller's voice filled the pickup cab again.

'Here we go, he's committing to that little road that feeds the bridge northbound. Coming your way, John, and whatever he's got in there is starting to slide out.'

Muller laughed and someone else on his team started laughing too and Marquez could hear the laughter was real. They usually had to work hard and still get lucky to get a glimpse of what was being shipped, and here Faesy's load might slide out the back on the steep climb up from Crissy Field.

From Muller's back and forth with his team Marquez gathered the load was wrapped in a white tarp held together with duct tape. On the climb up from Crissy it slid halfway out. He heard Muller's disbelief and an SOU warden speculating that Faesy would get out at the stop sign before entering the bridge traffic and close the back. But he didn't seem to realize it was happening and drove as if trying to lose a tail.

When Faesy reached the stop sign he barely slowed and the cars that honked behind didn't do so to let him know his cargo was sliding out. They honked because he cut them off and veered hard left as he passed the toll booths. The bundle was slung sideways as he swerved into the next lane and just before the south tower it fell out of the truck. The tape tore loose as it hit the roadbed and the contents scattered across the north and southbound lanes.

Brake lights rippled and traffic slowed to a stop

243

just as Marquez got onto the bridge. The SOU and Faesy were on the northbound side and trapped in stalled traffic. Marquez had an idea. He called Muller.

'Can you see what dropped?'

'No, my view is blocked by cars. I see Faesy is out of his truck and trying to get whatever it is back in his truck.'

'Can you get there?'

'I can't get anywhere. It's bumper to bumper.'

Marquez looked across at the northbound side of the bridge. Everybody ahead of the U-Haul kept going and was off the bridge and the lanes ahead of Faesy's parked U-Haul were empty. He looked at that and Muller spoke again. 'It looks like a couple of guys are helping pick up what spilled. What do you think?'

'I think I can get there. I'm going to cross to the northbound side.'

Marquez drove through the orange cones and then accelerated up the empty lanes. When he got to mid span he saw the U-Haul with the driver's door open. He closed in and saw Faesy and two other motorists carrying elephant tusks and wheeled his car around and parked just ahead of the U-Haul. He got out fast and stopped the clean-up operation, then took photos that included the U-Haul and the tusks. He counted twenty-two tusks and arrested Faesy and moved him next to the U-Haul before the CHP arrived.

The California Highway Patrol were all about clearing the bridge. They were ready to throw the tusks in the water so traffic could flow again. Fewer were in the southbound lanes and those got picked up and heaved over to the northbound side. They clattered and bounced as they hit the roadway and even with the salt air and a light wind blowing across Marquez smelled Africa. He smelled the elephants.

The first cars started moving southbound and the honking subsided. Marquez, Muller, and an SOU warden named Linda Rees, and two highway patrol officers loaded the rest. Marquez made sure they got laid into the U-Haul carefully, as if that somehow could change anything.

It wasn't a world that would ever come again or one that he believed any longer that he could help save, but he could slow down the destruction and buy time. He lifted an eight-foot tusk and slid it in on top of four others then slid the back door down and latched it.

Muller pointed at Faesy. 'You're coming with me.'

Linda Rees drove the truck off the bridge to the tourist overlook on the Marin side and Marquez listened as Faesy repeated that he didn't know what was in there and he was just driving the truck as a favor for a friend whose name he didn't remember. Marquez listened and then walked back to his pickup and sat a few minutes in the cab in the sunlight looking at the bridge, the backed-up traffic, the commute that would take another hour to adjust, though by now commuters were being reassured that whatever spilled was cleaned up and gone.

His phone screen lit up and it was Hauser calling for the fourth time in half an hour. Marquez let it go to voice mail. He didn't call

245

Hauser back until he pulled onto the freeway, and when he did he realized that Hauser was scared.

FORTY

Now he sat with Hauser on a white-painted picnic bench outside a bakery in Larkspur Landing. Hauser was unshaven and claimed he had slept in his car last night because he didn't have enough money for a hotel. Coming from a guy who lived as he did, that was hard to believe, but he said his wife had transferred everything from the joint accounts and frozen the credit cards. His company Visa card was no good anymore and he said he had not had a personal bank account in years.

'Let's get you some food. Go order what you want.'

Marquez pulled out his wallet, gave him a couple of twenties and called Captain Waller after Hauser was inside in line. Through the window he watched a woman in line behind Hauser wrinkle her nose and step back. At Fish and Game talking to Waller about reimbursements was called talking to the wall, but he had to bring it up now and he was going to try. 'Your source who lives in a mansion in Piedmont can't afford a hotel room? Give me a break. The chief isn't going to approve it either, but you can try him if you want.'

Marquez called Chief Ippolito and Ippolito

wasn't defensive but he didn't like snap decisions or being put on the spot.

'Hauser's there with you?'

'He is and he's got a throwaway phone now with thirty-minutes of time on it, after which I may not be able to call him.'

'Do you honestly believe he's out of money?'

'He might be temporarily and I don't want to lose contact with him. He looks like he has been sleeping in his car and we're at a bakery now where he's buying food and wolfing the free samples they have out. He's out of his house. His wife asked him to leave and got a restraining order. She froze their credit cards and bank accounts and he says he doesn't have anywhere to go.'

'What has he actually given us?'

'The pike plot and he's told us that the people behind it may be inside ENTR.'

'But no names. He's flirted with you on the phone, but he never comes through—that's what you told me. Why would we back him now that he's been accused of significant felony and after ENTR has found in his computer files the location of the second hatchery?'

'That's their claim. We don't know what's true yet. They haven't proved to me that he knew where it was.'

'His wife walked away from him. She knows more than any of us.'

Marquez didn't have an answer for that and watched Hauser pay for the food. In the minutes before Hauser came back out Marquez didn't get anywhere with the chief and ended the call as

Hauser walked out. He waited until Hauser was eating before buying himself a coffee and then sitting down across from Hauser again. Even with fear and anxiety in his eyes Hauser still figured himself for the smartest guy in the room and Marquez knew he was nearing the point where he would have to decide whether to keep playing along.

'Our department doesn't have any money to help you out and I don't make your kind of money, but I'll get you a room in the Corte Madera Best Western.'

'I'll pay you back.'

'The Best Western is close to here. I'll put a motel room on a card and give you money for food.'

'I'd rather stay at a hotel in San Francisco. I have one in mind.'

'I'm sure you do, but it isn't going to happen through me. I'll give you some gas money and pay for a week at the Best Western. That'll give you time to work something out with your wife. I want some things in return. I want you to call your biologist friend and—'

'He's not going to do anything.'

'Call him anyway and get him to talk to me. I want his name, but we'll keep him anonymous. I want his phone number and where he is.'

'He won't do it. Look what happened to me.'

'Then borrow money from someone else. You must have a friend or relative you can borrow from.'

He didn't answer that and put the sandwich down.

'I can't call him.'

'Give me his number and his name. I'll call him.'

'I promised I wouldn't.'

'We need him and there are other things that need to happen too. I'm going to bring Emile Soliatano to the motel and the three of us are going to talk.'

'Lieutenant, are you aware they're following me? They're watching us right now.'

'I just talked to the chief of the department. He asked, why should we help someone who hasn't helped us and who has tried to leverage every piece of information into something that helps himself? Basically, he said you don't care what happens to anything except yourself. You got yourself into a bad spot with your company and when you learned of the pike project it looked like a way to weasel out. He reminded me that you've made promises for three weeks and delivered nothing. He now thinks you're trying to use me and our department to get into a better negotiating position with ENTR.'

'I'm not.'

'Where's the third hatchery? Where's your biologist friend and what is his name?'

'All right, I'll call him. I'll give him your number and I'll sleep in my car.'

'What's his name?'

He hesitated on that. He looked at Marquez and then out across the bay. He probably did make the promise he said he had.

'Barry Peason. I'll call him right now.'

He made the call but Peason didn't pick up.

Maybe he didn't recognize the number, or maybe it was a bluff on Hauser's part. He called him again and this time Peason answered and Marquez listened to the conversation, to Hauser's apology and heard the loud voice on the other side. He took the phone as Hauser handed it to him.

'Barry, you've got to talk to me.'

'I can't take the risk!'

Marquez walked away from the table to tell Peason he got a call this morning from Washington Fish and Wildlife to say that they had confirmed a pike in the Columbia River; they were young fish and believed the stocking to be recent.

'They're scared. They think they may have thousands of northern pike in the Columbia. I need the third hatchery and more than that I need a way to get to whoever is behind the whole thing.'

'They'll destroy me.'

'We'll keep you anonymous.'

'They'll hack into your systems. They'll find me. Look what they're already doing to Matt.'

'You're a biologist. You know what'll happen if we don't stop this.'

'I don't know where the hatchery is.'

Marquez tried one last time.

'What you know may get us there. Let's meet and talk.'

Peason was quiet and then cleared his throat. 'I'll think about that. I'll call you back.'

'Stay on the line, Barry. The fish we found in hatchery two and those that almost went in the river from the first hatchery were all well along. The pike they are growing in the third hatchery

250

are probably a similar age. They can't hold them. They'll need to get them to a river. We can't wait.'

'You've done nothing for Matt.'

Marquez looked over at Hauser.

'We're doing everything we can for him.'

'I'll call you back in an hour.'

Peason hung up abruptly and Marquez knew there wouldn't be any call back. He wrote down Peason's phone number then walked back to the table.

'He thinks we haven't taken care of you, that I made promises to protect you that weren't kept. Did you say anything like that?'

'No.'

'I didn't think so. You would never say anything like that.' He slid the phone over to Hauser. 'Call him back and tell him it's a big misunderstanding.'

Hauser called several times and Peason didn't pick up. He emailed and texted him then laid his phone down and started eating again.

'You've got to get to him.'

'I'm trying.'

Marquez called the Best Western and read off his Visa number and gave them Matt Hauser's name. When he left Hauser was talking like a victim. Marquez looked back at him before getting into the pickup and knew that what the chief and Waller said about Hauser was true, but still felt they had to stay with him. Later though he would regret that and wish he hadn't thrown the money down for the hotel.

FORTY-ONE

Sorzak's call came less than an hour after he'd left Hauser. She was distant as she dictated where he needed to be tomorrow night, though the meeting with Rider wouldn't be until the following day.

'No other game wardens or police, nobody but you, or he said he'll hold me responsible. I don't like doing this. It's scaring me. I know the guys who burned the cabin were sent by him. There's no one else it could have been.'

'I'll take it from here.'

Marquez called Voight before calling Captain Waller to ask for backup from the Del Norte and Siskiyou wardens. Voight was right there, serious and interested, asking, 'What did you hear back from the FBI?'

'A James Edward Colson who worked for the Texas State Police disappeared while out on a night call helping with the aftermath of a tornado. He never showed up in the town hit by the tornado, but the tornado also touched down twice on the highway Colson would have used to approach the town. For months they thought the tornado got him and they expected to find him and his vehicle out in the brush or at the bottom of a pond.

'They did a wide search for him and in that part of Texas plenty of people will remember his name. He left behind a wife and a kid and eventually they pieced together that he took off, though some locals still think the tornado got him.'

Voight was quiet a long moment then asked, 'How did he get this far?' The question was general. The question wasn't really for Marquez to answer, but he did anyway.

'He planned ahead and was ready with a new social security number. His name is common enough sounding and he headed for a place where a missing deputy in Texas would never make news. He changed jobs. He changed addresses. He never had a run-in with the law. I'll call you when I get on the road tomorrow.'

'Where are you supposed to be tomorrow night?'

'At a bar in Crescent City and two of our area wardens will back me up.'

'That's not enough.'

'It's what I've got.'

'That's a lot of crap. If this guy really is who you think he is and he's fixated on you, you can't take it that casually.'

Captain Waller wasn't comfortable with it either. Waller was close to saying no, yet he didn't on the condition Marquez found more backup and a more cohesive idea of how the backup would protect him. That left Marquez the rest of today and tomorrow to make that happen, but for whatever reason as he got off the phone his mind turned inward instead and back to LA where this investigation first started.

Fifteen months ago in August in LA on a stifling

253

afternoon when the sky was white and the heat oppressive he waited in a shopping mall lot for another meeting that might or might not happen. The last one hadn't and after a half-hour here he drove out of the lot figuring he couldn't show weakness by waiting too long, and he wouldn't call them back this time. He wouldn't pursue. It would be on them to move it forward.

Then a new black Land Cruiser pulled alongside him and matched his speed. The passenger window lowered and the driver never looked over, but the woman in the passenger seat pointed toward the side of the road and they cut in front of him and signaled a right turn.

He followed them into an alley between industrial buildings and they parked and stood alongside a chain-link fence littered with trash at the back of a small parking lot. The air smelled of chemicals and the dry weeds on the other side of the fence.

'Call me Adam,' the man said, 'like the first man, like the one in the Bible.'

He laughed. He wore black pants that clung to his legs and a T-shirt from a bar in Portugal. He was energetic in a jerky nervous way that put Marquez on guard, the type of guy to pull a gun and shoot without warning. The man feigned amusement at how long it had taken to get this meeting together. But in truth it had all been one way, Marquez trying to make a buy and them digging deeper into who he was first. Twice the phone he was using got hacked.

'You seem worried, my friend, but what is there to worry about? Finally, we are meeting. You

want to buy. You need to buy. You have customers so this is a good day, yes? So what is it?'

'Let's just do it.'

'Of course, but first tell us more about your operation. Such a quiet operation you run, so quiet we couldn't find it.'

'And you couldn't get into my phone either.'

The man laughed. He smiled hard then stared at the woman he called Lia. Marquez took a longer look at her too, half Puerto Rican he guessed, not a face he'd ever seen. She was tall, long limbed, and looked physical. It seemed her role was to protect. With striking suddenness the man's eyes emptied, lost their depth and flattened. He reached and lightly touched Marquez's chest at his heart.

'Are you a buyer who will buy from us for a long time?'

'I am a buyer.'

'You have many clients?'

'Yes.'

'Where did you get these clients? You say you have a network of people you supply and we can't find anyone that knows you. The world is large so who knows, maybe you do. But it would be a very bad mistake to go forward if you are trying to fool us. The one we work for is very unforgiving.'

'I'm not worried; I brought a list and we need to talk logistics. I want to deal only with one person. I want to establish how I take delivery of the live product and separately the rest. I don't want to trade phone calls. I want a system and I'll pay on delivery.'

'You have yet to give me your name, but you want a system.'

'Call me John.'

'Like the John Doe the police find? Or like the John the whore sleeps with?'

'John Artura.'

'What do you want to buy, John Artura?'

'Live birds, snakes, turtles, everything on the banned list, and I have a client who will pay very well for a condor.'

The man laughed.

'A condor, yes, of course, a condor—and who is this client who is willing to pay what it will cost to get you a condor?'

'How much?'

'At least one hundred fifty thousand dollars.'

'He has the money.'

'Then maybe it's more.'

Marquez shifted stance and looked past the man through the fence. He was still being challenged so maybe this wasn't going to happen and he should back away.

'What else do you need?'

'Venomous snakes and as many parts as you can get—rhino horn, elephant tusks, big cat, and everything that sells into the Asian medicinal market. I brought a list.'

'Yes, you said you have a list, and you're prepared to pay as you take possession.'

'I am.'

Marquez pulled the list and the man didn't touch it, but said, 'Okay, my friend, let's move this conversation inside. Are you carrying a weapon?'

'A gun.'

'Where?'

'In my belt.'

'At your back?'

'Yes.'

'Take it out please. We'll hold it for you.'

He pointed to the building behind Marquez. 'We have an office in that building but perhaps you are afraid to go inside with me or with Lia who could kill you—and I have to tell you she once killed for me an old general who she was on top of and he was inside her and with him inside her she strangled him. But she has also killed much younger men, some bigger than you.'

'Do you want to make me afraid of you or do you want to do business?'

'I know already you are afraid. You brought a gun and that tells me you're afraid or you don't trust us or you are ordinary in a way we don't want to deal with. Lia will search you before we go in.'

Marquez pulled the clip before handing the Glock over. In the office the man methodically made certain the blinds were down and Lia threw the deadbolt on a steel door.

'Take off your shoes.'

'Why?'

'We need to know more about you. Take off your shoes, your socks and the rest of your clothes, or you have the choice of leaving now. If you are wearing anything that records the conversation, walk out now and never call me again. If you work for the Fish and the Game, then walk away. This is your last chance for that.'

Marquez stripped his clothes, stopped at his boxers, and then slid those off when she gestured.

'Lia will check you for anything small and taped onto you. She will want to look at your

257

hair and in your mouth and ears and it will be like your doctor, but she will also look in your eyes in a way that your doctor never has.'

Marquez faced the wall as told and her hands moved over him and she turned him to face her. Her touch moved up his body and without saying anything she hooked a finger in his mouth and opened it and with saliva from his mouth on her hands she felt the curve of his skull, moved her hands through his hair. Then she stood face to face looking into his eyes for long seconds before turning away.

'Do not dress yet,' the man said after he had stepped away and whispered with her. 'She is not sure about you. You are not easy to see into.'

'I had a hard childhood.'

He laughed. 'So did I. Very hard, so hard I had to cut the throat of my father to get away. She will look again in your eyes.'

'Come on, man, you can't be fucking serious about this eye shit. I'm going to put my clothes back on and leave. I can't deal with this.'

'Not yet.' He pulled a gun. 'I'm sorry, but not yet and it is still possible we will do business and someday laugh at this. I want her to look in your eyes again.'

Marquez allowed it and as she looked again into his eyes he wasn't at all ready for the pinprick of a needle and within thirty seconds he was on his knees and dizzy. Then he was on his back and unable to move his arms and legs as she hovered over him, a needle with a large syringe near his left eye.

'What she injects will blind you and will be quite painful,' the man said. 'I am not so convinced

but she says you are lying and I know if you could speak you would say you are a buyer with a large but quiet operation. So first one eye then more questions and if the answers are satisfactory you keep the other eye. If not, I'm sorry.' He shook his head. 'It's crazy the things we get into.'

He turned his back and Marquez saw the concentration as she brought the needle down and got ready and he tried to turn his head and then the man turned back and commanded, 'Wait! Lia, come talk to me again.'

Ten minutes passed with Marquez paralysed and lying on his back. As they returned he began to get control of his limbs again. There were apologies in the time it took for the paralysis to leave. Now Marquez was dressed but shaky on his feet. The man held out Marquez's list of what he was looking to buy.

'I can get many of these, maybe all of them. The supply of animals is less and more are fighting over what's left to sell. I know you understand this and it makes things more expensive and everyone is risking more, including the police. I think you can forgive that we came close here to taking your eyes. You must always remember that Lia was just seconds from blinding you.'

He reached and touched Marquez's head. 'Right now, you could be blind and in pain and they say the pain from what the acid does never goes away. Do you understand?'

'I hear you.'

'I'm asking if you understand.'

'I get that you stopped her.'

'Why did I do that?'

'So we can do business.'

'No, not that, but I am responsible now. I am risking that maybe you will work with us in a different way. Do you understand?'

'No.'

'We know who you are. We didn't take your eyes but we could find you again or find your wife. We want you to work with us.'

'Who am I?'

'You are in the Fish and Game.' He pulled his phone out. 'I will show you a picture.'

He did and when Marquez said nothing, he said, 'Tell me about this one who wants a condor. This fascinates me. We have other orders for condors now. Soon they will all be gone. If someone wants a condor it should be very expensive.'

He laughed.

'We will be in touch and tell you what we will pay you to work with us. I will tell you next time. But you should go now. You should leave and tonight get down on your knees and be thankful you can still see. You are a very lucky man.'

He laughed again.

'And do not worry, we will do business, just not the kind you thought.' His face hardened. 'Go now before I change my mind.'

FORTY-TWO

Way back when she thought he was so cool and limber and loose, Kevin told her he would one

260

day give her a thousand roses. That was before the constant fist bumps and the endless *what's up, dude* that came after he stopped caring about anybody, or maybe he never had. Maria watched him walk toward her, watching his body, remembering how he got when he was seriously annoyed like he was now.

He slid a chair out, sat down and said, 'I hate this place.'

'That's why I wanted to meet here.'

'So what's on the menu today, Maria? Are we going to talk the murders, your dad, or the investigator dipshit?'

'The murders were Sarah and Terry.'

'That's exactly what I'm saying, babe. They were Sarah and Terry. They aren't anymore.'

'What's your deal stonewalling Voight? Did you know they were basically attacked at a party held by one of your friends?'

'Look, they wanted to connect with some people along the river and I tried to make it happen for them. It wasn't visiting where weed gets grown that got them offed, and who in the fuck are you that you can ask me about this and then turn around and give it to Voight?'

'Sarah wanted to see grow fields. Who showed them to her?'

'A friend of a friend and I don't know where.'

'Voight says there was a knife pulled at a party and the same man came on to Sarah.'

'Good luck with that.'

'With what?'

'Coming on to her.

'You are seriously cold.'

261

'I'm the same. You changed.'

'You weren't like this.'

'They're dead, Maria. They got murdered. They're not coming back and I'm not giving Voight people I might need someday just so he can fuck with them.'

Sometimes when Kevin lied he did this thing with his right eye where he blinked; he did it now and she called him on it.

'You know what parties they went to with your friends up there. Why lie about it?'

'Keep it up, M, and I'm out of here and we're done with anything we ever had.'

'You mean after you tried to kill me you'll stop talking to me if I ask the wrong questions. What are you so scared of?'

'I never tried to kill you. I told your dad that to fuck with him. I knew you would be fine. I watched you. You can still ride.'

Kevin leaned forward so his face was right in front of her, the corners of his eyes all crinkly with lines and his mouth that used to smile so sweet now looking cruel. What he cared about was his dope business. It's why he wouldn't help Voight. She knew he wasn't going to remember anything that might help. He'd already made his mind up about that, but she wanted him to say it, to admit he could have helped more two years ago and he didn't because the people he would have named could have given up information about his business.

'When did you turn into a little bitch?'

'When you quit caring about anything except you.'

'I do business with some people up north and I put Sarah and Terry in touch with a couple of them. They got into a party or two they wouldn't have known about and Sarah got to see where dope is grown. That's what you already know.

'What you don't seem to get is that the local deputies don't trip out over people growing dope. The Feds do their flyover shit and they bust people, but growing isn't that big of a deal anymore and it's not like they took some big risk going out to a grow field. No one killed them because they saw a grow field. Didn't happen and it's a totally fucking stupid idea and I'm not giving up connections to help that fat slob Voight figure that out.'

She stared at him and he got on his business rant.

'Do you know what they're afraid of in Humboldt County? What they're afraid of is that dope will get legalized. When that happens the market will crash and all that will be left will be some plots of organic high-end specialty bud and a toothless white-haired dude tending to it.'

'So you did nothing.'

'Both of them got a look up a road and an hour hike in and out and that was it. They saw a big grow field and that was because the two guys who showed it to them were hoping to get laid that night. Where they went I've never been but it didn't work out for anybody and it doesn't have anything to do with them getting killed. These dudes don't want to talk to Voight and I don't want them to talk to Voight because they do know stuff about my business.'

263

'Is one of them the one who pulled the knife?'

'No.'

'You're sure?'

'I'm positive.'

'Then tell Voight that.'

'You'll tell him so I don't have to.'

'Who pulled the knife? What's his name?'

'Mack Ellington and he's a paranoid meth cook who lives out in the woods and is so scared of getting busted he doesn't own a car or a computer or ever use his real name. He didn't follow them and this is all dead-end bullshit Voight shouldn't waste his time with. Voight doesn't know his head from his ass.'

'So call him and tell him you know they went to parties and tell him the names of your friends who got them in. Then he can track them down and find other people who were at those parties.'

'And he's going to do this two years after they were killed? Are you telling me people who were stoned and drunk and usually can't remember the next day what they did the night before are going to remember what happened at a party two years ago?'

'They'll remember Sarah and Terry were murdered.'

'Why are you fucking with me?'

'I'm not. Why have you blocked Voight from getting to these guys?'

'I told you why.'

'You basically told me you didn't care enough about Sarah and Terry to let Voight talk to them. But it could have been someone they met at the parties and if these two were hoping to score

264

then they probably watched who else talked to them. They may remember that.'

Kevin leaned back. He was thinking about what he was going to say next, how he wanted to end this and Maria knew this was it. Everything else led up to this and this was the end.

'It's like this, little girl. Your friends got murdered and they're gone. Nothing can change that and I've got a business that's only going to last another five years or so because at some point dope will get legal, so I've only got so long to make as much money as I can and you don't get to fuck that up. I'm not going to let you.'

'Tell Voight you'll talk to him as long as he doesn't mess with you. He'll get it. I'm sure he's had to cut deals with all kinds of scuzzballs over the years. You got to do what you've got to do to get information.'

Kevin really didn't like that. He stared super hard at her and she knew there was never any going back from today. But that was fine. This is where it ended forever and it was better to make sure it was done.

'You only care about yourself, Kevin.'

'That's all anyone cares about, you stupid bitch.'

'When they were killed what you said was they ran into some bad energy. You're bad energy, dude. You suck the good stuff away from people. You live like a leach and you're a coward for not helping the investigator.'

'I'm gone, but here's the takeaway. If you mess with my business something will happen to you.'

'Something will happen to me? What does that mean? Are you're going to hurt me?'

'It means don't make a mistake. Go back to your bullshit job and never call me again and it means Voight better not call me after talking to you.'

'Or what?'

'Fucking find out if you want. Later, Maria, have a good life.'

FORTY-THREE

Marquez followed the Smith River down past Panther Flat and Middle Fork Gorge and finally to the Redwood Highway and Crescent City. He checked into a motel before driving to the bar where he was supposed to be at six o'clock. It was less than a mile from the Methuselah and he couldn't help think about that as he took a stool. He signaled the bartender as outside gusting wind turned into rain. The streets darkened with night and he nursed a beer and waited.

When the meeting time came and went and he was close to leaving, he signaled the bartender for one more beer. The bartender reminded him of a poacher they had busted in '04, who then did two years in prison and now a fire-breathing, blade-faced preacher way out in the desert in Nevada. His flock prayed for apocalypse and retribution to unbelievers. Not long ago he sent Marquez a YouTube clip of a sermon where he had sacrificed a lamb.

266

The beer came and he watched the bartender discourage an older fellow from anymore drinks with a loud, 'Get the fuck out of here, Charley.' The old boy cussed out the bartender then got down off his stool and left. Now, as it was just Marquez, the bartender moved over in front of him.

'I always have to run him off. He's a drunk and I don't like him in here.'

'I'm about to leave myself. What do I owe you?'

'Don't leave until we talk about tomorrow.'

'What about it?'

'I'm your ride at six in the morning.'

'Where are we going?'

'Wherever they tell me to bring you.'

'You don't know.'

'I wouldn't tell you if I did.'

Marquez took a harder look at him. 'You and I know each other, don't we? You've lost your hair since I last saw you. You were still a guard at Pelican Bay. That was in 1997. I came up to see a prisoner and the next time I came back they said you'd moved on to another prison. That was before you were arrested.'

'I paid for what I did and it's none of your business.'

But it agitated him and he got busy with his cell phone and came back with a photo on his phone of a newspaper article headline he wanted Marquez to see.

'That's the boy who testified against me.'

Marquez read: 'Disturbed Ex-Con Takes Own Life.'

'I look at that every day. That boy framed me and I don't care what you think about me. When you come out of prison there are no jobs. You make money however you can. They took everything from me for it. I had twenty-five years in and didn't end up with any pension. I'm sixty-three years old and if someone comes in here and offers me five hundred dollars to guide some asshole of a warden out a dirt road, I don't have any problem doing that and then forgetting where I left him.'

'Sure, not much different than when you were selling new inmates to prison gangs. You pocket the money and forget about it.'

His name came to Marquez now. York. Pierce York and one of four guards paid by a prison gang to get access to new prisoners they wanted for sex. It worked until one of the unwilling sex partners needed intestinal surgery following a gang rape. That was the young man in the headline Pierce just showed him.

'York thumped the top of the bar with a calloused index finger. 'Get out of here and show up in the morning or don't, I don't give a damn which.'

Marquez drove back to the motel. He cleaned his gun as he talked with Hauser. Hauser was at the Best Western Marquez had booked him into and had no new information and was very down. As cleaning fluid sat in the gun barrel, Marquez leaned back in the motel room's one chair and listened.

'I wish I'd never gotten involved. I've destroyed my career and my personal life.'

'Return the money.'

'I'm not a thief.'

'You gambled ENTR wouldn't go public with the missing money, but they surprised you. Now they have to tie you to the pike project and they're working on that and you still aren't giving me what I need to help you.'

'You want some real world, Lieutenant? Go online and Google my name and you'll see people questioning my microclimate models. Those questions weren't there a month ago. That's ENTR working at discrediting me. Do you know I was considered for a Nobel Prize?'

'I hadn't heard but I know you're letting a criminal case get built. Call your lawyer tomorrow morning and let him float some ideas by ENTR management. It came out of accounts you were overseeing. You're probably the one guy who could figure out how to get it back.'

'If it got returned tomorrow the pike in the third hatchery would get released into the rivers. Do you want that?'

'They won't get released if your biologist friend helps us.'

'He can't do anything without risking his career.'

'He needs to take that risk.'

Hauser hung up and Marquez reassembled the gun then phoned Voight and the two wardens who would back him up tomorrow. The Del Norte sheriff was also backing him up with three deputies. The wardens would be out of uniform and in a faded blue pickup carrying chainsaws. If Marquez was taken down a dirt road they would be there with the cover of being out there to cut firewood from deadfall. Marquez also had a small GPS tracker stitched into the tongue of his right boot and another in his coat. He made the call to Waller as promised and then went through his gear again, feeling nervous in a way he didn't usually experience.

He lay on his back on the motel bed and talked with Katherine before trying to sleep. At three in the morning just after he had dozed off his phone rang. He recognized the biologist Barry Peason's cell number, but when he answered all that was on the other end was someone breathing and listening. He tried for a couple of minutes to get Peason to talk and left the line open.

'We need your help, Barry. Talk to me. You can do that without any risk to yourself.'

Marquez paused. He listened and waited and the phone screen threw blue light on the motel room wall.

'The best thing you can do now is help us.'

There was a soft click as the line went dead.

FORTY-FOUR

There were rain showers in the early morning as Marquez waited in the dark outside the bar, but it looked like it was going to clear. When a pickup drove up it wasn't the bartender, instead a sun-weathered older guy who said he was a boat captain and that Marquez should follow him to the wharf.

Marquez talked to the two wardens and the Del Norte officers as he followed the pickup to a pier and a fishing boat. Ten minutes later the boat's diesels fired and the boat vibrated with the engines' thrum as the captain pushed the throttle forward. They cleared the harbor and churned south in good-sized swell.

After sunrise as the visibility improved a Zodiac came into view, and then ran alongside them. The captain slowed and put the boat on autopilot. He took Marquez to the crane used to bring supplies onboard and lift out the fish catch and told him to get in the basket.

'Why?'

'I'm going to lower you onto their boat.'

'Have you ever done this before?'

'Plenty of times with illegals and I've only lost a couple of them.' He smiled. 'When you lose one they don't pay you. I haven't done this in a while but you're fine. I haven't forgotten how.'

Marquez climbed into the crane basket and the boat captain swung him out over the ocean as the fishing boat pitched and rolled and the Zodiac alongside rose and fell underneath the basket holding Marquez. He climbed over the edge of the basket and they grabbed at his legs. When he let go and dropped he knocked both men down, catching one on the cheekbone with his elbow.

The Zodiac accelerated away, angling for the shore with Marquez seated at the bow. They put in at a broken-down pier, got out fast and hurried over to a green Suburban. Guns came out and a canvas sack went over Marquez's head. He felt the poke of a needle and heard a muffled, 'Have a nice sleep.'

He didn't remember losing consciousness but he knew from the sound of the tires as he came to that they were now on a smooth dirt road. He touched his coat. His phone was still with him. The bag was tied loosely at his neck and his face and hair were drenched in sweat. He slowly moved his left boot to his right. His boots were still on so the GPS tracker was intact.

He listened to the road and talking that was low and indistinct. The road climbed and he felt the curves and heard the engine pulling harder as it got steeper. They bounced in ruts that jarred and the driver swore, and maybe half an hour later they slowed and as they stopped the bag came off and he smelled pine and fir and felt the cold air.

'Out. Time to walk.'

Now it was just two men and him and a shadow of a trail climbing along a creek. They startled a black bear and the one in the front took a couple of steps toward it to get the big bear moving. An orange Coast Guard plane passed overhead and the man nearest looked at him and smiled as if the plane was searching for Marquez and the idea of finding him up here was a joke.

The trail steepened as it left the creek and under the brush and along the rocks was a few inches of icy new snow. They struggled upward and then hit another dirt track and followed that up and a mile later walked into an encampment that looked to Marquez like a back to the earth group inhabiting a failed settlement from a former century. Blue plastic tarps stretched over lean-to structures and the remains of cabins, smoldering wood fires, beards and beads, and faces turned toward them but the men leading him didn't say a word to anyone.

They walked through the encampment and picked up a trail through cedars that led to a cabin with a stout wood door and two guards. One held a shotgun, the other an AR-15 on a sling over his right shoulder. That man rapped on the door and said, 'The prisoner is here.'

Now Marquez was looking at an injured Jim Colson. His head was shaved. An angry red scar that looked very raw and was laced with black stitches curved in a half moon under the back of his skull. His left eye was also bruised and he looked weak and pale though his look was one of disdain. He motioned Marquez to a chair and the cabin door was pulled shut.

'You may have made a bad mistake coming here, but we'll talk.'

'What happened to your head?'

Colson didn't answer at first and Marquez sat down. The only light was a battery lantern and a dying fire in the stone fireplace.

'I've come close to killing you more than once, Marquez. I've got a twitchy sniper working for me, an Afghan vet, I gave the go to take you down in the Washougal Basin. Half of your skull would have been in the brush behind you if he hadn't missed.'

Marquez knew about the shot taken. He had

273

backed away fast. He listened as Colson explained a change he'd come to after receiving the head wound that he touched now with his left hand. His voice was deep and hoarse.

'I've had to reconsider many things since I got hurt and there is an opening here for you. There is a way we could do a deal. You won't like it and I'm not sure what I'll do with you if you turn it down, but if you want to hear it I'll lay it out for you.'

'Go ahead.'

'I have more than enough money and I could give you lists of people, networks, smuggling lines, shippers, law enforcement officers, as long as I have in writing a guarantee no one will come after me.'

'You want out.'

'That's right, I want out, but not a plea deal. I'm not admitting to anything and I want to leave with everything I've earned and a guarantee no charges will ever be filed.'

He said this without turning his head from the fire, but turned now, his eyes dark in the shadowy light, face impassive, his voice slow and soft.

'It's not a decision you're going to make, Lieutenant, but you are the one who can make it happen. It means you wouldn't hunt for me any longer and I wouldn't think about killing you anymore. I would go away and you'd have all the names.'

'How long have you used this place?'

'Hippies settled this place forty years ago. They tricked the government and ended up with a ninety-nine-year lease. They grow dope and ratty vegetables and make craft-type crap they sell at flea markets. Some were born here. I killed one of the natives when I first got here. He was a young man whose girlfriend I slept with and he wanted to fight to the death. He's buried down by the creek and they don't like me much here, but they don't dislike me anymore either. I give them money. I built a building with showers and put in a septic system so they don't have to shit in the woods. I rebuilt this cabin and use it when I need to rest.'

'Were you once a cop?'

'Did she give you that?'

'No.'

'Who did?'

'It doesn't matter who.'

Marquez took in the cabin. It was no more than fifteen feet by twelve feet. Stone walls, a stone fireplace, a cedar plank floor, a bed, a small iron stove and a grill in the fireplace that looked like it had been used to cook on. A five-gallon jug held water.

'This is where I figured out I was Rider.'

'And we've figured out who you were before.'

There was a long silence and then, 'Well, he doesn't exist anymore.'

'Where did he go?'

'You need me, Lieutenant. You can't get it done on your own. Everything you want to save is for sale and there's more demand every year.'

'I want to keep talking but I need to know more about you.'

'I left Texas after finding out my wife had an affair as long as our marriage and that my son wasn't mine. I would have killed the man who fathered the boy, but I couldn't then. I had to wait for that. That was a humiliation like no other. I couldn't stay there any longer. My ex lives in a trailer park on the outskirts of town now and waitresses at a dump that's been there forever and pays nothing. She's barely holding it together.

'I sent a man to make her feel better and bring her flowers at the restaurant and ask her out last summer. Over dinner on their first date he offered her a weekend job across the border in a Mexican whorehouse. He said her face collapsed, but I'll never forgive her. I'll track her to her grave. The boy never made it out of high school and does grunt work for a fracking company. He'll never go anywhere.'

'Who were you when you left Texas? I want to hear you say the name.'

'The man you're asking about doesn't exist anymore and doesn't matter in this conversation.'

'I want you to say your name.'

'It's Rider and I started into animal trafficking when I was a bartender. I bought illegal abalone and urchin for restaurants. Then a man I used to pour free drinks for connected me with a cartel that could deliver just about any Latin or South American animal. That worked into a relationship and an even broader pipeline. I developed Chinese buyers. They haggle over everything, but they pay their bills and they want everything. I can't come close to giving them everything they want. That's how much demand there is. Marquez, I'm offering you something you could only dream of and you're taunting me with this name bullshit. Why are you doing that?'

The cabin door creaked open and a guard apologized as a teenage girl appeared, sunlight shining from behind her. She spoke to Colson as if Marquez wasn't there, telling him she needed to see him today and he ignored her until the guard pulled her away and the door pushed shut.

'It's different out here. They grow up faster but they don't have much education. There are only so many things she'll ever be able to do.'

He stared at Marquez.

'Your vanity is you go places without enough backup. You think you're that good and your badge will cover the rest. You're wrong about both and you're a fool to offend me this morning.'

'I'm not alone out here.'

'Those two wardens got a flat tire. The Del Norte deputies got lost on a dirt road. You are alone. I could have you killed today and your body left where it will never be found.'

'You didn't bring me here to kill me and I'm interested in your deal but I have to know who I'm talking to.'

'That's a lie. You're fucking with me but let's get out of this cabin. Follow me.'

They walked down the trail back to the encampment with two guards following and one in front. Marquez saw a couple of kids in the brush, an old pickup settling into the ground, blue smoke rising from a faded tepee. They stopped at a fire pit ringed with stones in a clearing with split logs for benches out front.

'This is where the girl lives. Her parents first

sent her to me as a way of paying down the money they owe me.'

He gestured toward a small child who looked around the edge of a red blanket covering the opening to one of the lean-tos.

'These people think they're the start of a new civilization.'

He turned to look at Marquez, eyes opaque, a strange smile forming.

'Is a deal possible or is this just a waste of our time?'

'That depends on how badly you want out.'

'I'm offering to help you, Lieutenant. I'll trade immunity for what you couldn't gather in a lifetime.'

He reached slowly and touched the back of his head.

'This was a bad wound. I've been here weeks. I don't need this anymore. We can make a deal or remain enemies. It's your choice.'

'I want to know who I'm dealing with first.'

Colson took a gun now from one of his men and stood in front of Marquez and far enough back to where Marquez couldn't lunge as he raised the gun and aimed at Marquez's head. His eyes narrowed, his trigger finger tightened, and seconds passed with Marquez not looking away.

'I'm not going to kill you today, but if we don't make a deal I'm not going to let you keep looking for me. But you won't stop, so it's this or we deal.'

'Show me you mean that.'

Colson lowered the gun.

'I'll give you Lia and Arturo. She's the one who almost blinded you. They're in LA. I have an address in the cabin and I'll get it and then you leave and you get forty-eight hours to answer my offer.'

Marquez knew he was looking at Jim Colson, no doubt about it. He nodded at Colson and waited as Colson limped back to the cabin then returned with what he said was a way to find Lia and Arturo.

'We'll look for them and I'll be back in touch. If we make a deal then when we do your name has to come from you. No one named Rider is getting immunity from anything.'

Marquez left the encampment with the men who brought him here. They drove dirt roads for an hour until they came to a stop.

'This is where you get out.'

Marquez could see a long distance down a smooth Forest Service road. He saw where it disappeared into the trees.

'Take me to the highway.'

The man in the passenger seat turned and pointed a gun. 'Out.'

'You got it, bud. I'll walk from here and I won't forget you.'

FORTY-FIVE

Marquez walked for hours before the two wardens found him with the GPS trackers. But it was a call from Voight that let him know his cell phone was working again.

'Bad news, Marquez, the sheriff wants me to bring you in. You can bet that's about the election next Tuesday. He likes you for the murders. Do you want to let him go public with a warrant or do you want me to come pick you up and bring you in?'

'Let me call Harknell first.'

Marquez called the Siskiyou County Sheriff's Office and asked for Sheriff Harknell, figuring that Harknell would pick up and tape the call.

He picked up on the third ring. 'Lieutenant, where are you?'

'I'm waiting for Voight to arrive but before he does I want to make sure you and I understand each other.'

'I'm for that.'

'You're playing this game with me and I know you're going to say it's not a game but you owe me at least the true reason why.'

'You're right, Warden, it's not a game it's a murder investigation.'

'How is a false arrest going to help your credibility?'

'We'll let the courts decide guilt or innocence.'

'Call whatever TV and print reporters you've contacted and tell them you've changed your mind about framing me.'

'We're not backing away and I've got some advice for you: confess and let your attorney cut a deal that keeps you off death row.'

'Don't hang up yet. You need to know I won't let you get away with this. I told you that once before and I meant it. You don't get to make a quiet apology later and explain how you were going with the best information you had at the time. It's not going to work like that.'

'I hear that as a threat, warden, and I'll play this for the judge. Let's hold right there until we see each other.'

The sheriff broke the connection and Marquez didn't feel any better for having talked to him. The wardens dropped him in Hoopa and Voight picked him up there. Two hours later they slowed along the front of the SCSO in Yreka and in the lot were three TV vans and a half-dozen reporters.

'I'm supposed to pull up here with you in the back in handcuffs. He wants to make sure they get you on local TV so you can never work effectively undercover up here again. But we'll go in a back way.'

Harknell was stiff and tense with anger when he learned that's what had happened. He confronted Voight with Marquez ten feet away seated at a chair in an interview room with the door wide open.

'Why wasn't he handcuffed?'

'I didn't arrest him.'

'You'd better have a very good reason.'

'I do. I have nothing to charge him with.'

It got loud now.

'You have a double murder.'

'There's no evidence.'

'You're relieved of duty as lead investigator. I'm replacing you.'

'Then I'm going to tell you that you can't hold him or charge him.'

'I'm reassigning you to a night patrol unit but not until you get your weight within department

281

parameters. You're on leave until then and unless you can produce doctor's evidence that your weight is uncontrollable that will not be paid leave. You can draw from sick days and vacation. Do not take away any of the files relating to the case. I want everything related to it on my desk in twenty minutes.'

'My weight is none of your business.'

'I just gave you orders.'

The sheriff stood a long minute looking at Marquez and getting a hard stare back. Then he walked away without arresting or charging Marquez with anything.

The rest of it Marquez saw later that night on local TV in a Redding motel room. Voight must have delivered the files to the sheriff before walking out the front and gathering the news reporters, several that he knew, and telling the cameras that he had just been put on an indefinite leave of absence for refusing to arrest a Department of Fish and Game officer and falsely charge him with the murders of Terry Ellis and Sarah Steiner. He allowed that those charges might still come but guaranteed they would be dropped immediately following election day and dropping them would be followed by an apology that he didn't want to be part of.

Marquez's photo didn't run and the local TV angle was tensions in the sheriff's office boiling over ahead of Tuesday's election. One reporter speculated that Harknell had shot himself in the foot. Marquez called Voight's cell after watching the coverage on two channels.

'Thank you.'

'I didn't do it for you. I did it for myself. I thought it was bullshit last time he was so intent on getting you to the office so he could sit in on the questioning. He has moved me to the graveyard shift driving a patrol car. I'm done as an investigator as long as he's sheriff and the kid moving up has you as job one, so stay the hell out of the county for the next week. As soon as the election is over he'll lay off you. In the meantime he'll have everyone looking for you. He'll call a press conference and have a new angle tomorrow.'

Marquez flew south-west from Oakland early the next morning and sat with two LAPD homicide detectives then recounted what Colson told him yesterday. The detectives took him to the warehouse which was out near the border with Glendale in a white-painted concrete building in a rundown area that wouldn't attract much attention from anyone. He stood in front of the building and looked at the railroad tracks off to his left and the freeway onramp not a quarter mile from the building.

They showed him where the guard was found and apologized for calling US Fish and Wildlife first, but had reasoned the cache of animal parts was so large and varied they figured it was a Fed deal.'

'We've got a copy for you of what US Fish and Wildlife catalogued.'

'I've got that already.'

They showed him where the young Hispanic guard was shot. Inside the building it was cool and dark and he looked at the pool of darkened blood on the concrete and the spaces where the live animals were kept and the rooms where animal parts were stacked.

They drove from there to the address Colson gave him. No one answered but a neighbor volunteered that the two people who lived there had left in the middle of the night. The neighbor described a woman that she knew as Marianne so accurately that Marquez turned to one of the detectives and said, 'Different name, but that's Lia Mibaki.'

'Maybe this Colson tipped them.'

'Or they'll be back.'

'Or he tipped them and all this is to fuck with you.'

'He lost a warehouse here. It's more likely he wants to shed everyone connected with it. But he also sent me back with an offer to our department to make a deal with him.'

Marquez paused there. Colson had also given him something else and the detectives weren't going to like it and might react against it. But it could fit.

'He gave me one other name and that's someone he claims is inside your department who has been on his payroll for years. His words were, "I've paid this guy for a decade to watch out for me and he owes for the warehouse."'

'Give us the name.'

'Pat Tillerson.'

One detective said, 'Pat?' The other shook his head. 'That's impossible.'

'It's what he said. Who is Pat Tillerson?'

'Someone we work with.'

'I've got to head to the airport. Call me.'

284

FORTY-SIX

The Best Western Hotel in Corte Madera was just off the freeway, not that far from where Marquez lived. He liked the proximity and the rooms were reasonable enough to where he could get reimbursed or at least had a chance of getting reimbursed if he put an informant up here. Or that's the way it used to be.

When he couldn't reach Hauser by phone he stopped there, found Hauser's room, and knocked on the door. He knocked harder the second time and when nothing happened went down to the front desk and showed the Visa card the room was charged to. Even then they were reluctant to open the door, but after they did and he saw the bed was made and the carpet looking like it hadn't been walked on since it was vacuumed, he got the manager to check with the cleaning staff. A maid reported she didn't have to do anything in the room this morning.

Marquez took that back to his car and called Hauser. Behind him, he heard the low roar of the freeway as Hauser's cell rang. He answered on the fifth ring.

'I'm checking in with you, Matt. How are you doing?'

'Not well.'

'Where are you?'

'In the hotel room you rented for me and on my back with a bad migraine. I can't talk long.'

Hauser who hurt too much to talk long did a riff now on his wife and his wife's lawyer and the restraining order forbidding him to go near his house in Piedmont. He said his lawyer told him again this morning that he should quit cooperating with Fish and Game as it wasn't a reciprocal arrangement. Marquez didn't cut him off or interrupt. He listened to the whole thing and waited for Hauser to return to his headache.

When he did, Marquez interrupted before he could end the call.

'Where's Peason?'

'He's not taking my calls. I've made at least ten calls to him in the last twenty-four hours. I've got meetings later today. I've got to try to get some rest.'

'Tell me your room number there again? There's a place in that shopping mall across the street that has chicken soup that might help you. I'll get them to send some over.'

'The room number is 215 but if I eat anything when I feel like this I throw it up.'

'You're on your back in bed?'

'I'm in bad shape, Lieutenant. I can't talk anymore today.'

'I need you to try Barry Peason again.'

Marquez heard a loud exhale and then, 'You know what, Lieutenant, I'm going to follow my lawyer's advice from here. I'll check out of the room tomorrow and I'll pay for it. I'll have them reverse whatever is on your credit card. My wife and I have come to an agreement on some funds.

Even if you haven't been able to do anything for me, I appreciate your efforts.'

'It was never about you.'

'Maybe it should have been.'

Marquez thought about that last comment before pulling out of the lot. It was dusk and orange at the horizon with a clear cold night coming. He reached Ridge Road and turned onto the gravel drive to his house. There are things that can make you feel small and mistakes you make with an investigation that are born of believing a source is going to come through for you despite the apparent truth.

Marquez knew in the first weeks of talking with Hauser that Hauser was skirting giving him any real information. He just didn't know why. When after meeting him and Hauser was still reluctant Marquez knew he wasn't the source he hoped he would be, yet he didn't let go of him. *I needed him and I let him string me along and I should have let him go,* he thought. *I should have listened to Waller.*

But it goes that way sometimes. You work with an informant, someone with a grudge and information, you nurse the contact and most often they're in it for themselves and you work with that. You work toward the day when they give you the piece of information that moves the investigation. Other times that investment is a waste and you have to own up to getting burned or used or drawn into the world of someone who is emotionally troubled.

In the walk from his car into the house he let Hauser go. He got a beer from the refrigerator, opened it, and moved out on the back deck. He sat and took a drink and looked out over the dark of the trees below to the last red line on the horizon above the ocean. Where would he turn now? He tapped his phone and let it go dark as he weighed the risks and failure with Hauser causing him to doubt himself. Get over it, he thought. It happens. He picked up his phone, scrolled contacts, found Barbara Jones' number and called it.

'I was just thinking about you, Lieutenant.'

'Were you?'

'I'm up here in Siskiyou County and I just heard on the radio that an LAPD officer was shot by a suspect and that a SWAT team got into a firefight with two suspects wanted in the killing of a man guarding a large cache of illegal animal products in a warehouse in LA. It sounds like it just happened.'

'Let me call you back in a few minutes.'

He found the card he got from one of the detectives and called.

'Yeah, they came back for a duffel bag of cash they left behind and a surveillance team recognized them as they cruised the neighborhood before going into the house. They approached and knocked and the woman opened fire. One of our guys got hit in the leg. Our SWAT guys showed up and called them out and lobbed tear gas in through the living-room window. It looks like she shot her partner and then tried to get away from the gas by running out the back to a neighbor's house. They weren't going to let her do that and when she took a shot at one of the

SWAT guys they took her out. Look, I've got to run here but we'll be in touch.'

Marquez called Barbara Jones back and she answered with, 'You must need me.'

'I've got doubts about Matt Hauser.'

'No kidding, you've got doubts? I'd hate to be waiting around for you to ask me to marry you. You are slow.'

'My dreams die hard. Why don't you help me along?'

'Ask me what you want to know?'

'Do you know all ENTR employees?'

'There are one hundred and two employees. I know something about most of them.'

'Barry Peason.'

'He's a biologist.'

'Attached to what team?'

'You've got it all down now, don't you? He's attached to the one you're interested in, WPT, the Water Project Team.'

Marquez paused before gambling.

'Why isn't he at work?'

'Good question.'

'Where is he?'

'No one seems to know.'

'What's his connection to Hauser besides the team?'

'I can't talk about that but I'm working on it.'

'You need to talk to me about it. Didn't you say we're on the same side?'

'We are and I wish I could. I like you and I like the way you do your job. I make more in three months than you make in a year but you work harder.'

It was coming together for Marquez. More of the pieces were fitting and he felt the tiredness slipping away. He couldn't see anything close to all of it yet, but he saw more and he pushed now.

'How did Hauser transfer eight point two million dollars? How did he pull that off?'

'He was trusted. He was a team head and there are monthly audits. He knew when it would be caught. Everything he's done he scripted.'

'Wouldn't he need help?'

'How do you know that?'

'I'm making a guess.'

'Embezzlers tend to work alone.'

'But what if you're moving money inside the company to a project that's off screen and only a few people know what it's for, and then you move most of it again thinking the people behind the secret project can't do a thing about it without hanging themselves. What happens then? I'll make a guess at that too. Those who set up the secret project decided to play hardball with the embezzler. They created a phoney record of where the money was transferred from and then sold that to the FBI who then started investigating Hauser.'

'Lie to the Feds?'

'Sure, they're already in pretty deep with the pike project and they need to destroy Hauser's credibility. That's job one and they need someone honest like you who is boots on the ground and chasing the leads they've planted in phoney files uncovered in Hauser's impounded computers. Hauser tried to screw them and they're giving it right back to him. They upped the stakes.'

'That's your going theory, that Hauser was overseeing the pike project from the start and stole money allocated for it?' Jones asked.

'Yes.'

'And I'm a patsy being encouraged to investigate Hauser and find the third hatchery and the rest in the other states by the very people who set it up in the first place.'

'Somebody set it up, you agree with that, right?'

She was quiet. She didn't want to admit yet that Hauser was right in claiming the project originated at ENTR. She was that kind of loyal. She couldn't bring herself to say it. But too many fragments fit. Hauser was part of the original scheme and likely promised a lot of money to speed along the inevitable changes coming to the river ecosystems. Once in, he saw a way to get even more money and calculated that they wouldn't be able to come after him without revealing the pike project. It also explained the dance with Fish and Game.

'Of course, somebody set it up.'

'You hear me, right?'

'I hear you but your theory is wrong.'

'What was the name of the guy with you at the second hatchery? Wasn't it Ned Cowler? Go back to him.'

'You're crazy. He's worth a hundred million. He wouldn't take that kind of risk.'

'Ask him.'

'What else have you figured out?'

'That you and I both know where Barry Peason is. He's at the third hatchery.'

She was silent for a moment then said, 'Look,

we'll solve the problem. If it started with us, we'll solve it.'

'You don't know where the third hatchery is, do you? You're looking for it. Are you on your own with this or is Cowler encouraging you to look for it?'

'He is as serious about finding out the truth as you are.'

'I think he already knows the truth. You think about what I just said and maybe between us we can find it in time. Are you good with that?'

'You're wrong, but I'm in.'

When he hung up he wished he had said be careful. He almost called her back.

FORTY-SEVEN

About half of the twenty-five thousand registered voters in Siskiyou County turned out for the special election for sheriff that Mark Harknell lost by 617 votes. He was said to be reflective and not intending to ask for a recount so as to prevent the county from needlessly spending money. Marquez heard the results on an early-morning radio report and almost called Voight, but instead listened to a local radio station interview the departing Sheriff Harknell who would vacate his office today.

He spoke of standing up for a rural America under attack from outside forces, citing his opposition to the proposed removal of four dams along the Klamath as a stance in defense of farmers and ranchers. He painted himself as defending the county against special interests and radical liberal elements that wanted to impose their agenda on families who had lived for generations in Siskiyou County. He brushed over the unsolved murders and growing preponderance of meth labs and large-scale dope farms his opponent had hammered away at and sounded more like a man who had lost a run for Congress than a sheriff seeking re-election.

The call from Voight came soon after. 'Are you anywhere nearby?'

'Yeah, I can't get enough of your county.'

'I got reinstated early this morning by the new sheriff. He wants me to wait to go into the building until Harknell clears his desk.'

'Maybe you could help him clear it. Did you think he was going to lose?'

'No, it surprised me, but from the way he wanted to name you a suspect maybe I shouldn't have been surprised. Enough people must have felt he was overstepping his role. He told me once that Ellis and Steiner had no business being in the county supporting the dam removal and that what happened to them could have happened to anyone doing what they were doing. I don't mean to say he didn't want to solve the murders, but in his head your department is part of a bigger problem of outsiders imposing their will, so it's not hard for him to see you as a bad guy. Even if the murder charges didn't stick he wasn't hurting anybody that didn't already need hurting in his mind. Does that make sense?'

'You didn't let that happen and I owe you. I'm glad you got reinstated right away. That says people knew it was wrong.'

'Harknell overstepped.'

'Everyone does.'

'You're an ongoing riddle. Are you going to defend him? This guy was set on ruining your life.'

'I get where he's coming from. He had to turn his back as farmers pulled irrigation water even if it was illegal.'

'And killed your fish.'

'Not my fish, not mine, not yours, not anyone's.'

'All right, we don't have to get lost in this. I just wanted to make sure you knew he's gone. I've got to go now; we had a homicide last night. I'm on my way there.'

'Where was that?'

'A woman shot in her car. We'll talk in the next few days. You're still up here looking for that third hatchery?'

'I am but we may be joining forces with ENTR's security unit. They're better tapped into the information that will get us there.'

'Good luck with it—and call Sorzak. I can't get her to call me back.'

Marquez had planned to call her anyway. He did now and she picked up right away, asking, 'How did it go?'

'How much do you know about where he's living?'

'The cabin in the hippy refugee camp, is that where he met you?'

'Yes.'

294

'I've been there but don't worry for him. He's got very nice apartments in Vancouver and LA, and a house in San Francisco. He goes up to that encampment to hide and prey on the teenage girls.'

'When is the last time you saw him?'

'The morning he came for me to make the phone call to you.'

'Okay.'

Marquez waited a moment before saying, 'I'm going to change subjects.'

'Go ahead.'

'Did you hear about the shoot-out in LA?'

'No. What happened?'

'It was a couple, a man and a woman, and they were wanted for questioning about a murder of a young guy who was guarding a cache of animal parts and live animals in a warehouse.'

'Did you ask Jim about it?'

'I didn't know about it when I met with him. This went down yesterday. A shot was taken at an LAPD detective and a SWAT team brought in. Do the names Lia Mibaki and Arturo Borg mean anything to you?'

'No and why would they?'

'They may have worked for Colson. You never came across them?'

'I've never heard of them.'

'Never?'

'Not that I can remember.'

'Why are you avoiding Voight?'

'Because he lost his job and he's not the investigator anymore. It's news around here.'

'He got it back when Harknell lost the run-off.'

'Guess I'd better return his calls after all.'

But she wouldn't reach him today. The homicide that Voight was called out to was in an area with spotty cell coverage. Marquez learned that when Voight relayed a request through the sheriff's office that Marquez come to the murder scene.

The murdered woman was found by a rancher checking his fences along a rural road. She was at a turnout and slumped in her seat. Her car engine was running and the headlights on when the rancher found her before dawn. He drove past the car on his way out and saw it was in the same position when he returned an hour later, so took a look.

She was shot four times through the open driver's window and struck in the chest, neck, and head. The car wasn't opened until after Voight arrived and Voight didn't get a look at her wallet until the forensics team finished. Then he went through the contents of her purse and scrolled through her cell phone.

'One of her last calls was to you,' Voight said. 'She works for ENTR and we haven't told them she's dead, though the company has verified she's an employee. I want you to look at her before I give you her name or call ENTR.'

'You can't tell me her name?'

'I'd like you to drive here first.' When Marquez didn't answer he asked, 'Are you still there?'

'Yes.'

'What's up?'

'What kind of car?'

'A white Audi.'

'I'll see you there.'

She was out of the car and in the county coroner's wagon when Marquez arrived. Voight pulled the sheet back and Marquez felt a strong wave of sadness looking at the sightless eyes of Barbara Jones.

'You knew her?'

Marquez nodded. He couldn't quite speak.

'You're in her recent calls. What was that about? Why was she calling you?'

'She was looking for the third pike hatchery and we just agreed to team up to find it.'

'Could she have been killed for that?'

Marquez didn't have an answer for him or for any of his questions about who would kill her. He reached to touch her face and Voight pulled his arm back and then they looked at the car together as the coroner slammed the doors shut and backed off of the dirt turnout and drove away.

FORTY-EIGHT

Voight watched Marquez's reaction when he saw Barbara Jones' body. With his pike deal Marquez sided with this whacked and yet he was clearly disturbed by this ENTR employee's death. He treated embezzlement charges the climatologist was facing as some sort of side show, yet now he was saying that Mathew Hauser was in it from the start and double-crossed those who set up the

pike project. He claimed he and the victim here
had begun to work together.

Marquez took a step back and Voight knew he
was both looking at her car and trying to get his
head around how the murder happened. He
watched Marquez assess what evidence was left
in the dirt after the rancher and locals and deputies drove in and out of the turnout and tramped
around the car. The rancher brought his family
down here thinking they might recognize her.
They all walked around the car. It was pretty well
hopeless when he had arrived and worse now,
but Marquez looked like he was going to do his
pathfinder thing and squat down and scratch at
the dirt with a stick. Voight walked over.

'You're wasting your time.'

But if Marquez was anything he was stubborn.
Voight talked and Marquez questioned him about
the rancher's tire tracks. Now he was looking at
the deputies' vehicles. He turned back to him.

'Was she on her phone when she was shot?'

'She may have been but I don't know yet. Her
phone is out of juice and I need to get back to
the office to check with the phone company. She
was in the driver's seat and her window was
down. Maybe she lowered it for whoever shot
her or maybe it was already down. If you're okay
with one of these deputies driving your pickup
back to Yreka, I'd like it if you rode with me. I
want to talk with you about her. When did you
start working with her?'

'When I gave up on Hauser.'

Marquez handed over the pickup keys to a
deputy and walked out on the road, but there

wasn't going to be much there to see. Voight had already walked it. He gathered Marquez's missing hatchery was somewhere around here and after talking to the rancher he knew Barbara Jones may have parked here for the simple reason that this is where cell phones worked. That's what you did in this part of the county.

Voight had her laptop in his trunk in an evidence bag and figured to plug that in this afternoon and ask ENTR to get him past whatever encryption he encountered. Her car would get covered and towed. The forensic team had already loaded and left, but he was never in a hurry to leave a crime scene. He walked her car again and left Marquez out on the road.

When Marquez returned he was on the opposite side of the road and looking down like one of those diviner types who search for water. Voight saw him pause and called, 'What are you seeing there, John?'

'Let me show you something.'

Voight walked with him to a curve in the road near a small creek and then around the curve. They could no longer see her car, only the curve ahead with the brush on either side. Off the shoulder were a couple of footprints in the mud.

Marquez knelt.

'This is recent and it could have been one of your guys walking the road this morning, or it could be someone else walking toward the turnout.'

'It doesn't look like it goes any farther than here.'

'It does but let's look at this first.'

Marquez showed him what he called the first tracks, but it was just as likely a deputy who stepped off the road earlier today.

'This is where a car could have stopped to let someone out. That's what I'm seeing here. The heel is dug down because they got out fast then needed these next steps to get their balance and move left onto the asphalt. Meanwhile the driver accelerates away and drives past the turnout where she's parked. She sees the headlights go flash past.'

'That leaves the shooter hidden around the curve in the dark and on foot. He starts walking down the road and sticks to the edge because he wants to use the brush to hide it. He doesn't have a light and is letting his eyes adjust, but he steps off the asphalt in a couple of places because the edge of the road is uneven and the asphalt has degraded. You'll see it's the same boot print.'

Marquez showed him three more spots.

'Same heel print as that first one and that's a different heel than the deputies who were here earlier or the two still here.' He pointed at the heel mark. 'It's fresh.'

Voight nodded. He saw it now. Marquez was right. From the blood splatter on her phone and on the laptop the shooter had walked up and surprised her. The shooter knew she would be parked here. She was on her phone and turned her head when she heard the shooter approaching or her name was called.

'He walked up and shot her and the car that dropped him came back and picked him up,'

Marquez said. 'They knew she was going to be here and waiting. Somehow they knew.'

Voight agreed but didn't respond. He had his own questions such as why didn't the shooter take her laptop or phone. He got four casts made of the footprints Marquez found and then started questioning Marquez as to what he knew about Barbara Jones and the ENTR security unit she worked for, but unfortunately, Marquez's best source on her was Hauser.

'Hauser told me the security unit was five-person and she was the one most often out in the field. She was very confident. She told me she was in Siskiyou County looking for the third hatchery.'

Voight nodded. She was way out a rural road for a reason and driving back with Marquez to Yreka Voight heard everything Marquez knew or was willing to say about her and the people she was looking for and worked with. When they got to Yreka he picked up a sandwich and potato salad and Marquez bought coffee and made it clear he didn't want to leave yet. Whatever Barbara Jones had learned, he wanted.

But Marquez wasn't saying what he was looking for and call it a bad habit or a suspicious nature, but he had Marquez's steering wheel and door handles and several other spots in the car checked with luminal to look for trace blood. He did that despite not having any suspicions about Marquez and he liked it that Marquez cared about her. That showed when he saw her body and in the way he talked.

The laptop and cell phone were checked for

301

touch DNA and plugged in and charged up and Marquez was still here, though he had been in and out of the building and on and off his phone. Voight talked with ENTR without Marquez in the room and ENTR walked him around her laptop firewall and provided her login, but they didn't come across without a threat first. He went through files on her laptop and when he realized he'd need longer than today to do that, he brought Marquez back in.

'What are you waiting around for, John?'

'A look at her laptop and phone.'

'You can look at both. In fact, I'd like you to read an email she may have been writing you when she was shot. Here.'

Marquez leaned over and read it. He nodded as if he understood her writing it, but he also looked puzzled.

'What is she trying to tell you and why is it so cryptic?'

Marquez turned one of those big hands of his outward as if to say, who knows, then started talking.

'Any email she wrote could be read by the company. They all get saved so she took it to the edge of what she thought I might figure out but that someone reading inside ENTR might not. That could mean she believed the pike project originated inside the company and there was someone at ENTR she didn't trust.'

'What about the rest of it? How does it connect, and if these emails are getting stored why didn't she text you instead?'

'It's all the same. ENTR captures everything.'

'You know that or she told you that?'

'She told me and so did Hauser, as did a biologist I'm looking for.'

'What's his name?'

'Barry Peason.'

Voight slid the laptop closer to Marquez.

'What's the last part about?'

It read: 'Saw one of shoot-out pair last week up here??? Call me.'

Now Voight felt Marquez evaluating him. He had weighed Marquez as a possible suspect and it was as if Marquez was turning the tables.

'Marquez, don't go dark on me. Don't even think about doing that.'

'The shoot-out she means was in Los Angeles.'

'The tusk shooters?'

Marquez nodded.

'Does that make any sense to you?'

'Not right now but if she saw one of them up here it probably means she saw them with somebody she was watching.'

'I still don't get it.'

'I didn't say I did. Is that all you got out of her computer and phone?'

'No, there's something else you need to look at.' He slid her phone across his desk. 'Take a look under Notes.'

Marquez scanned the files and found a grocery list which literally read: milk, bread, etc. Voight watched him read through a holiday shopping list, gifts and names to go with them. He scanned a recipe for a Thanksgiving turkey and a file titled Juliet and after reading wondered aloud if Juliet was a girlfriend, or a lover, and went slowly down a to-do list that included 'leak at fireplace, buy new coffee maker,' and three entries under to-do: 'BP offer', 'possible meet with SH', and the last entry was just one word with a question mark, 'Rider?' It gave him a chill. He looked up as he started to get into her emails. Then he looked up alarmed.

'Did you save the files in her computer?'

'No.'

'Do it now. Emails are vanishing off her phone.'

Marquez clicked into Settings and tried to disconnect the phone from any network. He turned the phone off and it came back on and Voight was aware Marquez wasn't having any luck and his own fingers were trembling as he pushed a memory stick in and called to Marquez for help in getting into the docs and Marquez took over. Marquez wasn't fast but he knew what to do, but it was too late. Voight watched him try three times and then they just sat there aware that everything was gone.

'I'll get somebody to pull them off the hard drive.'

Marquez didn't answer at first then said, 'They're buying time to move the fish out of that third hatchery. One of her notes on the to-do list read "BP offer." That's not British Petroleum. That's Barry Peason, the biologist I mentioned.'

'Do you know him?"

'I've talked to him and I've been chasing him.'

'Who is SH? Is that Hauser's initials?"

Voight reached for his notebook, still stunned that everything on the computer was gone.

'Mathew Stephen Hauser,' he read. 'She was being clever using his middle initial.'

Marquez shook his head.

'I'm not sure it is him. It could be but there's another way to look at this. She and I talked about Siskiyou County and who knows what goes on up here. It's five times bigger than the state of Rhode Island and has forty-five thousand people living in it, so we talked about who's connected, who knows the area and the people and the name Sheriff Harknell came up. The date on this note is right after she and I talked. SH could be Sheriff Harknell.'

Voight sat on that one for a moment.

'What was she going to do with that idea?'

'She was going to call Harknell. He knows a lot about what's going on in the county and might have heard rumors about a hatchery and that's not to say he would know anything about what's being grown at the hatchery, just knows that it exists. She had some charisma. She might have gotten it out of him.'

Marquez slowly stood.

'I've got to go. Think about who could ask him and call me.'

'There's no one to ask him.'

'Then I guess it'll be me and you. Call me when you're ready.'

FORTY-NINE

The next morning fog was low in the trees and misting across the wet road as Marquez drove

305

the dirt track to the encampment. The road splintered as he neared the overgrown airfield in the meadow and he parked under trees near there. He crossed the wet grass of the airfield and walked up the dirt road that climbed to the encampment. He found the tented and tarped remains of the falling-down cabin where the girl who showed up at Colson's cabin lived. He wanted to talk with her first.

Smoke rose from the stone chimney and there was no door but he called and a woman who looked like she could be her mother pulled the tarp back. When she did the smell of tortillas and frying eggs was strong. She squinted as if trying to comprehend his presence here and then shook her head. She saw no reason for him to talk to her daughter.

'She's not here.'

'Is there a way I can find her?'

'She hasn't done anything wrong.'

She let the tarp fall shut as she went back inside and Marquez heard a man's voice and waited to see if he'd come out, but no one did and he worked his way through the salvaged iron and wood and rusted vehicles and past the scraggly crops at the center of the encampment and climbed the trail up through the cedars to Colson's cabin.

The young man standing guard was familiar. His gun rested against the cabin wall as he warmed his hands over coals glowing in a rusted barrel. He looked stiff and tired as if he had been there all night. He probably had. But he moved fast when Marquez pushed aside a cedar branch, stepped into the small clearing and identified himself. He held his Glock level and warned the man he wasn't alone. He backed him away from his gun then moved to the cabin door.

'You're Jason, right?'

No answer and Marquez broke the guard's shotgun open and emptied out the shells.

'There are six more law enforcement officers in the area and there's a plane overhead. It's not going down like last time.'

Marquez knocked on the cabin door with the butt of his gun. He knocked again, harder, and heard rustling inside as he turned the badge so Jason could read it.

'Where's your partner? I don't want him to get shot.'

'He's in the showers.'

'And Rider's inside.'

'Yeah, he's here. He's not going to like this though.'

Jason was a young man, mid twenties, some facial hair, flannel shirt over another shirt underneath, jeans, and would fit easily in a brew pub anywhere along the north-west coast. His coat was folded and crumpled alongside the camp stool and wet with fog drip out of the trees. He probably had been here all night but wouldn't last five seconds if someone came to kill Colson. The guard job was gratuitous make work or maybe Colson's head wound rattled his confidence and made him worry in a way he never had to here.

Marquez hammered the door again.

'Open up.'

Marquez couldn't see the encampment but blue smoke drifted through cedars toward them. It looked like an inch of snow fell last night. It was cold this morning. The door swung open now and the girl was there wrapped in a blanket. Marquez put her age at fifteen or sixteen. He saw Colson sitting on the bed in jeans and boots, no shirt, and a gun in his hand.

'Are you alone, Lieutenant?'

'No.'

'Where are they?'

'They're here and surrounding us and there's a plane if we need, but I'm here to continue the conversation. We're interested in negotiating but not here. We're going to take a drive and I'll need to arrest you and put restraints on. That's a condition. That's the only way you're coming in and that's from my chief.'

'You don't need restraints and I already knew you were coming.'

He sent the girl away and as she ran back down the path he pulled the clip out of his gun and left it lying on the bed as he stood. He gestured back at the gun.

'There. I'll get dressed and we'll do the deal.'

'I want you to say your name now.'

Colson stared at him.

'You're as fucked up as me, do you know that?'

'Say it.'

But he didn't. He stood with his arms at his side and then reached and touched the stitches along the back of his head and his gaze moved from Marquez to the door. He shook his head as if trying to keep a gnat or mosquito away from his ear and looked back at Marquez and said, 'James Colson.'

'Okay, Colson, get dressed. Let's go.'

'And what happens if we don't make a deal?'

'I bring you back here.'

Colson gave a thin smile. 'Like fuck you would.'

'Or I'll release you to the wild.'

'What does that mean?'

'It means your business is coming apart. I'm already hearing rumors of other people wanting parts of it. Some people think you're already dead. Word of your head wound got around.

I think you came to us because there are enough people out there now who want you dead.'

'Let's see your backup here, Marquez.'

'You're not going to see them yet, but I'll get on the radio with them.'

He pulled his radio and got Burwell and the Blanco and Colson heard enough to believe they were there. Colson pulled on a sweater, a coat, and shoes.

'There's plenty of backup this time but no one is going to ride with us. We're going to get a few hours of one-on-one conversation.'

'Where are we going?'

'To the sheriff's office in Yreka first. It's where this starts.'

When Colson didn't say anything to that, Marquez continued.

'There's some news out of the LA end of your operation. Lia Mibaki shot Arturo Borg and then tried to outgun a SWAT team and escape. Everything in your warehouse was confiscated, but you probably already know that. What you might not know about are the arrests US Fish and Wildlife has made in Florida, New York, Texas, and Virginia. That's part of what's getting the word out. There are other plea bargains underway.'

'I guess that means I should really make the deal that works for you. You just tell me what you need, Lieutenant. I'm just here to bend over for you, though I've never heard of a Lia and Arturo. They sound like folk singers. Is that what they are?'

'You gave me their names.'

'That will be your word against mine on that.'

'The Feds are leaving six messages a day asking for any information I have on your whereabouts and I get the feeling there are careers to be made on this one. Look, you made an offer and I took you up on it. I'm back and if you want to go forward with it, you've got to cooperate.'

Colson pressed close to him as they left the cabin said, 'I knew you would be back.'

Now they were back down to the untended airstrip and past the stained Beechcraft lodged in ferns near a windsock long since in tatters. Marquez led Colson to his pickup under the trees and loaded him in. He knew the guards and several others were hanging back watching for the wardens and any other backup, and the moment was tense and hung on Colson telling his guys to do nothing.

'Does a kid hauling elephant tusks in a taco truck mean anything to you?'

'No, and I don't feel much like bullshit banter

this morning. I get it that adrenalin has got you running a little high and you've got something you think is big in your back pocket to charge me with. But you can't imagine the money I've made and how easy it was. I can give you five hundred names—hunters, poaching teams, spotter pilots, corrupt cops, longshoremen, trucking and shipping firms I've used, and buyers, every day there are more buyers. Are you wired right now?'

'No and we're interested in trading. I haven't lied to you yet. I can't promise you immunity. I can't promise anything, but your tip on Lia and Arturo was legit and we're interested in talking. We've got two and a half million dollars in animals and animal parts that I can tie to you. We've got the kid who drove a food truck who has given us a list of names and agreed to testify against you. We've got Lisa Sorzak who is talking with a DA about charging you with rape. We want the California end of your operation, the buyers and the middle men.'

'Do you really think you have Lisa?'

'She says she'll testify and that you've threatened and abused her for a decade.'

'You don't know her.'

Colson coughed.

'What if I told you I passed along money that came through Sheriff Harknell and that it has nothing to do with animals? What would that be worth to you?'

'I'm a Fish and Game officer.'

'You want to know about this.'

'Then tell me.'

They started into the steeper curves and the

tires kicked up mud that chattered against the wheel wells and Colson's voice got stronger as he talked above it. Marquez knew later he should have picked up on that.

'I can help you with the sheriff, Lieutenant. I know he's got it in for you.'

'You've been in the woods too long. Harknell isn't sheriff anymore and why would I care about anything to do with Harknell?'

Colson's voice hardened.

'Shut up and listen; you aren't in control here yet, and if you lie to me we aren't going to have that conversation you want so badly. We'll never have it and my lawyers will get me off. Harknell knew I was dealing animals, trading skins is what he called it when he finally ran me down. This was about two and a half years ago in early March. He caught me when I was in his county and out with my people and he took me down hard. His boot was on my face and my face was in slush on a sidewalk when he told me he knew I was once a Texas lawman.

'He said that meant we could talk and if we could talk we could do business. The business was passing money on to the right people. The sheriff had someone who gave money to his campaign and he didn't say who it was or why he was doing this for them, but the donor was strong against taking any dams down. The donor wanted money to go on to people who didn't like having strangers up here interfering, and Harknell said I knew the right people to put an end to outside interference. He gave me fifty thousand in cash to stop what he said was growing into a

312

movement to tear down the dams. There was double that money if I made it happen, but it needed to shock the outsider types coming into his county and causing problems.'

'Are you going to confess to two murders?'

Colson laughed. 'I thought you were.' He went on. 'No. I didn't kill those girls. I lay on the sidewalk with his boot on my face and I'm thinking *fuck you, Harknell.* I knew he had his boat moored at a marina on Lake Shasta and thought one of my guys could get him out on his boat someday.

'He took his boot off me and told me we'd meet on his boat and indeed we did. We drank and talked and when we got back to shore I left with the first part of the money. I walked the dock with it.'

'Was it a warm day?'

'What kind of question is that? Who gives a fuck what the day was like? Yes, it was sunny and hot.'

Colson grimaced as they hit a pothole and it threw him forward against the dash and then back.

'Goddamn you, Marquez, take these off me.'

Marquez knew the dock where the sheriff's boat was. He pictured splintered dry wood, boards nailed in decades ago and rusted and creaky. In the drought years it loomed over the reservoir mud, shore dirt and rock. In the last few years the water was higher, but every year was different and he thought, underneath all of this it's about water, all of this. It was always about water.

'It was hot and you weren't wearing a coat and

313

you didn't know you'd be leaving there carrying fifty thousand. Maybe you thought you might but you didn't know and there was a good chance it was in hundred dollar bills or even twenties.'

'It was a mix.'

'Harknell is a fisherman, isn't he?'

'There are rods on his boat.'

Marquez nodded and another piece of it made sense now. Colson was the type never to forget anyone who had ever humiliated him. He went back for his ex-wife. He had her ex-lover killed. Harknell put a boot on his face.

'Did you walk off the dock with the money in the tackle box that got buried with the murder weapon?'

'Well, I'm impressed, Lieutenant. Maybe you are what they say.'

'Who else knew about Harknell's offer?'

He didn't answer that but they had hours more and Marquez took the long route. He knew Colson expected that. Instead of taking Highway 299 to Redding he drove to Hoopa and started up the Klamath River Highway. The road was one lane either direction and ran next to the river. Before they reached the interstate he planned to cross the Klamath and take Colson to the dirt road on the far bank and down to where Terry Ellis and Sarah Steiner were killed.

It was as good a chance as he would ever have with Colson and he drove slowly and there was no traffic and the river in the gorge below was dark green into white water at the bends and the slopes rich with pine and fir. Driving as slow as he was he didn't think much about the black

314

pickup that appeared from behind him. He assumed it had passed the wardens who were following and would also pass him. But it didn't and when it hung back with a gray sedan behind it he started tracking them.

He saw Colson watching the side mirror on the passenger door and tried reaching the wardens by cell, but the call dropped and his pickup didn't have a radio. He tried again a mile later and then slowed for road work ahead and tried again as the black pickup and the sedan closed in behind. A backhoe blocked the road ahead as Marquez checked out the road crew. He heard Colson clear his throat.

'Bridge isn't far from here,' Colson said. 'But I didn't kill them.'

'Did the sheriff pay a second fifty thousand?'

'It was never the sheriff's money.'

'Was it paid?'

Colson never answered and ahead Marquez saw a flagman start toward them. So did two others in the orange fluorescent jackets of a road crew and he couldn't think of any reason for that or for the two men in the black pickup behind them to get out of their truck. But they did and the gray sedan came up alongside the pickup and then turned and parked to block the rest of the road. Ahead he didn't see any way around the backhoe. The hoe arm was extended and the driver raised a rifle and aimed in their direction.

'You can jump out, Lieutenant, and run down toward the river, but I don't think you'll get far.'

'How about if I put a gun to your head and they move the backhoe?'

315

'I don't plan to kill you. This is all more complicated than you know. You should have taken me up on my offer last time.'

Marquez pulled his gun. No mistaking how outnumbered he was and Colson was quiet now letting him come to the conclusion that he couldn't shoot his way out.

'What do you want to do, Lieutenant?'

The second man from behind was alongside them now yelling at Marquez to unlock the doors. He aimed a gun through the driver-door window at Marquez's head.

'Unlock these restraints and then get out slowly and they won't kill you. We're going to take your truck and leave you here.'

Marquez ignored the yelling from outside.

'I won't kill you. I'll leave you here and then I'll be in touch. What I'll have to tell you will surprise you. Lay your gun on the dash.'

Marquez did that and got out slowly and one of the men helped Colson out while another patted down Marquez and at gunpoint led him over to the road shoulder.

Rider started walking toward a Chevy Suburban up ahead of the backhoe blocking the road and his stride said he was in control again. But he wasn't. The man behind him closed the gap before Colson reached the backhoe and lifted his gun and fired. Marquez heard three shots and saw Colson slide to the ground.

The shooter put four more shots into him and turned and Marquez thought, this is where it ends. But they didn't shoot him. They stripped him of his phone and took the pickup and his gun. He was standing near Colson's body when the two area wardens arrived and not long after they heard yelling from a white van parked fifty yards up the road from the backhoe. When they got there they found the real road crew locked inside and chained together, one with a bloody face and no front teeth left and another with a gunshot wound that blew out his knee.

Not long after, the first sirens echoed in the canyon.

FIFTY

The next day he rode with Voight to Harknell's house in Weed. Darcie Smith-Harknell, the sheriff's wife, opened the front door and frowned when she saw Voight. She stared at Marquez before turning back angrily to Voight.

'Is the sheriff expecting you?'

'He's not the sheriff, ma'am, and this isn't a social call.'

'He's still the sheriff at this house and I'll call him that just as long as I want.'

Marquez saw Harknell come out of a room and start toward them. He looked as if he had been napping and ran a hand through his hair and shook off what looked like confusion as he reached the small foyer. His eyes lit when he saw Marquez. With a hand he moved his wife aside and stood in the doorway.

'What's this about? Get out of here, both of you.'

317

'You want to talk to me,' Voight said, 'and Lieutenant Marquez is here because Jim Colson talked to him about you.'

He turned to Marquez.

'What did you talk about? Did he owe you money to keep his trafficking operation going? Is that why you're up here so much? There's nothing he could have said about me that wouldn't be a lie. I heard they picked him up off the shoulder like road kill.'

Marquez had an answer for that but it was Voight's lead and he kept quiet as Harknell and Voight got into it, Harknell telling Voight that he should quit and go back to LA, that he never fit here and was considered the department drunk. Now Harknell stepped out onto his porch, his face taking on a pink hue as his anger rose. He pulled the door shut behind him and got in Voight's face.

'You're an embarrassment to the department. It was Siskiyou County's bad luck that you landed here and now you think you're going to trump up something to get even with me. That isn't going to happen and I'll tell you something else that I've been thinking for a while. The man who murdered your child did it because he knew you wouldn't have the stones to do anything about it.'

Voight launched at him and Marquez got an arm between. When Harknell tried to push him away he gathered up Harknell's sweatshirt in his left hand and pushed him hard enough against the wall of his house that the breath wheezed out of him. He used his right to hold Voight off until

Voight stopped himself and laid it out for his ex-sheriff.

'If you don't want to talk to us that's your right, but I will be back. I will be back and back and back and I'll bring you in and question you until you have answers.'

'What in the fuck are you talking about? You don't make any more sense today than you ever did.'

'Invite us in and we'll talk.'

'I don't want the warden in my house.'

'He comes with me. I want him here.'

'Then we have a problem.'

Voight started back to his car and Harknell called, 'All right, we'll take twenty minutes in my office and we'll walk around the house to get there. I don't want Darcie exposed to this horseshit.'

They followed Harknell around the house on a garden path and into an office of much higher quality than the rest of the house. Floor to ceiling windows faced Mount Shasta where wind high on the mountain lifted plumes of new snow off the summit and spun it into funnels in the clear sky. The floor of the office was oiled walnut planking and the white-painted walls were smooth and clean. The chairs were plush, his desk suggestive of his ambition. Harknell directed them to a couch and Marquez took a chair.

'What have you got? Let's hear it or do you want scout here to talk first and tell how he found Colson, who I know for a fact has been paying him off for years.'

Voight asked a dozen questions about what

319

contact Harknell had with Colson and for how long and whether he had ever met with him at the cabin where Marquez arrested him yesterday.

'I've never met with him anywhere. I've never met the man or had reason to.'

'Did you ever make a phone call to Texas and confirm he had once worked for the state police?'

'I did after you got on to him and scout here. I don't have a date for you.'

'They have a record of you making an inquiry two and a half years ago.'

'Bullshit, they do. No one keeps records like that.'

'This is informal here,' Voight said, 'but if they send me what they've promised and I compare it to your phone records and it comes back that you lied to me, that's an issue.'

'What if I did make an inquiry? If you're sheriff and you're like me you want to know everything you can about anyone questionable. If I checked him or anyone else two and a half years ago and can't remember doing that it doesn't mean jack shit.

'Now, contrast that with you, Rich. You get up in the morning and if you're sober you come into work when you're ready and then sit at your desk until ten minutes to twelve and then go to that diner where you wolf as much as you can before you come back and shuffle papers around and nap in your chair ahead of going home. That's your day. It's busier as sheriff and if you don't want to take my word for it, talk to your boss after he's been in there a couple of months.'

Voight glanced at Marquez and that was the

signal for Marquez to get in. Marquez stood as he started talking.

'Colson will never testify.'

'That's for sure, son.'

'I went to his hideout.'

'I'm sure you've been there many times.'

'There's a young woman who lives there who has picked you out of a line-up. She's here in Yreka right now. She was brought in last night. Would you remember sleeping with an under-age teenage girl more than once or does that just get mixed in with the rest of the job?'

'Well, Scout, you're a man, you know how it is. I have wandered occasionally but I don't remember any teenaged whores. If you want to put her through that you can do that to her. You've got to remember a young woman can be fragile.'

'Set what you did to her aside for a moment. What's really going on here, Mark, is that your visits to Colson's hideout can be proved.'

'It's a lie.'

'Here's the next thing. I was on the phone with Barbara Jones not long before she was shot. I know why she called you.'

Harknell broke off staring at him and looked over at Voight.

'That's true. She and I talked a number of times.' He pointed a finger at Marquez. 'Several of those were about you.'

'I'm saying I know why she called you.'

Now Voight slid a copy of phone records across the coffee table and Harknell went to his desk for reading glasses. He picked up the printout. That her recent calls would get scrutinized couldn't be any surprise to him yet he seemed unsettled. He tossed the paper back down on the table, dismissing it, but the gesture didn't carry.

'Again, I talk to a lot of people.'

'You talked to her late in the afternoon of the day she was killed. I talked to her after you. She was looking for the third hatchery. That's why she called you.' Marquez glanced at Voight and gambled. 'You went out to meet her.'

'Gentlemen, excuse me for a minute.'

Harknell got up and left the room and they looked at each other wondering what was going on. Voight put on a gun for the trip out here and reached around and unclasped the holster. He didn't like the abrupt departure. When they heard a car engine start, Voight jumped up.

'He's running.'

They got outside in time to see Harknell accelerate away. Voight leaned into his car and got on his radio and a deputy picked up Harknell. When he turned onto the southbound I-5 onramp two highway patrol units moved in to help follow. But he wasn't pulled over because Marquez argued against it.

'Let's pass him. He hasn't been arrested or charged with anything and he's going to try to get on his boat. There may be something there he wants to lose. Get me there ahead of this convoy and I'll take care of the boat.'

Voight got on his radio and let the deputies know that he was going around and then hit the gas and the car leapt forward and they took the Shasta Dam exit and as they rolled through Shasta City the call came that Harknell had just exited and was three miles behind them and driving slowly.

'He's scared and he's unsure what to do, but he's headed to the lake,' Marquez said, and pushed Voight to drive the road hard. He figured he had five to ten minutes, probably closer to five after he got through the gate and onto Harknell's boat.

After Marquez got around the dock gate he reached in through the cabin window and got the cabin door open. Now he cut the ignition wires and pushed them up under the dash. He was back out the gate and off the dock as the strange convoy rolled in and a red-faced and shaking Harknell confronted the deputies. They kept quiet as Voight tried to talk to him.

'Goddamn you, you drunk fraud, so help me God, I'll have your job.'

Harknell turned to the highway patrol officer, said loudly, 'Eddie, your dad and I go way back and if you've got any questions about this bastard's insinuations call him. He turned back to Voight, his hands shaking as he fumbled for his key to the dock gate. He opened the gate and maybe he was unaware it didn't close behind him as he strode toward his boat or maybe at heart he knew it was over.

He cast the bow line off before getting onboard and two more sheriff deputies pulled in. Marquez stepped onto the dock and walked down to Harknell's boat. Harknell had a gun near his right knee and was hunched over the dash trying to figure out why his key didn't work.

Harknell turned.

'Step on this boat and I'll shoot you and I'll be within my rights.'

'I won't get on the boat, Sheriff, and you don't want to shoot anyone.'

His forehead was beaded with sweat, his cheeks red, eyes desperate and Marquez kept talking. Harknell started to rise then stumbled and sat back down in the seat, and Voight was now on the dock approaching with two deputies.

'You're a fisherman, Sheriff. You've got to tell me. You know what'll happen. Tell me now before they get here. Those pike are going to the delta. They'll kill off everything. You might hate me but you don't want that.'

Did Marquez expect anything? No. But was it worth a try? Why not? Just as Voight and the deputies arrived and a moment before Harknell was ordered to place his hands on the boat's dashboard, he whispered, 'One-Two-Three-One Burnside Road.'

FIFTY-ONE

The SOU team was too far south to get there but a Siskiyou warden and two SOU met Marquez at the cut-off to Burnside Road. He laid out his plan.

'I want them to think there are more of us. I'll go in first and five minutes later, you.'

He pointed to one of the SOU wardens and she nodded. The other two would follow her.

324

'I'm going to show you a photo I pulled off the Internet of a biologist named Barry Peason. I hope I got the right Barry Peason.'

Nobody laughed.

'I'm joking. It's him. He's a biologist and this other guy is named Matt Hauser. I don't know who else is here and I don't know if these guys are here either, but I'm hoping they are and we're not too late. I'll go in now.'

Marquez turned in at a mailbox on a gray redwood post with stick-on letters reading 1231. It was a ranch and as he saw three cars and the buildings his first reaction was that Harknell may have lied and this was a legitimate ranch. A Ford 250 was parked next to a Honda and beat-up Subaru all-wheel drive. He saw a barn, a house, two other out buildings, three horses in a corral, alfalfa in a field, things he would expect to see on a small ranch.

He didn't see Hauser's car or the white Prius registered to Barry Peason. He studied the barn as he knocked on the door of the house, and then knocked again. As he did, the door to the barn rolled open sideways and almost silently but for a mechanical whirr, and when he saw what was happening he called Sheila Braga. She was the lead warden coming in.

'I'm almost to you,' she said.

'Block the road and bring the others up fast. You're about to see a white Prius with Peason at the wheel coming at you. Don't do anything until there are three of you. I'll be there in a few minutes. I'm checking out the barn and I can see fish tanks. The set-up is a lot like the last one.'

He walked through and confirmed what he knew he would find, empty tanks, the operation being shuttered and Peason on his way out. He called Braga back.

'The pike are gone.'

'We've got him.'

'Bring him back here. I think the fish moved this morning. There are wet tire tracks in the barn and they're from a bigger vehicle, not Peason's Prius.'

Peason shook with nervousness and stalled and then blamed Hauser for everything. He didn't know where Hauser was and no, Hauser had never been here. He said no one else was in the house or anywhere on the premises and gave them permission to check. Two guys were southbound toward the delta in a pickup truck with plastic coolers carrying the young pike.

Marquez let Peason believe if he cooperated it might all work out for him and he could undo everything and start over. He said the truck with the fish left two hours ago but wouldn't release pike into the delta until dusk. There were multiple coolers and approximately three thousand fingerlings. They might release from a boat but he wasn't sure and got more and more vague about the actual release spot, repeating that it wasn't his responsibility.

'Whose is it?'

'I don't even know their names.'

'You don't know the names of the guys driving the fish to the delta?'

'The first time I saw them was this morning.'

'Who paid for this hatchery?'

'ENTR but only a few people know about it.'

'We'll need the names of everyone.'

'I'm not a manager.'

'You're a scientist.'

'That's right. You need to talk to the manager of the project. When I took this on it wasn't to dump invasive species into the delta. No one told me that's what was going to happen. I don't know anything about that part of it. This was an experiment to see if we could breed northern pike. The rest is something else that I don't have anything to do with.'

Peason was scared and shocked and his story shifted. Marquez figured they couldn't wait as he fumbled for a way out.

'Here's where you're at. You're the guy in charge of the California hatcheries and who knows where the Oregon and Washington hatcheries are. You're not a bystander watching to see if we stop this delta release. You are absolutely fucked if it happens.

'The first round died of a virus, the second was stopped, and this is the third. If it makes it into the river there's nothing we can do and you'll become known as the biologist who micromanaged a multi species die-off. You'll go to prison and you'll see a flood of civil suits that will continue after you're out of prison as the pike take over and the natives die-off. You'll never see a share of the money Hauser promised you, but the good news is you'll never have to worry about money again. You won't have any. How much did Hauser promise you?'

'I don't know what you're talking about?'

But he did and Marquez could picture Peason's role now. Hauser had promised him something substantial, enough to where Peason had hung on until the end. Peason had gambled and lost and couldn't accept that. He didn't see ENTR trying to pin it all on him and Hauser and the promise of money going away.

He gave Peason a few minutes and then stepped away and called Wheeler to see if he could get his plane in the air. Wheeler said thirty minutes. Questioning Peason could wait. All that mattered now was stopping that truck. He walked back over to Peason and sat down.

'Do you want to stay and help us or should we run you down to the county jail and get you booked?'

Turned out the scientist in him didn't need much time to do a deep analysis. Five minutes was all he needed to think it through. He wanted to help.

FIFTY-TWO

Marquez took Peason with him. He knew Peason hadn't told him everything and when Wheeler couldn't find a blue pickup with an orange tarp over the bed after flying Highway 99, his gut feeling got a little deeper. He watched Peason nervously adjusting his glasses and the zipper of his fleece coat and asked again, 'Orange tarp, blue Ford pickup?'

'Same as I told you before.'

'We aren't finding it from the air.'

'Maybe your pilot flew over when they were under a gas station canopy.'

'Or maybe they took a different road.'

'This is the highway they're supposed to drive.'

'Call the driver.'

'I don't have his number.'

'Someone knows where they are. Call them.'

'Your plane will find them.'

But the spotter plane didn't find them. It was Muller and four of the SOU team in the late afternoon who picked up on a white pickup towing a power boat, its bed covered with a gray tarp. The pickup pulled in at Brannan Island State Recreation Area and drove through and drove out and continued up the road to the Isleton Launch Ramp near the Ramos Oil Company. The two men in the pickup started to back down that ramp then changed their minds and pulled out and Muller kept two of the team with them as they checked out other boat launches before returning to the Brannan Island Recreation Area.

But they didn't launch their boat, and instead spread food out on one of the picnic tables and started a charcoal fire in one of the barbecue stations. Two steaks marinated in a shallow plastic dish as the coals readied. One of the men walked down at the boat launch and toed the invasive water hyacinth that had grown up the launch ramp while the other swigged beer and served potato salad onto paper plates and kept the sea gulls at bay.

Muller pulled out the SOU wardens just as the steaks were hitting the coals. He told Marquez they had another pickup to check out on a levee road above prospect Slough, and the pair at Brennan were cooking and eating, so probably the wrong pickup.

Marquez reached the delta soon after. He pulled off on the shoulder outside Isleton and turned to Peason.

'You're not going to ride any farther with me, Barry. I want you to get out and face the truck. I'm going to arrest you and there's a warden on the way who will take you to get booked.'

'Why are you doing this after I gave you the Oregon and Washington hatcheries?'

'You mean, why am I double-crossing you?'

'Yes!'

'I don't want you riding with me as we look for the pike you raised. I'm in a bad mood, Barry, and I don't trust you much. Turn around.'

Marquez put restraints on his wrists and a warden arrived and Marquez touched Peason's right shoulder. 'Stay here. I'm going to talk to the warden a minute before we get you loaded up. And I'm going to borrow your phone a minute too.'

He pulled a cell phone from Peason's coat as he stepped away and Peason yelled, 'You can't do that. You don't have the right. That's illegal.'

Marquez checked text messages and then forwarded the last dozen to himself. The last text Peason sent read: 'launching rio.' He read emails and scrolled through Contacts and forwarded several to himself. He pulled the battery from the phone and gave it to the warden after turning Peason over.

'Where's my phone?'

'I slid it back into your pocket. Have you ever been arrested before?'

'No.'

'You're going to have to give up your phone and wallet when they book you. Same thing when you do prison time, but they'll give it back to you when you get out. The warden has your phone battery. If you remember anything before you're booked and charged then call me and I'll sit with the district attorney's office and tell them in the very end you helped us. Or you could do that right now. What's "launching rio" mean?'

Peason shrugged and Marquez could only come up with one answer for the biologist to do this. Money.

He talked to Muller as he pulled away. 'I'm five minutes from the Brannan Recreation launch. Peason got a text off as we were driving that reads, "launching rio," and this isn't Rio de Janeiro.'

It was Muller's team and Muller's call about how to do this. Muller said, 'Hold on, John,' and got on his radio as Marquez passed a slow car and got back into his lane. Thirty seconds later, as he made the left turn into the Brannan Recreation Area, the driver he had passed sat on her horn and flipped him off as she went by. He wound along the narrow asphalt road and Muller came back with, 'Are you there?'

'I'm here and the boat is in the water with one guy in it and the other running down to the boat right now. He's going to get in before I get to him and I'm looking at coolers stacked in the back. This is it.'

The second man climbed on the bow and the boat chugged into reverse. They watched Marquez drive down to the boat launch and jump out and though they weren't looking at a uniform, they knew he was after them. One was Hispanic, one white, both young, the driver's gaze leaving him as he straightened the boat out and put his sunglasses on. The stern rode low with the weight of the fish coolers and the boat slowly started upriver.

Marquez didn't yell Fish and Game because he didn't want them to dump the evidence. He called Muller, who said they'd get a boat in the water, but what they really needed was a helicopter and all he could do now was follow the boat from the highway. He drove out of Brennan and the steel frame of the Rio Vista Bridge came into view as SOU recruited a fisherman's boat. Two SOU wardens got on-board and Marquez stopped at the Rio Vista Bridge.

He jogged out the pedestrian walkway and saw the boat with the pike upriver and read the uncertainty of the two men in it. Their boat slowed and he talked with Muller and said, 'I'm standing on the rio part. I can see the SOU wardens on a fisherman's boat and they're trying to hail the guys with the coolers right now.'

The pair with the coolers were probably expecting a call with directions on where to empty the coolers, how close to shore, how far apart. Maybe that call would have come from Peason, but they were on their own now and in trouble. When they saw the boat with the two wardens coming toward them they turned and accelerated downstream. Marquez read that as they were giving up and running back to their truck.

He ran back to his own truck, shoes clanging on the metal bridge and traffic slowing as a driver or two turned to watch him. Before he reached his pickup the boat passed beneath him. When he got to the Brannan Island Recreation Area he was ahead of Muller and any of the SOU and the two men were already out of the water.

One was unhitching the boat trailer and the other in the driver's seat starting the engine. He had them easily, but the boat was still in the water and he saw they had freed the ties holding the coolers and guessed their plan was to empty the coolers and then let them float off before dragging the boat out.

But he was wrong. They were leaving the boat behind. One man ran back to it just ahead of Marquez. He shoved the stick in reverse and jumped out of the boat into the water and made his way out as his buddy backed up to pick him up.

Now the boat was thirty yards offshore and drifting with the river as it spun circles in reverse. Stern heavy, it was taking on water and moving toward shoreline trees. Marquez ran down the shoreline, pulling his coat off. He kicked off his shoes and was in the cold water and swimming as the right rear of the boat tipped up against a snag. The engines whined as they tried to push the boat and it was heavy with water when he got there. He pulled himself onboard just before the props swung and caught him as the boat came free of the snag.

He climbed over the coolers, knocked the stick into neutral, reached for the bilge pump switch as one engine died. He needed to back out of the willow branches and now, and when the remaining engine coughed he went to full power and as the water-filled boat churned in reverse he thought *there's no other way, I've got to bring it around.*

He knew if the engine died here it was over but the boat came around and he got the bow pointed back toward the boat launch ramp. He made slow forward progress and the boat with SOU wardens closed in. He tied the line they threw to the bow just before the engine died.

The fisherman's boat had a lone Evinrude engine without much horsepower but it was enough to slowly drag the pike boat back to the launch. Then they used the trailer the two men had left behind. Marquez stayed with the boat as it was pulled out and under his hand resting on a cooler he felt the pike moving. He felt their force and the vibration of their movement, but it was a thing again to see them as they cleared the water and parked and opened the cooler lids. Thousands of pike finger-lings writhed over each other, and he stared and then looked at the warden on the phone with Muller who signaled now with a fist pump that the two men had been apprehended.

Now there was a debate about transporting the fish and Marquez cut it off. They had videotape and they could take samples. They had all the evidence they needed. He pointed.

'Over there in the grass.' He picked up one handle on one end of the cooler nearest him as one of the SOU grabbed the other handle and they dumped the first cooler in the grass. With everybody hauling the rest, sixteen coolers were empty in ten minutes. The pike fingerlings flopped in the grass and one of the wardens moved his truck closer and put his headlights on as the dusk came on.

Marquez stood in the cold in his wet clothes waiting for the last one to die. But there was no righteousness in that. There was only relief and when they were dead they shoveled them back into the coolers and the coolers were loaded onto the area warden's truck with jokes about the smell.

He walked back to his truck and found a dry sweatshirt and jeans and changed standing in the darkness. He started the engine and got the heater going, but he didn't leave yet. He pulled his phone and read the emails he'd forwarded from Peason's phone then went back over the text messages and sat there a long time thinking about Hauser and Peason and Colson and Barbara Jones and the sheriff. He thought about everything that had happened with Colson and it hit him. There was only one answer that fit.

FIFTY-THREE

A call came from Voight the next morning as Marquez got into Weaverville and drove past a huge stack of logs that steamed in the early sun.

Voight was huffing but his breathing slowed as he talked, so maybe he was coming off one of his morning walks.

'I won't string you out. We don't have enough to charge Harknell yet, but we're going in the right direction.'

'What did you find on the boat?'

They had found a locked waterproof first-aid cabinet with a box of ammunition in it, two folding combat knives, a disassembled Glock hand gun, fifteen hundred dollars in cash, a Droid X cell phone minus its battery and very water damaged. The cell phone's serial number did not match Sarah Steiner's missing phone and Harknell wouldn't say why it was there. In the cabinet was also a short club made of black walnut with a leather wrist band and a piece of steel inset into the fire-hardened head of the club. There was blood on the head of the club, enough to pull DNA samples.

'Do any of those items mean anything to you?'

'Are Ellis' and Steiner's names in the notebook?'

'They are and so are half a dozen groups and organizations that focus on water.'

'Send me a photo of the club.'

The photo came through a few minutes later but he didn't look at it yet. He parked. From here he could see the green metal roof of Sorzak's bar and the lot out front. There were no cars in the lot yet. It was early and cold and the air smelled of wood smoke. Now he opened the photo of the club head and thought about Harknell, who didn't keep this club as a defensive weapon, but rather as something to wield control. He enlarged the photo, studied the rounded head and saw the dried blood Voight talked about.

He remembered Colson leaning over, showing him the back of his skull. The rounded curve of the dark walnut was a good match for the wound. He stared at it and called Voight.

'It's going to be Colson's blood on the club.'

'That's what I think too, but why did Harknell do it?'

'Colson wouldn't pay him anymore. Colson wanted out. He wanted to quit his business and disappear.'

'Who killed him?'

'Whoever plans to take over his business.'

'And who's that?'

'I have a pretty good guess, but that's all, right now. I'll call you later.'

The slump-shouldered bartender's green Chevy Tahoe pulled in now and Marquez watched him get out, unlock, and go inside. He looked eager to get out of the cold. A few minutes later a white panel van pulled up and parked alongside the bartender's rig. Two men got out and one knocked on a service door and the other moved down along the side of the building as if looking for somebody hiding. Marquez put that down to caution. He reached in the glove compartment for binoculars.

Now he watched a third car pull in and as Lisa Sorzak and two men got out he started his engine. He moved closer and with binoculars studied the two men who arrived with her. He recognized both, no doubt about either. He got out now and walked down through trees to the backside of the bar building.

From here he had enough of a view to see into the white-panel van as they opened it. He wasn't quite close enough to make out their words but he didn't really have to. He saw the two doors at the back of the white-paneled van opened and Lisa got in and inspected as the pair who had arrived in the van stood to the side, one on his phone.

Now the two that came with her and the bartender backed her up as she negotiated, their voices rising, cash showing, the one who had been on his cell phone off it now, brandishing it like a weapon as he argued with her.

Marquez held the binoculars up and studied her face. It was hard, holding tough with these guys, hundred dollar bills in her right hand, the bartender with a big gun in his coat that was making the pocket hang outward. His hand kept going to it. This was not a done deal yet but she was taking over. They opened the second of the two doors at the back of the paneled van and he saw furs, bone, and cages. He watched the exchange of cash, the slow counting and recounting of hundred dollar bills, one of the two men who brought the product sitting on the back of the van counting bills to his left side in the sunlight as Sorzak stood with her hands on her hips and looked past the man at the product behind him.

When the counting was done one of the men got on his phone again. A few minutes later a Chevy Malibu with tinted windows pulled in and in jumped the pair who had delivered the white-panel van and just got paid. As that happened Marquez took a photo of the Malibu and sent it with a text to Muller, though he doubted Muller needed it. Muller's team was close already.

The return text read, 'We're on him.'

Now the two that arrived with Sorzak moved toward the car and Marquez texted the plates to Voight and a message: 'The tall black-haired one shot Colson. Looks like they're leaving.'

They were. There got in the car and Sorzak wasn't going with them. She closed up the panel van and went back inside with the bartender and Marquez called Voight.

'These guys are pulling out.'

'No problem, the Weaverville Police are working with us. You certain about the taller guy?'

'Yes, and the other one was there too.'

'And Sorzak arrived with them?'

Voight was putting it together.

'That's right, and they need to be very careful when they pull these guys over. How many units have they got?'

'There are Trinity sheriffs helping too.'

'Good.'

Twenty minutes later the bartender came out and left. When that happened Marquez was tempted to go knock on the bar door, but he didn't. He waited but without the excitement he felt on his first animal trafficking bust years ago. He felt now like he was dealing with something inexorable and thought about the man sitting on the back of the panel van in the sun counting bills like a small shopkeeper readying the day.

What do you do about that? And what do you do about Ugandan military helicopters entering Garamba National Park on an elephant hunting expedition, or a Chinese restaurant that only serves endangered species?

His phone buzzed and his thoughts shifted. It was Voight sounding excited and happy. 'They're in custody, no one got hurt, and we're getting another bonus out of this. One of the guys connects to your stepdaughter's ex-friend, Kevin. He's driven loads for him and is eager to trade.'

'Good. I want to be there.'

'Where are you?'

'I'm still at the bar but working my way back to my truck and waiting for her to move.'

'Maybe she's there for the day.'

She wasn't. The bar didn't open until five and she wasn't going to leave this van in the lot. He had the other thought again and came close to telling Voight but didn't. Half of Muller's SOU team would follow the pair back to wherever they came from and Marquez planned to stay with Sorzak.

He climbed quickly up through the trees to his truck and when he got a look again Sorzak was out of the building and moving to the van. She headed east out of town, crossed the river and then took the narrow highway toward Hayfork and the Mad River. So the rumor was probably true. She had a place there somewhere.

He called Muller, gave his position and within thirty minutes three of the SOU were alongside and ahead of him, and they gave her a long lead. For miles ahead there were few places to turn off this road as it wound through forested range, climbing and falling and then climbing again. An hour and a half later Sorzak stopped at the converted trailer that was Mad River Burger. It was one of the better burgers places Marquez knew of though he had no appetite today and watched her order and eat and then backtrack toward Ruth Lake.

He let the SOU wardens know. 'We're getting close so let's tighten it up.'

And if they hadn't closed they might have missed her turn onto the dirt road. Marquez switched to radio when he lost cell reception following her onto the dirt road. He guessed out on this road was a house or a cabin she owned. The road followed a creek for a mile and then climbed through oak and into the hills. Two and half miles in he saw the house and moments later she parked. Now the white-paneled van and a jeep were side-by-side in front of a small modern house.

Maybe the jeep was hers or maybe someone else was there as well. They could sit on the house and wait and keep following the van as it moved again. Or they could approach. She ended that debate for him by unloading the birdcages and doing it alone which suggested no one else was there.

If they drove straight in she would see them coming and Marquez decided to do it that way, but not until she had a bird cage in either hand. Then they came fast and she turned as she heard the engines and opened the door but couldn't get back inside before Marquez reached her. She looked shocked, then fine. The recovery was liquid and quick and she smiled.

'I was hoping I'd see you again.'

'Well, you got your wish except that I'm here to arrest you.'

'That doesn't work for me.'

'I didn't think it would.'

She took in the three SOU wardens, and Marquez pointed toward the panel van.

'Do you want to show us what else is in there?

She shook her head.

'There's not much in the van and I want to talk alone with you first.'

'We can do that, but put the birds down first.'

'They need water and food and that's inside. Do you mind carrying them in and I'll get the food and water?'

'This is bigger than what's in the van, Lisa.'

'I know it is.'

He carried the cages in but not before holding his hand up for the SOU wardens to say, *if I'm not out in five minutes, come in.* He put the cages down on a counter and instead of coming back to the cages with food she came at him with a gun.

'If you pull the trigger they'll come in shooting.'

'I want you to take the gun out of your shoulder harness with your index finger and thumb. Pull it out by the grip and lower it to the floor and do the same with the one at your ankle.'

He did that.

'Now tell me what you've figured out.'

342

'The wardens are just a couple of minutes from coming through the door.'

'You and I may be dead by then.'

'You made a deal with Harknell and then you took out Colson. One of the men who arrived with you this morning was the shooter. He's in custody.'

She leveled the gun at his head. 'We're going to take your truck and drive away.'

'There's nowhere to go, Lisa.'

The SOU wardens saw the gun at his head and radioed for help and trailed Marquez's truck as it slowly drove past. Sorzak sat across from him with a two-handed grip.

'You got fifty thousand dollars from the sheriff for Terry Ellis and Sarah Steiner. What did you get for Barbara Jones?'

'I didn't kill her. Harknell must have shot her. And I got a hundred thousand for the girls, not fifty. I did it for the money and so Harknell and I could start working together before I took the operation away from Colson. I was sorry for the girls. They really didn't want to die, but they had chances I never got and they shouldn't have been where they were anyway.

'You and I could still make a deal, Lieutenant. There's no proof about these other things. We could make a deal and both of us will make a lot of money when I take over. It could be worth half a million dollars a year to you.'

'That's not going to happen.'

They came around another turn and were looking at a green California Fish and Game truck blocking the road. Marquez slowed to a stop. He didn't see the warden.

343

'Get out. We'll take his truck.'

When it didn't look like that was going to work she leveled her gun, aimed at his head, and the first round came from the hill above and caught her in the chest. She still managed to get off a shot before a second round tore into her throat and the gun fell from her hand as she tumbled. Marquez reached her in seconds and saw she was dying. He knelt and took her hand and couldn't have said why.

He laid her hand down after she died and sat in sunlight wrapping gauze around his right arm where the shot she got off grazed him. They reported her death and a pair of wardens and Marquez searched the house and van.

Trinity County deputies arrived and it was late afternoon before Marquez left there. The four birds in cages rode with him. He propped their cages so they didn't move much in the curves and the birds seemed fine with the drive. They chirped and fluttered and talked and were good companions on the long ride home.